RACHEL WYATT

SUSPICION

COTEAU BOOKS

Edited by Edna Alford
Cover and text design by Tania Craan
Typeset by Susan Buck
Printed and bound in Canada at Friesens

FSC
www.fsc.org
MIX
Paper from
responsible sources
FSC® C016245

LIBRARY AND ARCHIVES CANADA CATALOGUING IN PUBLICATION

Wyatt, Rachel, 1929-
        Suspicion / Rachel Wyatt.

ISBN 978-1-55050-517-7

        I. Title.

PS8595.Y3S87 2012   C813'.54   C2012-903808-3

Issued also in electronic format.

10 9 8 7 6 5 4 3 2 1

2517 Victoria Avenue
Regina, Saskatchewan
Canada   S4P 0T2
www.coteaubooks.com

AVAILABLE IN CANADA FROM:
Publishers Group Canada
2440 Viking Way
Richmond, BC, Canada
V6V 1N2

Coteau Books gratefully acknowledges the financial support of its publishing program by: the Saskatchewan Arts Board, the Canada Council for the Arts, the Government of Canada through the Canada Book Fund, the Government of Saskatchewan through the Creative Economy Entrepreneurial Fund, the Association for the Export of Canadian Books and the City of Regina Arts Commission.

For my brother Stephen,
with love

"Suspicions amongst thoughts are like bats amongst birds: they ever fly by twilight. There is nothing makes a man suspect much, more than to know little."

– Francis Bacon

ONE

Hi people. Friday, so I'm up early. I like to be ready when Maj comes. I know it's a nuisance for him to set me and the chair down near the lake on the way to the clinic but it's the light. On these fall mornings it's mysterious and I want to photograph it, before Jack Wilson ruins the landscape. I'm planning a series for the club show next spring. It's almost impossible to paint this light, Simon says. But great artists have captured it, this kind of grey mist on water. Turner and Monet for two.

You never know what you might see at this hour. Birds are migrating now. People walk their dogs. Perhaps illicit lovers meet. Maybe I'll catch Hayden with her though I know that was over months ago. He has to be at work early today, so he said. And no, Boris, I don't use my camera for blackmail purposes. I'm not exactly able to climb ladders and look in windows. Besides which, I'm not a snoop.

By the way, Lauren, I don't think you should blame George 2 for responding to your comments about Clive. You brought it up. This *is* a *chat* room.

TNT *Marguerite*

•

You can't dance to that music. Yes I can, Stefan! As he moved slowly round the kitchen conducting the invisible New York Philharmonic, Jack looked forward to the coming weeks when, every day, he'd be the first to leave the house again. He knew it was wrong to think like that in these times but couldn't help it. Last one out had to do the breakfast dishes and make the bed. If

1

they had kids, he and Candace, two or three of them might be getting ready for school now. *Have you got your lunch? Did you finish your homework?* He could see himself making sandwiches. Peanut butter and jelly for the girl. Sliced cheese for the boy. Whole wheat bread. Crusts cut off for her maybe.

He looked at the clock. 8:05. Idleness at this time of day was for layabouts or thinkers or the growing number of sadly unemployed. And that was another thing. The protestors wouldn't see that the company was creating jobs, local jobs. Those men and women, mostly women, were deaf to logic. For them it was all about trees and scenery and fear of change and to hell with economic reality. He sat down with his coffee and listened to the last phrases of the symphony. Dvorak, a displaced person in his New World, built melancholy into hopefulness. Longing in there too. He was grateful to Stefan for taking time when they were at UBC to teach him how to listen. Playing tapes to him, luring him to concerts, opening his ears. His friend had seen it as fair trade for help with his school work. Heating systems for symphonies. Building codes for concerti. All the engineering Jack had taught him went for nothing in the end though. He didn't even do his own renovations. In third year, after Jack had to go back home, Stefan moved over to Fine Arts and quit that too after a few months. Both of them dropouts but doing okay, thank you.

The CD played itself out. How did a man or a woman know to put this phrase here, those notes there, to make the work a classic, a pure, good, lasting thing? Like the project. Like Pine View. A wall here. A window there. Everything in its perfect place. And it too would be a pure, good, lasting thing. He removed the disc from the player, dusted it and put it back in the case. On the crowded top shelf it stood between *Rusalka* and *The Spectre's Bride*. How had he and Candace acquired so many of these little plastic boxes? Rows and rows. Abba, the Beatles, Celine Dion. Jazz from everywhere. Dvorak and Tchaikovsky, the lonely classics. But who was to decide "classic"? People mainly, he supposed. The Beatles, Dylan, were up there too. So did it all come down to popularity like a beauty contest? And the truth was the composer had no idea whether he was creating a classic or whether his symphony would last beyond the first concert. Jack picked up his jacket and keys. Circular thinking could drive a person crazy. The dishes would wait and his mother always left the beds to air. Something to do with mites.

He drove past the arena. That too had caused protests and ill will and now was accepted as part of the town, another good thing. The naysayers had become proud of it, pointed it out to visitors and went to the games, glad of the comfortable seats. The museum, renovated and handsome now, was a small Parthenon set back its own park, putting to shame the old, shabby library across the road. Work needed to be done there but all public funds for renovation were on hold.

He squeezed the pickup into the last free space and walked down Corwin past Fashion Now. Erica was standing in the window like a mannequin, looking out. She wasn't usually at work so early. He waved but she didn't wave back and likely would have made a gesture at him anyway. Well screw her! There'd been times when he might have liked to do just that. She was a sexy woman, nice shape, sharper edged than her sister, than Candace, his wife.

•

Erica had seen him go by. The destroyer. The unbeliever. Her brother-in-law. Nearly a decade ago but still clear in her mind was her impulse to rush up the aisle of the church at the wedding and pull Candace away from him and take her place. Not that he was handsome, Jack. His face was marked by being outdoors in all kinds of weather. He wasn't even all that tall. But in his suit that day, with his aura of confidence, of simply "knowing", of superman strength, he was irresistible. Simon beside her had put his arm round her shoulders thinking she was overcome with the emotion usual at weddings. Her mother, had she told her, might have settled the matter Solomon fashion. She smiled at the gruesome thought.

She'd come in early to sort out yesterday's delivery. They'd been sent the wrong kind of sweater again. Not the colours they'd chosen either. And yet the order had been made clear. I have a degree in art history, Erica thought, as she compared the list on the computer with the invoice and went to the phone. It was after 11 a.m. in Toronto.

Inefficiency had settled over the world like a toxic cloud. Creeping in like a spy on a secret mission it had invaded stores, businesses, homes, and spread across the country. Perhaps it had ruined ancient civilizations and caused the downfall of dynasties. *I want to go to Isfahan while it's still there before some pilot, carelessly given wrong coordinates, bombs the place to bits.* She keyed in the number.

"Hello. Trends Inc. Moira speaking," a chirpy voice said.

"Well listen carefully, Moira. This is Erica from Fashion Now in Ghills Lake. You have sent us the wrong order again!"

"That's not my department, Erica. I'll put you through to dispatch."

"It is not the fault of dispatch, Moira. It's the fault of the person who packed the boxes and did not check our order correctly. I would like to speak to that person now, please."

In Isfahan, there is an ancient mosque.

•

Candace couldn't believe it. The date and time were logged in her BlackBerry. Marie had called two days ago to remind her of the appointment. And here she was, at 8:25, standing in the street, looking at a notice that said, "Closed till Monday."

She counted off the days on her fingers. It *was* Friday, October the sixteenth. There was no excuse for this. Damn! She kicked at the door and hurt her toe. It was a dark brown wooden door with a narrow stained glass panel set into the wall beside it. A design of green lilies made it impossible to see through to the reception area. She stared at the flowers as if they might have an answer for her.

Perhaps Dr. Chan's mother had died, or he'd had an accident. But then the receptionist would have let her know. Or maybe the good doctor had looked into Marie's eyes, picked up two free toothbrushes and run off with her in a wild moment of uncontrollable passion. He could have suffered a breakdown: "I will drill no more," he cried as he took off his mask and stuffed it into the open mouth of his last patient. Whatever! The door was locked. Crossly, Candace set off towards the office.

She wasn't expected at work for another hour and the system was likely still down anyway. She could take time out. A walk would calm her. She hurried past the building where her colleagues would soon be deep into sales strategies and product evaluation while they waited for the computer technician to return and correct yesterday's mistake. The damaged window of Tiny Tim's Toys was still boarded up. No one had yet figured out what the burglars wanted with six teddy bears and three plush beavers unless, as Alys had suggested, they wanted to fill them with pot and smuggle them across the border.

As she moved further away from her usual day, she felt lighter, like a child with an unexpected holiday. She could have lunch out if she found a café at some distance from work. Buy a magazine, *House and Garden,* or something on art, and read it while she ate like any other leisurely person. Looking at the pictures she could pick out a couch for the living room, and a decent dining table. Nine and a half years had gone by and somehow she and Jack had never found time to go out together to buy good furniture. And maybe that was part of the problem. Their house looked like a dump for the rejects people put at the ends of their driveways: Free. Please take. But it could be a kind of insurance: Once everything was perfect in the house, there would be nothing to aim for, no projects, no saying, "One of those would be nice," when they saw an ad on TV, and the marriage would be over. As it might have been if she hadn't told Hayden she didn't want to see him any more. She didn't even like him much. That whole few weeks had been like a virus, an attack. Short code words on the phone. Little meetings. Grabby encounters. Yuck. Filed away now under "What was I thinking?"

She slowed her pace and strolled past the school. The bell hadn't rung yet and kids were rushing around playing their games and shouting. The promise or threat, depending how you looked at it, to replace the old brick building with a modern, stream-lined structure full of every electronic device for modern, streamlined children with chips for brains, was on hold. Not enough kids in the area now and money was tight. She walked down the path towards the lake. A couple of boys were dawdling on the shore and would turn up in class with sand on their shoes and damp pebbles in their pockets. *I have time to notice the details of life.*

A whole day off would be a cure for all the irritations of the last few days. Dental emergency. Toothache. Sore face. She had a litany of excuses to offer Alys on Monday and Alys would believe none of them but who cared. After eight years in the job and no history of taking time off without reason, she was entitled to a few selfish hours. She would be silent, speak to no one, gather in her thoughts and consider her life to date, her life that could easily have ended last Friday. "You're a lucky woman," the cop said, standing there in the road. "Another few metres…"

Wiping the bench of the picnic table with a Kleenex, she sat down and got a pen and a scrap of paper from her bag and began to make a list. At the top she wrote LIFE.

She wasn't sure what to put next. Things to do to change her life around? She wrote that down because it sounded right. *Things to do to change my life.* Beneath that she wrote *couch* because a comfortable place to sit in the living room would make a difference to their leisure hours and perhaps even to their sex life. At Alys's a couple of weeks ago, she'd lounged on a soft L-shaped mound of comfort and found it a sensual delight. I'm getting rid of it, Alys had said. *He* used to lie there to watch baseball. You're welcome to it. But Candace knew that hers and Jack's must be carefully chosen, new and not harbouring the crumbs of other people's lives. Besides, Jack would have seen the gift as charity.

She underlined the word "couch." So what next? This would take time and the breeze off the lake was chilly. Her hand was cold. She wrote, *buy new gloves* and decided that so far her list was pathetic. There had to be larger ambitions. If she couldn't save the world she might at least make an effort to move it in the right direction.

Over there was the building site. She stared at the ugly pile of old tires that would deaden the sound of blasting. The idle crane and backhoe were animals waiting for a signal to pounce and destroy. When the digging started up again dust would fly in both senses and Jack – Jack would be a happy man back in his uniform; old clothes and hard hat. And she would love him again. She did love him, had loved him, but he'd become an obsessed and absent man. The aggravation of having his big plans, his dream of a lifetime, delayed and delayed again, had made him incapable of entering into any other part of life. At the same time, when the building began, Erica would become even more distant and full of cold words. Family life was a seesaw.

As she looked across the lake's choppy water at the island, it occurred to her that she herself, Candace Wilson, who had taken her husband's surname on her wedding day because she was escaping from her family, didn't have a lifetime dream. This was it. Day-to-day in this small town. My one and only life. She felt revealed and hollow. Getting off the treadmill even for this brief hour had led to a recognition of emptiness. So this was why a person kept on going to the office every weekday. Shop and clean and socialise at the weekend. Every Monday, repeat the cycle. Did people continue in their ruts for fear of being nothing, of having no strings to attach them to life? Was this really and truly LIFE? This unexpected gift of a free day was maybe a sign, like the accident last week, a nudge from the Fates to make a change, to take a leap, to be fantastic.

Who am I? Family and friends saw her as steady maybe. She wasn't excitable like her sister, or aggressive like her late mother or ponderous like her now slow-moving dad. Only occasionally, and only if provoked, was she driven to random unkind acts. Putting Jack's favourite sweater in the garbage last week had been thoughtless. So far he hadn't noticed.

She would have liked to be able to consider herself "good" but as of those few dismal weeks last spring the word hardly applied. A new direction might move her towards reform. It moved her now to get up and walk towards the fence. If Jack was there, she would suggest they go out to lunch later or make love. He would have no idea that things were about to change. There was no need for him to know. He hadn't noticed that there was anything wrong. From now on, she was going to be supportive and true. Her sister, intent on trying to persuade her to betray him further by joining in the protests, had made her see that there was only one right way.

She could not, though it had crossed her mind, say to Jack, Look, it was only a few times and he's not that good. It was an act of mercy, okay. She could only erase her sin by behaving well.

The block-like trailer beyond the fence reminded her of those two family holidays down East that she and Erica had tried to forget but laughed about now in their rare moments of harmony. She pushed at the wire gate. It was locked. Jack was probably still at home working the phone to make sure the council members stayed on side. Disappointed that her first step towards being a reformed person was thwarted, she turned away. A whole day with nothing to do suddenly became an exercise in loneliness. How was she to change if she couldn't cope with being on her own for an hour?

She went back to the picnic table and sat down to take off her running shoes and put on her smart brown boots. To the office she would go, to Alys's bitterness about her partner's defection, to finding a magic formula to improve sales figures and cut costs at the same time. Without her, they would make a hash of the new advertising campaign and accept the first idea Brent suggested. Alys would put weasel words into the proposal and add a let-out clause about time and staff. "Just in case" was her favourite phrase. At least there'd be coffee and muffins because it was the end of the week. She felt hungry as if she'd walked for hours. Later she'd make a plan to go to Vancouver, to spend a whole weekend considering her life and what might be done to improve both her and it. Dark nights of the soul had to last longer than forty-five minutes.

In a hurry now, thinking of what to say at the meeting, she crossed over the bridge and took the shortcut across the grass towards the road. Her heels dug into the softened ground tilting her backwards and she wished she'd kept her flat shoes on. She heard a cry and turned and fell, fell down inside a well, a hole, a trap, and landed on her side. Pain shot up her left leg. She tried to feel the edges of the space so she could climb out but there was nothing to grasp.

"Whoever you are," she yelled, "get me out of here. You'll pay for this."

TWO

"It's about risk. When you have kids, you can't take risks. Kids are a risk in themselves," Gary said. "Mine are."

Kids. Kids. Mine. The words struck at Jack's heart. He said nothing but wished that instead of fantasizing about imaginary sandwiches for imaginary children, he'd made a real one for himself. Then he could have stayed in the office now checking timelines and deliveries instead of half-listening to Gary and wondering what was the least fatty thing on the menu. Beyoncé in the background was singing "Broken-hearted Girl."

"But there's no risk involved here," Gary went on. "Look at the list of investors. Solid. The market's rumbling a bit but we're safe. We've got two-thirds of the money."

Candace had said Caesar salad was fattening. But it was all lettuce so had to be healthy.

"What you were saying about the height of the toilets, Jack, I don't think it matters. We're not expecting a lot of elderly people to buy. I know you're the expert when it comes to plumbing."

The music from the speakers suddenly became a scream.

People stopped their ears and yelled at the waitress.

"For goodness sake!"

"Turn it down!"

The song stopped altogether.

"Where was I?" Gary asked.

You were reminding me that I was a plumber by trade who has moved up into the developing business and maybe should be grateful.

"I don't know. That awful noise went right through me," Jack said.

"Someone must have turned the dial the wrong way. Anyway."

"I'll have the soup of the day and a grilled cheese sandwich, please, Mandy."

"Me too," Gary said. "And another coffee, please."

"You too what?"

"I'll have the same. Soup and a grilled cheese sandwich, please."

Mandy, thin as a stick, who obviously didn't eat in the café, slouched towards the kitchen as if they'd asked her to provide a six-course meal. She'd wanted to be a doctor but had failed her pre-meds twice and refused to go for a third try. Now she sulkily helped out her sister three days a week. Althea had only ever wanted to own a café, to feed people, to know everything that went on in her part of town. Some said the booths were miked.

"The investors, Brian Hampson in particular, will want progress reports."

Gary Streicher talked on while Jack recalled the day he'd told his father that he was happy being a plumber, really wanted to keep the family business going, and his father had hugged him as if he'd known it was a lie. But by then the old man didn't know much any more. Early Alzheimer's had taken his mind and, soon after, his life.

The soup came, and he paid attention to the man sitting opposite because, after all, he had given him the opportunity to hand in his electric snake and sell the van with "Wilson and Son. All-Purpose Plumbers. Your Pipes Are Our Business" written wordily on the side.

"Right," he said. "I'll make sure they're on time. Bill's a good guy. We won't have to worry."

Gary had the shine of a successful man about him. His skin shone, his jacket had the sheen of costly fabric. His clear eyes belied the fact that he drank wine as if all the vineyards in the world might suddenly get the blight. And he had an extra layer of fat that spoke of lunches with other successful men. He liked to talk about his first major project, the conversion of an office building to apartments in Kelowna, and was doing so when Hampson himself came in and shouted to them from the door.

"Hi, guys. How's it going?"

"It's going," Jack said before Gary could launch into a blow-by-blow account of the coming week's possible schedule.

"Great." He came over and talked to them about markets and possibilities and the fact that Bernanke said the recession was over.

The grey-green soup tasted bitter. Jack, reminded of lonely times in Vancouver, pushed it aside and hoped for better from the sandwich.

•

Important to remain calm, Candace told herself. The walls of this prison were strangely rough. She wanted to stand up but her leg was too painful. The break, if it was a break, was halfway down her calf. There was no bone sticking out as far as she could tell but the tissue was tender. She was shaking and wanted to stop. She tried to draw on calmness as if it were a garment that she could pull over her head and shake down to her feet. She felt her leg again. Her bag was lost or had been taken.

"I have to get this fixed," she shouted but no one came. It would be getting dark before Jack, Erica, Dad, would know she hadn't been at work. Alys would assume she'd gone home after the dentist's and taken painkillers. Though she should have called for her input on the Driver file. It was her baby. She'd spent weeks checking costs and looking at the artwork. She called out "Help" again. People had to be going by. Were they all freaking deaf? Were they all dead? The ground had opened up. The great Fault had opened its maw and swallowed every single person in the town. No! That was ridiculous.

But she wanted to hear voices. I am afraid. Cowardice is my middle name. Easily sounds like Candace. What were they thinking, Adam and Eve, when they registered her birth? In fact, they said, they'd named her after an ancient queen. At school, she'd been Candy. To her first slobbering boyfriend, she'd been Dace. In her meaner moments, Erica called her CanCan. What was wrong with Mary, Ruth or simple, beautiful Ann? But I am Candace. Candace Alison Wilson. C.A.W. A crow's cry. A crook not yet caught. Or only in the mesh of her own weaving. A thread of security that had been a lifeline since childhood had been cut.

Soon it would be time to shout again, to yell, I am here. Lights would appear above and there would be a stretcher and warm drinks and loving arms. Whose? Her dad's? Jack's?

They would search. Unless they assumed she had gone away, run off, found another lover.

She'd supported Jack against Erica and Simon as well as half the people in town, and was entitled to – to pleasure where she could find it. So she had thought eight months ago. And so she now regretted. The pain shot through her leg again.

What had she been thinking this morning: that she needed time to sort out her life? She'd wished too hard and time had been given her. Sensory deprivation. That's what this was. Nothing to hear, nothing to eat. It smelt of – well, earth. Damp earth. She looked up and could see a sliver of daylight filtered through a tangle of roots. Had she fallen into an animal trap? Even as she told herself there was nothing worth trapping so near the lake, she could see something dangling above her. She threw a pebble at it and another. It was her leather bag. She stretched up to grab it but the bag was a few mean centimetres out of her reach.

So she would be forced to think because there was nothing else to do until they came. As soon as they realized she wasn't home, they would come.

"Ja-a-a-ack!"

•

Candace was late home and Jack was glad. It would give him time to sort out his thoughts. These long useless days had been a kind of torture. Misgivings had crept into his mind: Had he been right to sell the business to go in with Streicher on this scheme? It had seemed exciting at first when everything was going well. But surely, surely, they would be able to restart on Monday. If he could have summoned a god, he would have prayed to him or her or it. Churches were listed in the yellow pages but not deities, not as such. His dad used to say there were too many gods in the world and as all of them were proclaimed to be The Superior Being by their adherents, you might as well invent one for yourself.

He'd talked to the councillors on Wednesday, and to Dan Bright, and they all said the same thing: We're very much in favour of this, Jack. You bet. It will draw business to the town. People with good incomes, professional people, will want to buy the homes. That's what they said. But how much were these seven men and women to be trusted? Gloria Pavel usually looked at him with unforgiving eyes through her steel-rimmed glasses. Her fine gold hair framed a doubting face. Yuri Beslov wavered as though trees and frogs could, at any moment, become more important to him than progress and he might be out in the park waving a banner like Erica and Simon and the other protesters. Well screw them! It would go ahead. It had to go ahead. Too much time, effort and bad feeling were invested in it for it to close down now. Dan, as mayor, had been on side from the beginning and the free pass to the planned golf course was a very small bribe. One other little matter, he'd said on the phone. A detail. Making it sound like nothing. But Jack still feared that at this last moment it would all come tumbling down. *Expect to be disappointed* should have been his daily horoscope.

Three years, one false start, and now, finally, they could begin.

Buying the property and raising the money had been easy compared to pushing the idea through, getting permits, persuading more than half the concerned citizens that it was good for the town. Truly, it was uncertainty that drove men crazy.

He went to sleep nights imagining the finished houses. Neat places, "sleek," Marcus had called them. Odd word but it was right. The sloping roofs, staggered balconies, every one of them private, no neighbours staring in. They were building something he'd like to live in himself if he could afford it. The most up-to-date appliances. Every kitchen with a centre island, double sink.

He moved round the room to his own music, saying the words, "Marble-topped counters, remote-controlled lighting, optional bidet, heated bathroom tiles." Then he noticed the breakfast dishes and stacked them into the dishwasher among, he saw as he put the last spoon in, plates and cutlery that were already clean. He sighed and began to unload the racks.

He and Gary would get the go-ahead today, set it all up over the weekend and have the men back to work on Monday morning. Some of the guys were already doing odd jobs in Chilliwack and Abbotsford. Barb and Wayne were getting paid to sit around the office. At least Wayne was using the time to bone up on the properties of cement for his next exam. But if the delay dragged on, the whole project would become a non-profit charity. Or the prices of the houses would go up and they'd have to take the word "affordable" out of the ads. But everything was affordable to somebody. Multi-billionaires could buy on Fifth Avenue, New York. People from Vancouver, tired of the drug and gang problems of the city, would come out here and imagine they were buying tranquillity. Men and women who worked from home would move in too and give new life to the town. An army of computer wizards. Stock brokers. Handsome, friendly people with kids who played hockey and liked horses. New life. New blood. An "invigoration". He doubted that was a real word but it was what he meant. And the buyers couldn't know that the gangs were making their way out of the city and finding havens in these smaller places.

He poured himself a cup of cold coffee, put it in the microwave and noticed the shopping list Candace had left on the counter. Why had she left it behind? Organized was her middle name. Maybe she had a duplicate. Or maybe she wanted him to pick the stuff up.

She hadn't said. She hadn't said much to him for days, come to that, and this weekend he was going to take her out to dinner at Peroni's and pay attention to what was on her mind, apologize for being distracted. Once it all begins, he would say, I'll be right there, with you. And where was she now? Probably at the beauty salon having unnatural blonde streaks put on her perfectly fine brown hair. His cellphone was vibrating.

"Where are you?" he snapped and then said, "Sorry."

"Jack. Is Candace okay?"

"Was when she left here this morning, Alys."

"When was that?"

"About eight. She was going to the dentist. She's not home yet. I'll have her call you."

"She didn't turn up for work."

"Ah. You sure?"

"I work there, Jack. Next desk."

"Sorry, Alys. It's weird, that's all. She didn't call in?"

"No. I tried her cell and your home number. No reply. I emailed her too. Any messages there?"

"I don't think so. I'll check."

"There'll be one from me. I called this morning about ten."

"Well thanks for letting me know. I'll check around. She's probably at her sister's."

"Have her call me when she comes back, please. I need to talk to her. We had to go ahead with the Driver project because of the deadline and she won't be happy about it."

"Okay, Alys. Thanks."

He turned the phone off and called out, "Candace!" She could have come back from the dentist's and fallen into a drugged sleep. He looked in the living room, the dining room, out on the patio as if she might be sitting there in the cold. He ran up the stairs and looked in their bedroom, the spare room, the office. Went back to their room. He looked through her closet as if he was familiar with her clothes. Hanger touched hanger. Jackets and blouses hung shoulder to shoulder. Slacks and skirts dangled by loops. If she'd packed a bag, she couldn't have taken much. Maybe she'd gone off with a rich guy who promised her Paris, fashion, Italy. *Don't bring anything, darling. We'll go shopping.*

He sat at the computer in the office and checked her email. Six messages. Three were from Amazon suggesting she shop now for Christmas. Someone called Robin advised her to book early and come to Florida for New Year, promising sunshine and relaxation. Alys's message was, *If you're reading this, call me.* The sixth was in some kind of code. *On the thirteenth day of the tenth month...*

He looked up the dentist's number and listened to the rings and then to a recorded message: *Dr. Chan will be in his office on Monday morning at 8. If this is an emergency...* Please let it not be. He checked his cell for text and voice mail. The usual harsh voice promised damnation if he went ahead with Pine View. An excited woman offered him a vacation in Mexico. But no familiar voice said, *Look, I'll be home a little late.* The land line yielded nothing either. Only Alys's message. Why hadn't the damn woman called him in the morning to say Candace hadn't turned up? She'd left it till the end of one whole day to let him know that his wife was possibly in danger. Nine hours.

He called Marcus first. The chances of her choosing to spend the day with her sister were slim.

"She can't have gone far," the old man said as if there were no planes, no trains, no rental cars to carry his daughter away. "Did she drive?"

"Her car's still at the shop. I offered to drive her but she likes to walk."

"Can't've gone far. Not very far. Maybe she's with Erica and forgot to call."

"I'll check right now."

"Well let me know. Can't be far. Can't have gone far."

Jack sympathized with Marcus's need to repeat himself. As well as being invisible, old people were often ignored when they spoke . And the old guy was laying a layer of comfort down in case. Well, in case what? How far could she have walked in those high-heeled boots of hers? *High-heeled boots, officer, grey jacket with fake fur collar, three-quarter length pants. Not sure what they're called. They wear them with boots.* Was it too soon to involve the cops and let the whole town know that Candace Alison Wilson, formerly Brandt, had, possibly, walked out on her husband?

He looked again at the shopping list: Onions, peppers, eggplant, zucchini, eggs, mushrooms, milk. There was nothing there that spelled out, "Goodbye, Jack."

He couldn't avoid calling his sister-in-law. It would be wrong to let her hear about Candace from anyone else.

"She can't have gone far," Erica said.

"She's had all day. She could be halfway to Europe by now. In Toronto. New York. There are any number of places you can get to in a day from here."

"But without leaving a note?"

There was a disaster-filled pause.

"You have to tell the police."

"They won't do anything for twenty-four hours, or maybe it's forty-eight."

"My neighbour's girl met someone on the Internet and just went off."

18

"She was a kid. Your sister is thirty-seven and sensible."

"Well, look. If there's anything we can do. I'll talk to Simon. I'm sorry, Jack. I hope she'll turn up and say she just decided to go to Vancouver for the day and do some shopping. Retail therapy. And maybe she tried to phone and... Bye."

She had all the answers, Erica. Retail therapy! Damn stupid. As for useless Simon who could have had a real job working on the site if he'd wanted, who needed his advice!

What neither of them had mentioned was the possibility of her running off with Hayden Cosgrave. That was over. Over!

The phone rattled again.

"Candace?" he pleaded.

"It's me," Gary said. "Dan, our beloved mayor, called. They have one last query and I've got a dinner to go to. They're meeting *in camera* around seven. I realize it's dinnertime. It should all be over by now but we have to clear this up. Can you make it?"

"Okay. I'll be there."

"It's just a matter of reassuring them, Jack."

Gary always had to act like the senior partner, bigger office and, since he put more money into the development, more control. Jack could have said that his wife was missing but later, when Gary understood that he'd attended the meeting in spite of that, it would be a small, smug victory. That is if she hadn't turned up by then as she surely would have. *Don't do this now, Candace. I'm on edge as it is.*

He scrawled a note and left it on the table. Crossed out *If* and wrote *When you get back, call my cell, please. Home in an hour. J.* At the door he turned back and inserted *Honey* after the please and then wrote the time at the top.

The phone again. The little screen announced his father-in-law.

"You said she's missing."

"Candace. I don't know. It seems so."

"What are you doing about it?"

"I'm on my way to the police station."

"Right. Well. She can't have got far."

"No. I expect she'll turn up soon."

"There wasn't – she didn't hit her head in the accident last Friday? No concussion? No after-effects?"

"No. Her shoulder still hurts a bit, that's all. She was lucky."

"Well then."

"Got to go, Marcus. If she turns up at your place, call me. You've got my cell number."

"Written on the wall here."

Missing was a heavy word. Jack wasn't prepared to allow it yet. When he got back, she'd be there. Or there'd be a message asking him to pick her up from the bus station. He called the body shop. Her car was still there, yes, Ralph said. They'd promised it for Monday and on Monday it would be ready. Right!

●

Marcus took off his red sweater. The hole in the sleeve wasn't getting any smaller. Not that it mattered most days what he wore round the house. But this evening was different. He got his dark blue blazer out of the closet and brushed it down. This was a time to look serious, not like some shambling old man who'd given up on appearances. Cops might come. Maybe Mounties. Why think of that! Candace was fine somewhere, lost in the mall or having a massage and a facial, forgetful of time, on her way back from a shopping trip in Vancouver. He looked in the mirror and got out the tweezers to remove another nose hair. An old man looked back at him. Lines on his forehead and down the sides of his mouth. But hair, he still had hair.

He tidied the living room, straightened the cushions on the

couch and wished now that he hadn't glued his collection of coasters to the wall so soon after SHE had died. It was an act of defiance to HER spirit, a mad response to grief and relief that he now regretted. Taking them off would mean repainting and once you started on that there was no end to it. So many memories though in those little squares and discs: A neat mosaic reflecting days of love and rose petals, pain-free walking and sound sleep. It was a history of nights and travels before he married and after: The ones on the lower level reminded him of happy times spent with his beloved Sheila before she became SHE, the irritable woman for whom nothing was right and who suspected even her friends of secret treacheries. What hope was there then for her daughters?

He'd tried to pinpoint the moment of change in her but it had been a gradual downward slope into a kind of grey pit from which the previously pleasant Sheila rarely emerged. Not exactly depression. She was active enough, way too active, some might say. A pursuer of the weak and needy all over town, at home she became a relentless seeker of dust and stains and faults. When the kids were little, the free spirit in her, left over from the sixties, had made her jolly, fun to be around most of the time. But when some demon had driven her to irrational acts, he'd taken the girls away for a day two till their mother calmed down. I should have known medical attention was required. Guilt set in too late.

He waited a month after her death before he took the coasters, all marked with the date and place and kind of beer or wine drunk, out of their boxes and began to glue them onto the wall. First he made a frieze, then diagonals. A few were in small clusters but the green octagon advertising Big Rock Ale had a space to itself. In that few days at High Pines, he and Sheila had shared brief hours of tender love and had murmured words like *always*.

From the hall, without his glasses on, the whole wall looked like an arty collage and one day maybe a collector would come in and photograph it and then take it to a museum. Wouldn't be easy to take it off the drywall. You've never drunk in all those places, Wendy had said. He'd just smiled. Let her think what she liked.

There'd been no need for Jack to shout just now as if he was deaf or stupid. He understood that Candace had not gone to work. But perhaps she had run towards happiness, a lover better in bed than Jack, a man not intent on ruining the landscape, a millionaire, a multi-millionaire. But there was that for Candace. She'd never been greedy, liked to work and pay her way. Even when she was at school, she fixed her own clothes and earned money. Independent. And maybe stubborn. Staying out of history class because she said Mr. Rawson was a racist and wouldn't apologize. Nearly got herself expelled.

He tried to imagine a few types who might have tempted her to run off so suddenly. The opposite of Jack: A guy half-shaven, the way a lot of them look nowadays as if they can't afford a razor. Maybe one with a beer gut she'd want to reform. There was probably enough of SHE in her to try that dead-end route. He comes in the door and she says, "You've been out looking like a clown." Or was that an echo of memory?

And then, oh God, she might have gone off with a thin-faced dreamy artist whose promise was yet to be fulfilled, like her sister.

At any rate, she would turn up soon for sure and right now it was time to read. Four pages a day would get him through the *Shorter Oxford* by the end of next year.

No dammit, I'm not trying to expand my vocabulary which is large enough, thank you. I like reading about words, right! Words are currency. What comes out of our mouths affects our lives every minute. If I could speak Russian, I'd read that dictionary too though they probably call it a lexicon. So shut up!

He said that to SHE whose jittering shade was never far away, picking on his decisions or singing some silly song cobbled together from bits of old musicals. Occasionally her invisible self lay on the bed beside him so that he had to get up and take a sleeping pill.

Now he could hear her saying, Candace is your daughter. Do something.

Hell! SHE was right again. Candace was their child. No DNA test required. Her eyes and mouth were Robinson to a T, to the teeth, and her straight nose was a gesture to the Brandt gene pool.

He glanced at the book on the lectern: "Breviate." He spoke the word aloud but couldn't concentrate. The pages would have to wait.

So Candace had not come home. He ran his finger along the shelf and picked out the battered book that had made her laugh so much when she was small. He'd read it to her and Erica a zillion times. What was that animal who reacted to danger by "making a loud noise until rescued"? A talking donkey, that was it: Eeyore.

Firstly though, was she in need of rescue?

Reasons for so thinking:

She had not been seen since breakfast time and had apparently left no message anywhere.

She had not called him to see if he was okay, as she often did around lunchtime on Friday.

Her car was at the body shop having the passenger door repaired. *There are no accidents.* Who says? It wasn't her fault that an idiot in a grey sedan had made a left turn too soon. And now she seemed to have disappeared. Were the two things connected? Some other smart person had stated that there were no coincidences either. How far could she have gone? If she had gone.

She'd never done anything like this before. Had Jack looked for her passport?

He sat with his head in his hands conjuring up an image of his daughter's face, her shape, the sound of her voice. And he hoped she was making a loud noise whether she was in danger or in bed with a lover.

•

Candace knew she must have slept part of the day in this awful place with her back resting against the muddy wall. Shock most likely. She was stiff and damp and cold.

No one had left her any food. If I am a kidnap victim. She groped around and found a bottle of water. Was it hers, the one she carried in her bag? Or had *they* left it for her. She took the cap off and sipped to moisten her throat. It was important to ration it. In camps they rationed everything.

She called out, "Help! Please, help." The words echoed back to her. "Whoever you are, if you have any humanity, take me to a doctor. My husband has no money. It's all invested in the development project. You've mistaken me for someone else."

Her hands were sore from trying to scrabble back out of the pit. A useless effort because she could put no pressure on her left leg. Climbing was not an option.

She felt tired again and thought of the way Jack had smiled at the hotel in Lucca right after the argument when she'd hurled the Italian dictionary as well as all her euros off the hotel balcony. He'd picked up his digital camera and taken a photo. And she'd admired him for not rushing down at once to retrieve the money.

She gritted her teeth. After all, she had seen real suffering. She'd travelled to that hard northern place where death was so easily come by, where no plants dared to stick their heads more than a few centimetres above the ground and where in winter the cold could kill. And she had not kept her promise to go back there as a teacher, as a politician, to help the people. Was this her punishment?

She called out again and would keep on doing so till someone replied.

Then she heard the ringing sound. Cellphone. In her bag. Stretching up as far as she could, shrieking from the pain in her leg, she could almost touch it.

If she'd had her iPod she could have listened to music while she waited. By eleven, when she hadn't turned up for the meeting, Alys should have called Jack. A search would have been set in motion. Soon she'd be home having a shower, a cup of coffee. Kindness. There would be kindness. Her eyes filled with tears.

THREE

Simon was grating carrots. Life had to go on apparently. He wanted to go out and search for Candace right away, and would later. Erica felt that the kids needed normalcy but this was not a normal time. If anything ever was. Was it "normal" to live in this nowhere town ninety minutes drive from the city? Some days he felt like an outcast in a dark forest seeing glimpses of light through leaves only occasionally. In Toronto and on trips to New York, he'd heard fine symphonies played by the best orchestras in the world and visited museums for nourishment. That was before marriage, before children. That was before he'd given up his office job to paint. Even getting to Vancouver to the galleries was a challenge now. His three-year bargain with Erica and the Fates would be up next March and then – and then unless he could sell more of his art, he'd have to look for work. His father had suggested that given the state of the economy he might start searching now. But that made no sense when so many others were out there looking for jobs. By spring next year they said, the people who wrote about markets and money said, it would be better.

And right now he had to focus on Candace. She was missing and he feared for her.

The police had rejected his instant offer to search. It was too soon. First thing in the morning, they would be glad of help, they said, but the darkness must be left to them. They were in charge of the night. They made that clear. And in any case, his sister-in-law, they implied, had, probably, simply left her husband. Happens all the time.

Erica said, "I think that's enough."

He pushed the mound of orange shreds into the bowl with raisins and mayonnaise and washed the grater.

"Cabbage?"

"No."

He put his hand on her shoulder and she touched it with the hot spatula.

"Ouch."

"Sorry."

She still admired him, he knew, and defended him from the slighting comments of her family. But compared to love, admiration was the silver medal. He hadn't yet been given the chance to stand on top of the podium and look down at the cheaper metals on either side. He liked, though, standing here in the kitchen, close to Erica, mixing the salad, knowing the kids were in the house, safe. On many days it was enough.

"I think we should be out there looking," he said.

"Where? North? South? To the lake?"

He wished she hadn't mentioned the lake. It was deep and cold.

"Burgers are ready."

"Wash your hands, kids."

Erica turned from the stove and smiled at him. He wanted to shake her and shout, Love me. I am lovable. But she would only have replied, I do love you, silly, because she didn't really know what true love was. Scars from her childhood had never fallen away.

She was mistrustful. Unafraid physically but an emotional coward. Too harsh a word, that. She touched up her blonde hair now and was no longer a slim girl but a lovely woman. Magically ripe. He smiled back at her. "Candace will be fine," he said.

Their son and daughter came into the kitchen, the one tall and usually cheerful, the other small and sad, both a little worried now. He had failed to keep the monsters at bay.

Erica passed a rare hamburger to him, half a well-done one

to Tannis, and for herself and the boy, a medium one each. The lonely half would be up for grabs.

"Carrot salad again, Dad?"

"There are tomatoes."

"When are we going to do something?" BJ asked.

"We have to wait till morning."

"But she might be lying bleeding."

"Like in one of your paintings, Dad."

"After dinner, I want to know you've done your homework and then we'll play Monopoly," Erica said.

Four eyes turned to her. Was this a kind of madness? BJ wanted to play "Mountain Men" on his computer and Tannis had to email all her friends every night and especially now when she had an important story to tell.

"Your mom wants us to have a family evening so that we don't sit about worrying, each one of us on his own," Simon said. "We all want to know what's happened to Aunt Candace. And it may be that she's perfectly fine and has left a message that got lost somewhere. So there's no point, till we know what's actually happened, in imagining bad things. It's 6:30 now. I'll clear up while you finish your homework and Mom will set the game out. We'll start around 7:30 and whoever's richest at 9 is the winner."

"This is so dumb," Tannis said.

"And I'll make popcorn."

Simon realized he was moving the dishes quietly as though he were in a place of mourning. The whole house felt grey. He could see Erica opening up the board, stacking piles of coloured money and putting the tokens at the starting point. A tiny car for BJ, a silver bear for Tannis, a boat for herself and the frog for him. But there was a mist in front of him. I am afraid, he said half-aloud, and he wanted to go and paint his fear to allay the demons before they got to Candace.

As he put the last of the dishes into the machine and pressed the numbers on the panel, the phone rang. It was his mother saying that she and his dad would come by for the children in half an hour.

•

Around and above her Candace imagined armies marching, tanks rumbling. It was war. No human voice reached her, no insignificant cry for help could echo when the machines of war rolled into action. She, a prisoner, was entitled to be treated according to the rules of the game. Water and plain food were her due, her right. Rice perhaps or oatmeal, hard bread. There would be complaints when she got free. Escaping was encouraged. She tried to kneel on her good leg so that she could stand up, but the pain made her cry out and she rolled back onto her behind. Her hand was wet. She licked her fingers and reality returned.

No sound of any kind enlivened the muddy, watery hole. I'm alone. There's a possibility of rats. If anything could push her up the sides of this slippery pit, it would be the appearance of a small brown creature with sharp teeth and beady eyes.

"No," she said, and began to cry. "What if the place fills with my tears?"

"Crying won't help." That was Dad reading aloud to her and Erica. "Crying won't help, you know."

Pray, Mom had said. Her head above them as they lay in their twin beds turning from side to side, crying. We must all pray. But praying wouldn't put the bear together again. *In the morning, I will sew it up.* But it was night. And in the dark, with her flashlight, Erica had led the way into the garden and they had buried the two halves of the toy tied together with ribbon. Both had said sorry to the bear as it lay there and then had taken turns to cover it with soil.

The hole she had scrabbled out was too small for her hand. A pebble came loose. She wiped it on her coat and put it in her mouth and sucked on it. *I am not dead. This is not a grave. This is not a grave.*

•

Jack tried Candace's phone again but there was no answer. He walked past Hair Today and then backtracked. The salon was still open. Maybe she'd had an appointment. The window was partly obscured by rows of bottles and canisters. A woman was staring out at him. Another was wrapping strands of a customer's hair in pieces of foil. It wasn't Candace's head, not her hair. But he might as well check. He went inside.

"My wife, Candace Wilson. Did she have an appointment today? She's not home yet. I wondered."

Oh wrong, wrong question! He should have walked on.

In their six eyes, he was instantly an abuser, a harasser, the pursuer of a woman who no doubt had bruises all over her body and had fled to a sanctuary but not in time.

Angrily, he said, "Look, I'm worried about her. I need help."

Wrong words again. They likely thought psychiatric help.

The receptionist looked in the book on the desk.

"Actually she had an appointment at lunchtime but didn't make it. Didn't let us know. There's a charge of fifty percent."

"I'll tell her."

"Maybe you should go to the police," the customer said.

"I expect there's a message at home, by now," he replied and left the salon as fast as he could without running.

The particulars taken down at the police station were as follows: Eyes brown. Shoulder length brown hair with some light streaks. Height, five feet seven inches. Slim. And before you ask, there were/are no problems in our marriage. Except that she's gone missing. And that's why I'm here.

He knew the desk officer was marking Candace down as a

happy runaway and himself as some sexually inadequate loser or worse, much worse.

Marak wasn't there, only the sergeant at the desk, an older guy he didn't know.

Defiantly he said, "We've been happily married for years."

The guy nodded and smiled. Bastard had seen everything. Heard everything. And had a knowing look on file for every goddam event: lost souls, purses, cars. Possibly on the take besides. And had the nerve to guide him to the door with a hand on his shoulder, saying, "It's too early to look. She'll turn up." *Under the floorboards of your house, right!*

The municipal hall was an ugly stone structure marked as a heritage site for no better reason than that it had stood where it was for ninety years. One day, someone would find a use for the space, maybe set fire to the building and put up something fine and modern. He hurried into the meeting room on the ground floor, trying to smile as if there was nothing at all wrong. And there probably wasn't. He had to believe that. Candace is fine. She's okay, he told himself as he glanced round at the seven city councillors: Grumpy, Harpy, Sleazy, Doc, Whiny, Dopey and Gruesome, aka Yuri, Gloria, Bill, old Rogers, Robert DiLazlo, silent Briony and the mayor.

"Jack," Dan said. "Thanks for coming over."

"Right."

"So what we're thinking, and we're all agreed here," he paused.

Get on with it. Every day those machines are idle is costing the company.

"Our thinking is that given the units that are sold already and the plans for the new gym taking shape in expectation of custom, not to mention the expansion of the hardware store, you should be able to go ahead."

There was slight applause from round the table.

Jack nodded waiting for the *but*.

"One thing. The concern of some of the local people including your own sister-in-law and her husband has to be addressed in some way."

Addressed to hell!

"The problem there partly," Jack said, "as Gary told them at the public meetings, is that they see the noise and the disruption but they can't imagine the finished houses, nice gardens and the golf course."

DiLazlo said, "Some people hate golf."

"Then they don't have to play," the mayor responded.

"And the golf course, "Jack repeated. "The other matter that they don't seem to see is that the Ben Henrikson High School will be allowed to remain open. You know that. We've had meetings with the school board. They'll wait to look at the numbers of kids moving in before they take action."

"And if none do?"

"A, that's highly unlikely. And B, if none do then they'll close it in a year as planned. No big deal. And C, we're creating jobs here at a time when some people are getting desperate for work."

Yuri had to speak. He was twitching like a kid who's put his hand up in the classroom and needs to pee. Smart and mean, wearing a sweater that didn't come from Sears and a silver cowboy buckle on the belt round his jeans, he leaned forward to deliver what he figured was a right hook.

"You know me, Jack. I tell it like it is."

Like you wish.

"We've looked at this from every angle and it comes down to trees."

It comes down to dollars and cents. That's what it comes down to, you fool.

"I understand that, Yuri."

"So," Gloria Pavel said. "That nice stand by the water. It gives shade to the picnic tables and it's very pretty. A lot of us have great memories of evenings – I might say nights – in that spot."

"Not all of us had your – advantages," Dan put in.

Gloria glared at him and said, "Some of us know how to appreciate nature."

"I do recall," Briony began.

"They have to come down anyway," Jack said before they could start on reminiscences of teen sex under the birches. "We got an arborist out from the university to take a look. He says they're diseased. They're old for that type of tree. Won't last more than a year or two anyway. And for every one we take down, we will plant two."

The phone jiggled in his hand. He looked at the screen. Blank!

"Where are you?" He knew he was shouting. There was no answer. The light on his phone went out. The battery had gone.

"Geez," he said. "Dammit to hell."

All seven of them were looking at him. Well the whole town would know by tomorrow if she hadn't returned.

"My wife," he said, "appears to be missing. Didn't turn up at work today. Hasn't been home."

There was a moment of silence.

Dan said, "We could've called this off. You must be worried sick, Jack."

Gloria looked at him with appalling pity. She would be on the side of those who thought that, at last, Candace had come to her senses. Yuri would have taken him in handcuffs to the cops that instant. Briony touched his hand in a kindly way that made him want to hug her.

"I didn't know till a couple of hours ago that she hadn't been at the office. So, you know, I don't know what to think. The police said to give it twenty-four hours. She's not a child."

"We are all children in this violent age," old Rogers said. "Vulnerable. Cut down like wheat. Sinners."

"I wanted to come," Jack said, "because you've all put in a lot of work on this. You want to do what's best for the town and so do I. We've had the public meetings and the general feeling is now in favour. We all love this place. But I don't think it can continue to exist without expansion. It needs an injection of twenty-first-century growth."

Gloria said, "It's not some twee little theme park, Jack. It's a hopping town with a population of nearly eighty thousand." Then, because she'd spoken sharply to a man in distress, she added, "Sorry. You must be out of your mind."

"It's only a day," Dan said. "She could have gone shopping maybe."

"More'n likely," Yuri added. "It's what they do."

Jack made his way to the door. The mix of sympathy and speculation was more than he could stand.

"I'll get the men back to work, Monday, and email the arborist's report to you, Dan."

"I appreciate that, Jack."

"Hey wait a minute," Yuri called out.

"When we plant the trees, Yuri, you can come to the ceremony. Get your picture in the paper. We'll let you hold a spade."

Dan said, "And if there are protesters on the site on Monday?"

We'll mow the fuckers down.

Their murmurings followed him down the hall: She'll be home when you get back. Don't worry. My wife once went to the Island and forgot to tell me. Let us know if there's anything.

As he walked to the car, Bill Janson ran after him and put a hand on his arm.

"Let me know if I can help."

"Thanks." Jack knew that gratitude was going to be his watchword until Candace turned up. There would be offers and kindnesses and even, he feared, casseroles. Bill was still smiling at him. "I'll call you tomorrow."

He turned the corner and looked back. Bill was doing a little jig in the sidewalk. Once they got back to work on the site, the man would be earning good money again. Enough at any rate to pay down his casino debts. The casino! That sinkhole should never have been allowed, so close to town. Flashing lights down the highway brought people from Vancouver, from Abbotsford, from places and homes where there often wasn't enough money to begin with. They'd allowed that and were kicking up all this fuss about an asset to the town like Pine View. He and Candace had gone to protest meetings about the casino but money won. And chance. And hope. The great hope of the big life-changing win.

He drove out to the site, still and dark as it was. Some instinct made him get out of the car and walk round to check the safety gate. The first foundation holes had been dug two months ago before the antis had insisted on another delay. Unseasonable warm weather had stopped them filling with water. But it was time now. He imagined the houses that would stand there, the families that would enjoy living so close to the lake. They were all happy families. Trees would be replanted and flourish. The gardens and the fountain over there would attract visitors. The whole project was a model of eco-sensitive development.

He heard a cry. A seagull? A crow? There was nobody around. The gate was locked. The site was secure. No way she could have got inside there. Candace was surely home by now. There'd be a message on the land line or else she'd be in the kitchen wanting to know why he hadn't put the lasagne in the oven. And he would try not to yell, "Where the hell have you been?" like some angry parent.

●

Candace knew she was smiling. She was describing every detail of her adventure to the men and women in the office. *I heard someone call out and then I turned and took a step back.* They would be gathered round her. Celia would find a felt-tipped pen and they would all sign the cast on her leg. Perhaps they'd have bought her flowers and would take turns to do little chores for her, fetching coffee, going to the printer. She'd have to be careful not to put on weight.

The walls of my cell were rough. People in dark uniforms came and went. No. That wasn't true. No one had come and gone, and if she stretched her arms out she could feel both sides of the space. Therefore it was perhaps five feet wide. She spent a few minutes trying to turn that figure into metres.

She wanted to close her eyes, but pain was keeping her awake. For no reason, the image of her mother strutting round the house naked saying, "Today is my birthday and this is my birthday suit," flicked across the walls of the cell like a TV image. She declared many days in the year her birthday and there was always the dread of finding a pubic hair in the food.

Her fear of eating had made both parents look at her with alarm. But for the cost and the fact that she managed to sustain her weight of around a hundred and twenty pounds, they would have sent her to a psychiatrist. The other reason was the fear that she would sit there on the doctor's couch and say, "My mother walks round the house naked."

After all it's a small town, she said to herself. But not that small. Where the hell is everybody?

"Everybody!" she yelled.

It would soon be time to turn on the TV to watch the news at ten.

Staring upwards she could see one star. A single star to wish on. Get me out of here, God, please. I will be good. Now I have to pee again and the place will stink. It stinks already.

This is what fouling your own nest means. Think of something cheerful. They will come soon with flashlights and a ladder and warm blankets.

Last night she'd watched a documentary about a young teacher at a poor school getting a choir together to go to a competition in China. The effort they made. The setbacks, the uniforms designed by themselves. When the students finally got on the plane to Beijing, tears were rolling down her cheeks.

When I get out of here, God, I will build a school in Namibia. She imagined the outline of Africa but couldn't pinpoint Namibia.

She bent forward to pick up another pebble and the pain in her leg made her scream. But no one came. She drew herself in to save her resources, folded her arms over her chest and put her head down and murmured, "They will come soon, they will come soon."

•

"I'm an acolyte," Erica murmured to her dream husband, Charles, who would never allow himself to be called Charlie or Chuck. Especially not Chuck. "My life is less. Others are reaching top places and I will always be half way up the staircase to success. Unless I come into money or win the lottery, the store will not become a boutique with branches across Canada from Vancouver to Halifax. Even a branch in the Interior, maybe Kelowna, would be a start. Tourists come through there. A different crowd."

Simon called to her, "Should I make coffee?"

"No thanks," she shouted back. "I need wine."

She put on her black underwear. The kids had gone off happily with Simon's parents. It wasn't the second Friday but this was an unusual time and the old folks thought it was the best way they could help. The Ghills Lake grapevine was already at work: Candace Wilson is missing.

Tannis and JB loved the chaos of the Belchuk household. Granny B. always had her hands in some kind of dough, either clay or pastry depending on the time of day. She'd modeled their heads and allowed them to play in her studio. Their grandfather cooked Mickey Mouse pancakes for breakfast and told them jokes that were older than time.

She'd never allowed the kids to stay overnight with her own mother. Not that Mother was a monster, she'd only behaved monstrously now and then and there was no calendar to predict her better days. Was she pushed over the edge by unfulfilled ambition, sexual deprivation or a brain tumour as the doctor suggested too late?

"Charles," she said. "How do I look?"

The mirror responded, "Wow but shouldn't you be thinking of your sister who might be lying dead in a ditch or suffering on some nearby roadside?"

"Sure," she replied, "but we're alone tonight and this is a rare chance for unbridled lust. And Candace will turn up any moment, a big smile on her fat face, saying, 'You didn't get my message?'"

Simon hugged her and said, "You must be worried, sweetheart." She pressed herself close to him and he stroked her hair.

She dimmed the light and lit the candles in the living room.

"Think of history," he said as he handed her a glass of wine. "Candy's previous behaviour. Let's go through it."

"Okay. Well. She did once run away from home because of something Mother did but she didn't go far. Didn't miss a meal even. She hasn't seemed depressed lately. I mean they argued but who doesn't? And everybody in town knows about her affair if you could even call it that."

"Jack must have been angry with Cosgrave."

The phone rang. Erica waited and heard Simon say, "Thank you. Yes. We're doing all we can. I'll let you know."

As soon as he'd hung up, it began to ring again.

"Damn Alys Steen. She must have texted the entire world. Ignore it."

"We can't, Errie."

"Yes," he said to the caller. "Thank you. We're hoping to hear from her very soon."

When he sat back, he sighed. "There has to be some clue to where she's gone. There usually is. Somebody knows something. Has seen something."

"Well no one's saying anything. We've asked everybody we know that she knows. Jack and the police are onto it and I don't think there's a thing we can do right now, Simon."

"All right. But I feel bad sitting here like this when she could be anywhere. In danger. In a mess. Frightened. I'd pray if I knew who to pray to. What I'm wondering is, did she go over to the site when she found the dentist was out and maybe look for Jack? It's pretty deserted at the moment and all that machinery. Anybody could've been hanging around. And she's not that big. She should've taken one of those martial arts classes, and you should too, honey."

She leaned against him and let him comfort her, aware that he was saying all the things she should have said herself. He stroked her hair and said, "If you ever disappeared, I'd search every house, look in every cellar and attic. I'd run up and down the streets shouting your name."

She pressed her body to his and put her hand on his thigh.

He stood up, letting her fall back, and began to pace.

"This is a nice town," he said. "It's a peaceful place. I know the dealers are moving this way from the city but still it's pretty safe. And the cops found that huge grow op last month. But there hasn't been a murder, intended murder, for six years, and that was bikers killing each other. And now, it's as if a monster has invaded and is stalking us." He was silent then, probably seeing images. Erica knew the signs.

Everything, especially things he felt deeply about, incidents, emotions, got processed in some kind of mental blender and became a subject for his art.

The phone rang. "Yes, thank you," he repeated. "The police are organizing a search tomorrow morning if she hasn't turned up then."

She went into the kitchen and poured herself another, larger, glass of wine. There'd be no sex tonight. Candace, taker of toys and candy, had done it again.

"But I am worried," she said to herself. If Candace were dead? Tears came to her eyes and she sat down at the counter. A funeral. People back to the house. Whose house? This one obviously. A wall of sympathy like that tsunami drowning villages in Samoa would wash over them. She imagined them swimming in it, trying to keep their heads above water. They couldn't invite the mourners to their father's house. Not since he'd gone crazy and glued up his coasters. And Candace and Jack lived in a kind of planned discomfort as if they didn't want people to stay too long and would prefer to have no visitors at all. Yet they'd had money before Jack had invested it in steel and concrete. Anyway, he couldn't cope with arranging food, getting in wine at such a time. It would all be down to her and Simon. We'll do it right for you, Sister. But hey! Candace would turn up later tonight. Maybe tomorrow morning early, wondering why they'd all been so worried. Laughing perhaps. And they'd feel like idiots for making a fuss. Or maybe, maybe, years from now they'd find her body in a place close by. A place they should have searched and had walked past time and again. She shuddered and fear overcame her.

●

The house was still empty. Her coat and boots were not in the hall. Jack turned on all the lights.

He put the dish in the microwave guiltily. He had no right to hunger. He had no right to drink but poured himself a shot of

Scotch. The world might expect a headless chicken reaction from him, a rushing about, a wailing and gnashing of teeth, but it was too soon for that. He had to believe that the next footstep he heard in the house would be hers. *I left a message. I sent an email. I asked Celia to call. I assumed...*

The cheese on top of the pasta had turned to rubber. He switched on the TV and saw '12 hours missing' written across the screen and jumped up. But it was the show about the FBI searching for lost people. A story. His life was about to fold into a story in which the first forty-eight hours were crucial and the word "victim" came into play. His heart began to pound. He was afraid, afraid to think.

The phone rang. He pounced on it.

"Yes?"

"Am I speaking to John Wilson?"

"Yes. Yes."

"Hello. How are you today? My name is Emma. Last year you donated fifty dollars to the firefighters' burn fund."

"Fuck off," he shouted and threw the phone across the room.

He didn't want to get through this by drinking, but he gulped the whisky and poured another glass.

Calm. Calm. He was talking to himself as if he were a dog. Be still, Spot.

The handset had come apart and the battery was loose. He put it back together and listened for a ring tone. Nothing.

He went upstairs to bring the other phone down from Candace's bedside table.

Books. What was she reading? She'd tried to tell him last night about some brilliant insight and he'd told her to shut up, he wanted to sleep. Now, he would have listened, should have listened, will always listen in future.

Three books and a magazine. The top one was called *Highways to Heaven*. Had she, without him noticing, taken up with some damn fool religion and gone off to a crazy cult group expecting a kind of rapture? He turned the pages of the book gingerly as if a demon might leap out at him. The photograph on the cover was of a wide road going off to nowhere. *When you drive from San Francisco to Los Angeles...* And further on, a picture of huge rocks. *Leaving Portrush, you might think...*

A travel book! So she was planning a trip? Trying to tell him where she wanted to go and he'd said, "Shut up."

The other two books were fiction, one a mystery, the other a copy of *Moby Dick* she'd been trying to finish for years. And *Gourmet* magazine. The road book was the only one with any kind of a clue to it, but he wasn't going to mention it to anyone. The air was already full of conclusions for people to draw on at will.

He picked up *Moby Dick.* It was a paperback with a few black-and-white photos in the middle, one of a ghastly, tattooed, shrunken head. *'Against the wind he now steers for the open jaw,' murmured Starbuck to himself...*

Jack picked out a few more lines and wondered why she'd begun the novel in the first place.

And wondered. Wondered where she was. Where are you, my love? I will listen. He took the book downstairs with him. When the doorbell rang, he took it with him, clutching it as if it were a talisman and Candace would be standing on the doorstep.

FOUR

He woke up hearing her voice. She'd called to him in his dream. She was in a strange house, trapped. Animals that looked like stuffed toys were barking at her and she was barking back. But her bark had an echo, his name. He hated the hollowness of it. There was only an echo if there was empty space. If there was empty space.

It was six o'clock in the morning. He'd been in bed less than four hours. He had a shower and then pulled on his pants and a T-shirt and went downstairs. He looked at the grounds in the coffee pot and thought that there was a lot to be said for instant. Instant any damn thing. He cleaned out the cone, put in a new filter, threw some beans into the basket and turned the machine on. He opened the front door but the *Echo* came late on Sundays. But this was not Sunday. Only Saturday. A month of time seemed to have gone by. He held back from thinking till he had a mug of coffee in his hand. While he was waiting, he wiped the counter, checked the dates on the milk carton and the juice. The machine was making a strange sound. He'd forgotten the water.

He took his juice into the living room. This space is fine the way it is, he thought as he sat in the red upholstered chair. Simon's picture, bought by Candace in a fit of family affection, had grown on him. At first he'd thought she was mad. *Loving,* it was called: Two naked figures entwined round a globe-shaped map of the universe. Green, blue, brown for mountains, shaded the male and female bodies. Jack saw it as a statement about the world and the need to accept others however hard that might be. He'd never said this to Simon in case he was wrong.

He tried to make sense of his dream. Animals. Spaces. Echoes. No way she could have fallen into the foundation. It was secure and besides, she could have probably climbed out on the bit of scaffolding that was already in place. Messy, it would have ruined her clothes, but she could have got out and, anyway, couldn't have got in. Containers. Storage lockers. Cellars didn't usually echo and besides, why would she be in someone's house. Pedophiles, who should all be jailed for life, sometimes kept children in their houses, hiding them. But Candace was a grown woman. She was fit and could have fought back unless...

He heard the thud of the paper as it landed on the step and went to fetch it. He flicked through the pages looking for her name but it would be Sunday before people read, *Candace Wilson, wife of Jack Wilson, partner at Streicher and Wilson, has not been seen since she left home to go to the dentist's on Friday morning. If you have any information, please contact the police.*

By then she would be back. All the same, the imagined words dug into his soul. Responsibility for Candace's well-being had passed into the hands of others. Who would come forward? Has not been seen. Left home. Had she left home? The truth, when it came out, could be unwelcome.

The school board wanted to ban a kids' book that had the word 'breasts' in it. The man caught climbing into a basement window said he was looking for a place to sleep. Number of homeless increased since same time last year. We are building homes but not, alas, for the homeless. Maybe one unit could be given over to street people. He could hear Gary yelling, "You out of your mind?"

He turned the page and saw something he hadn't been looking for but feared. *A woman was attacked on Giles Road in the early hours of yesterday.* They were loose. All kinds of goddam men who struck out at weaker people, at women, at kids, at gays, were prowling the streets of his town.

He threw the paper down and got up and looked outside. He

put on his jacket and boots and went to the car and drove to the site. Had he locked up the house? He couldn't recall and did it matter now?

I'm not afraid of the dark. But this dark held evil. He checked padlocks on the gate and shook the fence.

"Come to make sure?"

Jack held back a scream. "What the hell?"

The hooded figure of Death had come for him.

He recognized Bill.

"What do you mean, make sure?"

"That the site's secure. What d'you think I meant?"

But both of them knew and Jack shrank away.

"Yeah. I was rattling the gate. I can't help thinking there might be a gap."

"We've checked and re-checked, Jack."

"So what are you doing here at this hour?"

"Same as you, I guess. I woke up thinking where she could be. And I wanted to check one or two things. Come on. Let's go make some coffee. It's freezing."

In the trailer, they looked over the worksheets but without paying much attention.

"Years ago," Bill said, "Mandy wanted to go to the Bahamas for a couple of weeks. I said no, we had to wait till we'd got a bit more put away. I begin to think you have to seize the day in case there isn't a tomorrow."

"That's not making me feel better."

"Sorry, man. Right. Well there'll be no vacation now till the building's up. The men are happy. It looked like there'd be no Christmas there for a while." Bill stopped talking as if he realized that with every word he was putting his foot in it.

Jack looked at him, a kind man about his own age. Moved from the States with his parents in the seventies. Hated working indoors. Gave up on architecture in year two. A practical, dependable man who liked to make things happen.

And Jack thought that he might have loved this man if love in that sense were permissible. Love in the sense of deep friendship. There was no way he could use the word or even express his feelings without being misunderstood.

He put his hand on the other man's hand and said, "Thank you for sticking with the project."

"Hey, I might want a marble countertop in my bathroom one day. See you Monday."

A knock on the side of the trailer startled him. All Jack could see from the window was the top of a wool hat. He opened the door carefully.

"Alys? What are you doing here?"

"I often go for a walk early."

"Come in and have some coffee. There's no milk."

"I don't take milk, thanks."

He waited. She'd come for a reason. He wasn't sure, as he handed her the mug, that he wanted to know what it was.

"I just want to say, Jack, I'm sorry."

He waited again but wasn't prepared for the woman to throw herself on her knees in front of him. He leapt away. She pursued him on her knees across the floor.

"I'm just so sorry," she whimpered trying to catch hold of his legs. "I should have called your cell on Friday morning. It's my fault. My fault. To tell you the truth."

"Alys! For God's sake get up." He was backed up against the desk.

"To tell you the truth, I was glad she wasn't there. I wanted the Driver account for myself. I never thought. I just thought she'd gone home after the dentist's and taken a Tylenol or something. But she would have called me. I know. And now she's probably dead. And it's all my fault."

He shook the woman off and she lay on the trailer floor, whimpering. Bill came in and looked at both of them.

Jack took hold of him and whispered, "She's having hysterics."

"Ah," Bill said. "Then..."

He moved to the tap and filled a mug with water. Alys screamed when the water hit her face.

"Bloody women," he said as she ran outside, crying. "You'll have to watch out, Jack. They'll be after you now. You're vulnerable, like a wounded deer, and they'll come to feed off your flesh."

Jack shuddered. "What did you come back for?"

"I saw the tracks of a predator. I have this sixth sense."

They laughed but not for long. Both of them quickly recalled that it wasn't a time for laughter. But Jack patted Bill on the shoulder and thanked him.

"I wanted to say I heard about the search and I'll be there," Bill said. "Don't worry about Alys. She's okay really. She's a desperate woman right now, that's all. See you at the school."

Jack followed Bill out and drove home. Desperate? What had made Alys Steen desperate? Was Candace desperate? Erica? His mother? Didn't they know that men could be desperate too?

●

It was daylight again. Her throat was dry. Candace picked up the bottle and took the cap off and, as she did so, it slipped from her hand. Quickly, she dipped her finger in the water and put it on her tongue. It wasn't enough. They must come. Where were they? Food she could do without. Sleep too. But water. There was a Kleenex in her pocket. She reached over and dipped it in the pool by her knee and then put it in her mouth and sucked. It tasted of mud but it would do. She must ration her calls for help. It was maybe time right now. Saturday. Kids might be going to play by the lake.

"Help," she called. "It's me, Candace Wilson. And I am very

cold. Please. Help!"

There was a clunk beside her. Something had been thrown down.

"Hey," she said. "You. Get me out of here. Right now."

It was her bag. The big old leather bag that held her life had been released. She groped about in it, shoes, the Driver file, make-up case, wallet and, at last, her BlackBerry. She pushed the keys. No light came on. She had no tears left. There was such cruelty in this: To give her a dead lifeline. And the new, streamlined laptop that connected her to the universe was sitting on her desk at the office.

•

In her right mind, Candace would definitely have left a note. Erica was sorry she'd spoken sharply to Jack. He must be distraught. Possibly guilty? Feeling guilty at any rate. Candace had complained that he was spending all his time on the new plans. Not surprising considering the huge investment involved. And there were plenty of people in town who thought he'd bitten off more than he could chew. Had she complained to him once too often? She drove the words away, that kind of thinking could spread and lead to danger. She keyed in his number.

"Jack, dear, I'll come round when I've dropped the kids off. I have to pick them up from Simon's mom's."

"I'm going out to the search and then to the office."

"You should be waiting in case she calls."

"I've got my cell. I can't just sit around. I have to be doing something."

"I expect you know best. Let me know the minute you hear anything. And come to supper. I insist."

Simon had gone to join the search. She'd wanted to go too but he'd said it would be hard for her and anyway one of them had to drive the kids. She felt, stupidly, left out of the action and still mad because he'd stayed out so late last night when she needed comfort.

My sister took my toys. My best toys.

That day when Candace had dressed Grizzly Bear in a frilly pink skirt and made him look ridiculous, Erica had screamed at her. Kids argued all the time. How could that argument at that moment on that day have driven their mother so far over the edge. Candace dancing round singing, "I'm the Queen of Ethiopia and you're a shrub." Erica hitting out at her and yelling, "Give him back to me." The memory of their mother wielding the knife still stopped her breath. Both of them had shrieked but too late.

I do love my sister.

As far as she knew, Candace hadn't ever talked to a therapist about her mother. And neither had she. To Simon, she'd told everything as if her childhood and that incident in particular would explain away all her faults and shortcomings forever. For weeks he wouldn't let her see his painting. And then it had sold at a local show. *The cloven teddy bear.* A reporter had said it showed a warped imagination, a damaged psyche, referring of course to the artist. Simon hadn't included the pumpkin that was on the kitchen table that day twenty-three years ago. If only their dad had been there, he would have been carving the jack-o'-lantern instead of their mother. He'd always said it was a man's job.

And if only Candace had given the bear back to her when she asked.

But none of that explained her absence now.

Okay, Sister. We will look for you.

She called Glynis and said she would come in to work after all. There was nothing she could do. Sitting around at home watching the phone would lead to desperate imaginings. She tried to be calm. When she picked the kids up, she thanked her in-laws and said no, there was nothing yet but she was sure they'd hear soon.

She dropped BJ off at the rink then took Tannis to her friend

Sam's house. She and Sam were to make a map of the town for school, showing its principal features. They would mark in Jack and Gary's blasted development there by the lake. For better or worse it was part of the town now. And although she'd protested against it, she knew that it had to be completed, otherwise it would remain a reproachful eyesore. A great muddy hole. Sometimes though there was divine retribution. For heaven's sake! What was she thinking! God, even if she believed in Him, had nothing to do with their little lives. She parked the van in a small car space and hoped the driver on the other side had room to open his door but didn't bother to check. At a time like this, there was also, possibly, a relaxation of the rules.

Erica liked it best when the store was closed and she could go around checking the stock, folding sweaters, enjoying peaceful moments among the clothes. The lightweight pantsuits that would have to go into the November sale might as well be marked down now. She took down a black one and without thinking held it against herself, then hurriedly put it back. Harriet Albrey had called about the dark tan check suit in the window. The green skirt with darker jacket could go in its place. And maybe move that yellow sweater out altogether. Yellow wasn't everybody's colour.

She was proud of the display. The window was hers, her creation. Dry leaves, she'd said to Glynis, were ordinary. Pumpkins were obvious. Swathes of brown and orange material she'd borrowed from Buttons and Bows gave a sense of fall and a promise of warmth and would soon be changed for Christmas glitter and the inevitable red and green. She despised elves.

Glynis held her against her soft body, wool of her sweater tickling her neck, as she asked about Candace.

"I'm okay," Erica said finally and drew away.

"No you're not. You should go home."

"I want to be here. The kids are out. Simon's searching. I can tidy the racks. I need to check the coats."

"We've got to get a better system," Glynis said. "I swear Betty Bright put that blue sweater on and walked out with it. She was wearing that big coat of hers. Could've put three sweaters under it."

"We should use security tags," Erica said. "Why won't you?"

"It's a small place. Do we want people to think we don't trust them?"

"Yes!"

"I'd rather write off a couple of things than create that kind of suspicion."

"But you suspect her anyway. And she's not the only one."

"At least people are spending again, looking for bargains but spending. They say in a recession women still want to look nice and go on buying jewellery and shoes and getting their hair done."

"Let's hope they start coming in here."

The bell chimed and Glynis went to hold the door all the way open to allow Verlyn Cosgrave to wheel herself into the store. She had her camera round her neck as usual and wanted, as Erica knew, not to buy but to scrounge information.

"I've just heard about Candace, Erica. Jack must be out of his mind," she said. "I know I would be. Unless, of course. And then. I just wanted to say that when I called her Thursday about the book group, she seemed a little anxious. Not quite herself. But how can anyone know?"

"I've got some new shirts in just your size and colour," Glynis said.

"They're a good price too," Erica added.

They stood over Verlyn like two hawks, giving nothing, willing her to leave.

"I'm going to wait for your sale next month," she said. "I really came to tell you, Erica, that I know how you must be feeling. When someone goes off like this you always have to ask yourself, was it something we did? Something lacking in her life? It's sometimes our nearest who don't see the signs."

"She was perfectly fine. Is fine. And has probably left a message somewhere that we've missed. She often goes to see her friend in Vancouver at this time of year."

"We don't always know, do we, what's seething underneath that calm surface. She was seen to kick at the door of the dentist's surgery. There must be anger there. Possibly rage."

Erica was saved from pushing the woman out on to the street by the entrance of Hayden.

"There you are, sweetheart," he said to Verlyn. "Not spending all my hard-earned cash, I hope. Erica. How're you doing? You're right to come to work. There's nothing to be done at these times except wait and, of course, hope. Hope for the best. We're thinking about you, you know."

"I was just saying," his wife went on. "You have to come at these things from a psychological point of view. Was she in distress? Had she gone to someone for comfort, for advice?"

Hayden took hold of the handles of the wheelchair and propelled it out the door.

"If there's anything we can do," he said.

And Verlyn echoed, "Anything!"

"I suppose she can't help it," Erica said.

"She can help it, "Glynis replied. "Just because she's handicapped now, doesn't mean she can say what she likes. You'd think it might have made her saintly, the accident, but it seems to have gone the other way. And you must be out of your mind with worry."

"They're searching. It's just hard to know where to look. We have to think she'll turn up soon."

"That Verlyn, pretends she's birdwatching, taking photos. We know what she's watching. The whole damn town is what she's watching."

The doorbell rang again. It was going to be a hectic morning.

Some of the customers expressed surprise that Erica was there. Others sought details, offered sympathy. There were six of them in the shop at one time, riffling through racks of slacks and jackets and buying nothing.

Gloria Pavel, eager and important as she was, whispered, "She'll turn up, dear. Just when you least expect it. By the way, I'm looking for something in tweed. A nice jacket."

Betty Bright said, "You're being very brave, Erica. I don't think this is quite my size." She was holding up a skirt in a truly unsuitable shade of red. "But I'll try it on anyway."

"Please don't do up the zipper," Erica told her. "It's too small for you, you fat cow."

She knew then that she'd been absolutely wrong to come to work. Taking her purse from the locked drawer in the back of the counter, she whispered to Glynis and walked out. They could make of it what they would. And they would no doubt have a field day.

She didn't want to go straight home but there was nowhere else for her to go. The town she'd lived in all her life, except for three years at UVic, was suddenly a foreign place. Streets and houses taken for granted had become alien. What language did they speak here? What lurked behind those doors? Who was staring out the blank windows? The only safe place was the lakeshore but it was a cold damp morning. She decided to walk home the long way round. Althea's café was off-limits. All public places were closed to her now. She could hear the words if not the voices. *Candace Wilson has disappeared. What do you think happened? They say he... They say she... And there's her sister. Well they didn't get on. But that's no reason.*

RACHEL WYATT

Candace had been seen walking towards town. She had also been seen at the airport in Vancouver. There was the road and, on the left, the path to the picnic area. The path over the bridge led to the marina. Had her sister sailed away with a buccaneer in his big yacht?

As she went past the arena, Erica looked up at the sign. Ghillies playing a home game tonight. 7:30. BJ would want to go. She wondered where her skates were. A long time ago, reading *Anna Karenina*, she didn't get past the scene where the man Levin was skating with his princess. And he, unlike Simon, was the much better skater of the pair. *Hang on to me.* She'd read that scene over and over and never wanted to go further because there were hints that Kitty's snooty mother was about to spoil the romance. One day, she'd get the novel out of the library and read the rest. She hoped it turned out well for those two skaters. She'd met Simon at the rink, the tall thin stranger in town trying to skate with his toes turned in, fearfully, a real beginner. She'd stopped him from falling and had fallen for his strangeness. His charm. The guy from elsewhere whose parents had moved into town when they retired. A good son, he'd come to check the place out, and stayed on.

The new arena too had stirred up a fight three years ago. *Why spend all that money? The old one's been good enough for thirty years.* But here it was. The Elmer Ives Arena. Opened by Dan Bright last Labour Day. A joy to behold. Modern. Metal and glass. Smooth ice. Perhaps, too, Jack's townhouses...

The stream that ran into the lake, full now, disappeared under the road. She watched the running water for a moment and then turned towards home. Until she could figure out a way to face people around town, she'd be a prisoner, playing patience on the computer, cooking, waiting. *Has anyone seen my sister? Please! I'm going crazy. Candace, come home!*

•

54

The likely places, Jack thought. What about the unlikely? They were to search in all the likely places. But how did they know what those were? Last night, he and Simon, driving morbidly around, not having any idea what they were looking for, had stared through the pickup windows at shadows. They'd stopped at the railway station but there was only one train a day in each direction after October 1 and the office was closed. The bus depot. This woman? Have you seen her? Did she buy a ticket? They turned off the Trans-Canada onto the Coquihalla and glanced to either side as if Candace might have been standing out there all night waiting for a ride, holding up a sign that read, Take me to the Interior. Before they turned back, Jack had got out of the pickup to look along the shoulder. She might have thrown a boot or her bag for a clue as kidnappers bundled her into a trunk. It was hard to tell Simon that it was nonsense because it possibly wasn't. He was the one who should have been panicking and he'd been letting his brother-in-law do it by proxy.

They hadn't got home till two and now, after a few hours of non-sleep, here they were with a group of neighbours, friends, the curious, strangers, a man with a German shepherd, standing in the schoolyard waiting for instructions.

Marak murmured to him that they didn't usually start searching for adults till after forty-eight hours as if beginning now was a big favour. Jack said thank you and wondered whether he should be kneeling down and crying out, Please find my wife. It all seemed distant as if it were happening to someone else in a kind of fog. He was a spectator and didn't want to be here milling about among these staring people who'd gathered on his wife's behalf. There were dozens of them. He tried to count heads and wondered if this was a good number. Did other missing people draw larger crowds? Would he have to thank each one of them separately? Write notes? All of them were wearing raincoats or jackets and a few had on rubber boots and were carrying sticks.

Yuri and Gloria from the Council were there and he could see
Bill with some of the crew, all of them standing about muttering
like crows in a field. Candace's friend, Kathy, came up and put
her arms round him. "I've emailed the rest of the clan, the hikers,"
she told him. "We'll find her."

He caught sight of Alys, the woolly tuque on her head. He
kept away from her. It *was* her fault that a whole day had gone
by before he knew about Candace. Candace. Candy. My wife.
My love?

At last they were called to order and divided into three groups
by the small cop called Berry. Marak addressed them. It wasn't
easy because more people were straggling along to join the crowd.
Twice he had to begin again.

"Thank you all very much for coming here this morning.
When you're searching, go slow and spread out. If you see the
least thing of interest. It could be a shoe. A footprint. A thread
caught on a twig," he said. "You come to one of us. Don't touch
it. You all know which group you're in? Right. Group A go
towards the lake. Group B to the area behind the mall. Group
C around the school. Ms Wilson could simply have fallen somewhere and hurt herself. If you find her, call us. Don't try to
move her.

"This is a narrow search for now but from experience we
know that people are generally found close to home. Officer
Berry will remain here so anything you find can be brought to
her. I'll drive around to the various points. Remember. Every
minute counts."

The guy's watched too many cop shows, Jack thought, and is
making this up as he goes along. He walked for a while with the
others, fanning out, looking up, looking down. They were seekers.
Who would be the one to impress teacher? He and his group
came to the end of the vacant lot. Houses reared up before them.
She could be in a house, taken there by some freak. All windows

held secrets. He wanted to bang on the doors and yell, "Is my wife in there?"

He felt a hand on his shoulder and started.

"Sorry about your wife, Mr. Wilson." It was the clergyman, vicar, priest, whatever he called himself, from St. Michael's, new last year. He'd turned up occasionally at protest meetings as if to represent God.

"Good of you to come and help," Jack said, ready to lash out if the guy mentioned lost sheep.

"Least we can all do."

Jack tried to remember his name and couldn't so he said, "Thank you, Vicar." And hoped the title wasn't offensive.

"We'll pray for her tomorrow. And, of course, every day."

The man was maybe his age, nice face, sincere look. A believer but not one of those with a sickening smile. Jack shook his hand.

"You'll be welcome in our House," the clergyman said, "if you want to join us in prayer. My name's Reaver. Robert Reaver. You were a grade ahead of me at school. You won't remember."

Jack remembered. This was the weedy kid they'd teased because he couldn't throw a ball straight or ever get his stick onto the puck. Kid they'd driven to tears sometimes.

He felt a mixture of shame, guilt and anger. In his time of weakness here was the despised nerd Robby Reaver offering him love.

"Thank you, Reaver," he said. "Everything helps. Every little thing."

His heart was ripped apart and again he was having to be gracious.

"Well, Wilson," the Reverend replied, "in everything that happens there is some meaning. Something we can learn about our lives." Then he moved off quickly as if sensing danger.

Jack watched him go. They could have predicted, he and his friends, that young Robby would turn out to be a smooth, slimy bastard. He stood still for a moment. He'd judged the guy too quickly, probably unfairly. No doubt for those who needed him and his God, he did a great deal of good. But all the same he was likely a smooth, slimy bastard. And the more he thought about that "something we can learn" the angrier he got. He stopped by a tree and took a deep breath. What was the lesson here except that Candace was gone!

Some of the searchers had turned to go back, staring at the ground, retracing their steps in a zigzag fashion. It began to rain. Jack pulled his hood up and moved away and hoped the others wouldn't think he was afraid of finding something. If they did, they'd be right, in a way. And yet, and yet, as he felt his heart, whatever it was made of, contracting at the thought of what might have happened to her, an irrepressible leaping fish of gladness reminded him that work on the site could begin again in two days time.

Gary and Wayne were to meet him at the office. There was a lot to do before Monday and there were plenty of searchers. It was a futile exercise in any case. He knew they would find nothing. It was too close. If she'd fallen and hurt herself round here, she would have crawled home on her hands and knees. But then... He walked away quickly and heard footsteps behind him.

"Just a word, Mr. Wilson, please."

It was the kid reporter from the *Echo*. Jack resisted the impulse to yell at him. He was a marked man now, watched, a subject for gossip.

"If anyone knows anything about my wife's whereabouts, I hope they'll come forward."

"You don't have any idea where she might be?"

"If I had," he was shouting and lowered his voice, "I would look there. Now please."

The kid was following him saying, "Do you think this has

anything to do with your development? I mean the protests."

Jack got into the truck and drove off.

He imagined a flock of vultures outside his house, microphones, cameras, and suddenly felt sorry for the Queen. The boy went off no doubt to make up a lurid tale.

To settle his thoughts, he made a plan for the rest of the day.

He wouldn't go to Erica's for supper. Guilt would be served with wine: He'd neglected his lovely blame-free wife and now she'd gone God knew where. The second course would be sympathy, and finally there would be a swamping takeover as Erica moved into the space left by her sister and tried to organize his life for him. It was important, he knew, to keep his independence in this situation.

A clear head was key. Focus. Next thing. If, and it was impossible, she had willfully gone away, had she tapped into their joint account? He had to park in front of the laundromat. One day, maybe next year even, they'd be able to tear down this ugly outdated strip mall and build something modern, enticing, enviable. He went to the ATM inside the bank. The amount in the joint account was unchanged from yesterday. She had her own account too and that would have to be checked if she didn't return soon. Credit cards. She'd resisted a debit card. Too easy to steal the numbers, she said. Better call Visa right away. But what if she'd gone away and needed money? Tomorrow would be soon enough to cancel that. This was all new to him. He needed guidance. He needed to look strong.

He marched into the office building as if he and Gary owned it, and they might come close if the townhouses sold and the golf course and – but that was down the road and there were sand traps and Candace had been missing since yesterday morning.

Gary came to meet him and led him past the other offices to his own larger space and closed the door and gave him a hug.

"Jack. I am sorry about Candace. I heard this morning. You should've said. I could have gone to the meeting last night. Had you any idea?"

Jack wanted to walk out then and there.

"Any idea of what?" But he knew what the guy meant.

"Well, that she might up and leave."

"We don't know yet that she has. She might have had an accident. Or —"

He let Gary figure out the or for himself, allowed a measure of dread to settle into the room.

"I'm trying to go on as normal," Jack said. "I need to work or else I'll be hanging around at home smashing up the furniture. Waiting is a killer. Imagining things is a killer."

Why had he used that awful word? "Let's just get on with it."

"Course. Right. Well then. Let's look at these figures. Council gave the go-ahead, right?"

Jack nodded.

"The delay already means we're looking at an extra $500,000. With what's going on." He stopped. "I mean right now, what with, you know, I bet the protesters aren't going to mobilize and lie down in front of the machines."

"Foundations for stage one are half finished," Jack said, ignoring the man's crass comment. "Would've been done by now if it hadn't been for the Save-our-towners."

"Sots I call them."

"They have their points, I guess, even if wrong-headed. And who knows, when they see the houses, some of them might buy in."

"Right. So, ducks in a row and get going. What can we expect by Christmas?"

"We'll only be two months behind, and Bill can maybe get some overtime out of the guys."

"Unpaid?"

"Come on, Gary! "

"We can save on some of the fixtures."

"Not the marble countertops or the bidets."

They checked over the figures, the available men, the one woman, Nicola, who said she'd been working on building sites in Italy since she was fourteen. To show her strength, she'd lifted Gary off the ground and squeezed the breath out of him.

Gary said, "Candace will turn up. It could be amnesia, you know. She's sitting comfortably in a hospital bed wondering who she is while you're worrying your guts out."

"We checked the hospitals."

"I mean further afield. She could've, bewildered, got on to a bus. Could be in Calgary."

"Thanks." *For nothing. For worse than nothing.* "I'll stay here for a while and go over the plans and make some calls for Monday."

As he walked towards his own office, Gary called after him, "The cops'll want to check the site, I guess."

He might as well have thrown a hammer at Jack's head. He stopped still. Why had Gary said that? Did he think the unthinkable? He wanted to go back to him and take him by the throat and say, "Do I look like a murderer?" Instead he went into his own office and sat down and stared at the wall as if, by staring, he could make some magic words appear that would tell him where she was.

Hayden Cosgrave put his head round the door.

"I saw you come in, Jack. I just wanted to say that Verlyn said you should come and have supper with us. It'll be simple, you know. Best she can do."

"That's very kind."

"We eat at seven."

"Thanks. I'll be there."

Hayden stayed in the doorway like a damn wrong-way-up bat, as if there was something he wanted to say but couldn't. As if there was a secret trying to escape. Finally he said, "If there's ever anything you need to get off your chest, remember I'm a lawyer."

Jack said, "I'll see you."

"Right," the bat said, and still hung there.

What was that all about? He didn't need to proclaim his profession. He was Jack's lawyer. All kinds of meaning could be read into that last sentence of his. It was almost a threat. What did the guy know?

"And listen. You really must come to dinner. Verlyn asked especially. She gets a bit stir-crazy. Cabin fever. You know."

He was going to talk about his marital problems.

"I've just remembered. I'm going to my sister-in-law's. But thanks. I appreciate it."

"Tomorrow then. You need to keep your strength up. But she'll be back. Maybe now when you get home. There'll be a call. A friend. Somebody. Well. Anyway."

"Thanks."

"Call me if there's anything I can do."

Leave my wife alone for a start. But that was truly over. And anyway, it had been a brief, ridiculous nothing. For a time, he'd wanted to strangle the guy, but the best revenge was to be polite, even nice. Let him choke on it.

"So you're on for tomorrow unless –"

Jack understood that 'unless.' Hayden would no more invite Candace to his house than a herd of rats. A condition: Come dine with us if your wife's still missing.

Outside, in the house, in bed, everywhere, was a blank space where Candace should have been.

"Wayne," Jack called and the boy came out of his box, his face a wry mix of sympathy and promised efficiency. "The file on first materials, please."

"Right. And Jack."

"It's okay. I'm here for a half hour or so."

"If there's anything."

"The thing is, Wayne, a lot of people are waiting to go back to work and I think I have to sort that out. You know. And it's Saturday. You don't have to be here. Haven't you got a hockey game tonight?"

He looked at the kid and wondered whether he himself had ever looked so young and so bright. Wayne's one tiny ear-stud was his only concession to the current body-decorating fashion as far as Jack knew. Under the buttoned shirt and jeans there might be grotesque tattoos from neck to heel and metal in places he didn't want to think about.

"You're okay, then?"

"Thanks, Wayne. I'm going from hour to hour. All I can do."

If he sounded stoic, Jack couldn't help it. All his words were going to be interpreted for good or bad. The fact that he'd come to the office could give the impression that he was a cold, calculating man instead of one whose heart was filled with dread. And there was no way he could start saying to people, "My heart is filled with dread."

He hurried through the paperwork wanting really nothing more than to spend the whole day working on figures and plans, clearing a path to the future, hiding from the present.

When he got home there were no messages from Candace. Six kindly people had left consoling words. *If there's anything we can do...* Find my wife, dammit! That's what you can do.

He called Erica and told her he was going to dine with Hayden.

"Tomorrow then," she said.

The police are searching. I have absolutely no idea where my wife is. The recent coolness was due to the images she'd seen on his computer, but for God's sake he was only looking. Look but don't touch. Demeaning to women, she said. Okay! Okay Candace. I'll go sit in the park with my laptop when I want to go into that world but how about coming back now?

Had she felt underappreciated? A major factor in the sadness of women, maybe of all people. The Society for the Prevention of Underappreciation. SPUA. Start one up. Get a grant for it from some idiot government department.

Bess in her shadowy dress whispered in my ear and led me astray but briefly, briefly, Candace. And you were never meant to know. But the town spy felt it best you should be aware.

Coffee. The cure-all. He didn't want it because he knew it would clear his mind of all the cluttering thoughts he'd set up like a wall, and make him consider the many different things that could have happened to his wife. Fear and Dread, like vampires, were waiting to grab him by the throat.

A boy was going door to door with a sheet of paper in his hand. It was the Eckert kid, Ben, from the end house, collecting money to sponsor himself for the half-marathon. Charity. Jack reached for his wallet and fished out a twenty. It was a time for generosity. The 21.24K was a long run. The kid was next door now. A scrawny boy who looked as though a few trips to McDonalds wouldn't hurt. No one in at the Aspers. He was going back down their path. He walked towards Jack's house, hesitated, then kept on going and went to the Burkhardts on the other side.

Jack called out, "Hey Ben!" But the boy paid no attention as he tucked money into his pocket and held out his sheet for Mrs. B. to sign. Then he moved on to the next house.

So much for the neighbours then. They had already presumed him guilty. Well screw them all. I'm the neighbourhood monster like some pedophile. He shuddered. At Halloween, the kids would be told not to come near number 2039, the killer's house. More than anything that bit into his soul. He wanted to go out and shout at all these silent accusers. He kicked at the wall. He wanted to scream. The kid walking by like that, the deliberate avoidance, said more than any accusing cop or lawyer could do. This was no more his town. He went inside and felt as though he had slunk.

When he heard a knock at the door, he hesitated. Would they begin now to throw things at him, stone him as soon as he appeared?

He pulled the door open slowly, ready to slam it. But standing there was small, unthreatening, Ms Eckert holding a casserole dish wrapped in plastic.

"I thought," she said, "that you probably weren't eating. We're all so sorry about your wife. I told Ben not to come to your door because, you know, you might not feel up to giving anything right now."

He was ambushed by her sympathy and tears came to his eyes. She set the dish down on the step and gave him a hug.

Stunned, Jack picked up the dish, thrust the crumpled twenty into her hand, said thank you and closed the door. She knocked again but he didn't answer. Possibly she thought he'd paid her for the gift and was insulted. He was too confused to care.

He put the dish down on the counter and realized he was hungry. Pastry. He cut a chunk of the chicken pie and put it on a plate, got a fork from the drawer and took it back to the desk.

BJ had shown him how to find those little video clips about the daily news. Tiny talking people. They were company of a kind. Here was a man telling him about floods in Indonesia. So many washed away and what had their lives been before? Poor maybe, but alive, with relatives to love them and to love. Were people ever so poor that they had no strength left for love? He knew the answer and felt like a rich bastard taking more than his share of the world's goods.

When the bell rang, he rushed to the door. Candace had lost her
key. Was standing there. Returned after a day of shopping, a night
in Vancouver. Didn't you get my message?

But the visitor was tall and in uniform. And there were two
of them. The other shorter, female.

"Hi Marak. Come in."

"Jack, this is Sergeant Berry. Jack Wilson."

"We met this morning."

"We had to quit the search for now. This rain."

Jack offered them coffee and then asked if there was news,
knowing at once that he should have done those things in
reverse order.

"Not yet. Just a few questions." Marak sat down comfortably
on the rocker as if all kitchens were his kitchens and he had a
right to any chair he chose. He looked round, sharp-eyed, at the
cookbooks, the ornaments, the floor. A hidden weapon.
Bloodstains.

"You really have no idea where she might be?"

"A couple of times when we argued, she went to her sister's
even though..."

"Even though?"

"Even though they don't really get on."

"Why's that?"

Jack didn't answer.

"More we know, the better chance of finding her."

Crazy if they suspected Erica.

"It goes a long way back. Sometimes they were okay. It had
to do with a teddy bear. I mean it wasn't all the time but her sister,
Ms Brandt, was anti the new development and that brought it
all on again. The old quarrels." Stop talking, Jack. But he was on
a track. "You'd have to ask their dad about what happened when

they were kids. Their mother was a bit weird."

"Their father said they had a harmonious relationship."

"Marcus. Well you must have noticed. He's getting a bit senile. He has obsessions. If you've been there, you've seen the coasters."

"Great design. So your wife's friends, colleagues. No one she's likely to have confided in? Anyone who had it in for her?"

"My wife," he paused and let his mind wander through her day as she walked down the familiar street, glanced at the lake, picked up a latte from Althea's, entered the building and went to her office, turned on her computer and checked the dating sites. How in hell did that last thought come into his head! "My wife is a lovely person. Everybody loved her."

"Except her sister?"

Another gap for guilt to seep into the situation.

"Any family has arguments. Doesn't mean there isn't – well affection. Ties." He hadn't spoken to his own brother for about three years. Did Jason care? Did he? Their mother tried now and then to restore loving harmony. "They loved each other. They just didn't agree on things. Some things."

"Tell me about yesterday morning. She left early."

"She said she had an appointment at the dentist's."

"But now we know he was closed. Taking a day off."

"And that's weird because she is a very organized woman. It's not like her to have written down the wrong date."

"Unless that was an excuse and she's taken off."

"You're making assumptions, Marak."

"It's my job. Jack, we wouldn't even be in on this at this stage if – well I've known you since grade school and you're kind of somebody everybody knows. "

The other cop glanced round the room as if searching for clues, then she left and Jack could hear her going down the basement steps, clunk, clunk, clunk. He wanted to shout, "Take your boots off, dammit. There's new wall-to-wall."

"She can't just go down there."

Marak said, "We have to get the bottom of this. People don't vanish. She is somewhere."

Jack felt very tired and wished they would leave. But the only way was to go on telling the guy what he wanted to know. He was the one wearing a uniform and carrying a gun.

"She read the paper a bit. Made toast. Spilt coffee on her green sweater and worried about getting the stain out."

"Her dad said she was wearing red."

"What the fuck does he know! He wasn't here. And then she picked up her purse and left. So what are you doing about it?"

"We're going to widen the search area, Jack. We've got extra help coming in from Abbotsford. We'll put something out on TV. If you want to be part of it, that's fine."

"Me?"

"It's usual. We'll get a lot of weirdo calls but often there's something useful."

There was a pause, a moment that felt like a silent duel, then Marak said, "Her bag, Jack. Her purse?"

"Oh. Yes. She always carries a big shoulder bag. She's had it since university. I offered to buy her a new one but she likes it."

"Maybe you could tell me what it looks like. What was in it?"

"In it? It's brown and kind of battered-looking. I mean it's got to be fifteen years old or more. There'd be her wallet and her cellphone and papers from work. Stuff like that."

"We haven't come across it and maybe that's a good sign. Soon as anything turns up, we'll let you know."

The other cop emerged from below and followed her boss down the path carrying a load of suspicion with her.

"She never wore red," he called after them but they didn't turn round.

He went inside and closed the door though he wanted to keep it open slightly. The house should be welcoming, lights on, heat high. She complained that he kept the thermostat too low. He turned it up to twenty-five and then sat down to consider what the cops had said and what they might have made of his responses.

Red! Perhaps her lover liked her in that colour. She did not have a lover! Having sex with a guy a few times didn't make him a lover. And that was all over. But if she had met someone new. If he had been violent. If he had. Jack cried out. It was all impossible. Yesterday was part of a previous existence when all the pieces of life fitted into place, a neat picture, and his only worry was that there might be an unexpected holdup on the work. But today he'd moved into the province of unknowing where there were no fixed rules and anything at all could happen.

He took the file from his briefcase, the worksheets, and sat down but didn't look at them. Instead he picked up *Moby Dick*. Maybe if he read it, she'd come back. Like a task in a story, it could be something he had to do before he could rescue the maiden from the tower. And there might be clues. There were a few pages of quotes and then Chapter One. *Loomings*. He got down to the bottom of the first page, *Circumambulate the city of a dreamy Sabbath afternoon*. It was a language from another time and not one he wanted to learn.

FIVE

Marcus sat down with the *Ghills Lake Echo*. Headline: *Highest unemployment rate in twenty years. House prices down by fifteen percent. Two children swept away in raging torrent.* Tragedies in newspapers all the time. What they thrived on. Stories of the lost, the kidnapped, the shot and the stabbed and the just plain miserable. But these things weren't meant to happen to Candace. Not to your own family, only to other people. Though you didn't wish these things on other people either. He tried to stop his mind going down that route. But of course you hoped tragic things happened to *them* instead of *us*. Only saints thought otherwise.

On page three there was a piece about Pine View. A sly reference to Gary Streicher's bankruptcy five years ago. Hint of shifty goings-on. Cheap journalism. *There is no truth to the rumour!* They asked a question and all you had to do was shake your head and they had their answer. Oldest trick in the book. At least Candace hadn't become a story yet. Please God let her be found before her name is part of a black headline on the front page. And don't let me appear weeping on TV and saying, "If you've seen my little girl, please call this number." And then the police would be swamped with calls, most of them hysterical garbage.

Candace wasn't a child.

When they were little, she and Erica, they'd laughed with him, loved him. That sweet stage was too soon over. There were quarrels, a big argument over a bear and SHE there with a knife cutting pieces out of a pumpkin. This same grey time of year. If he hadn't been away so much it would have been different. It was a father's job to carve the face on the pumpkin.

He looked out the window. The clouds were broken, cleft.

Happier all round maybe if I'd stuck to teaching here in Ghills Lake, but Ghills Lake didn't choose to stick to me. If he'd gone back and apologized as Sheila wanted him to do, maybe he could have gone on till retirement at Jordan High and saved himself years of soft recrimination from her. Rarely mentioned but always there, in bed, in the living room, in the garden: His failed career. Their lost benefits.

The students were the problem. Shouting, "I have nothing left to give you, you useless little dickheads," and walking out that Friday morning had probably confused them, maybe even frightened them a bit. If it had provoked even one of them to smarten up and read a book now and then it was worth it. But they just sat there, all those boys and girls, day after day, birds with their beaks open, making no effort, gazing at him the way they gazed at their computer screens, waiting for worms of wisdom to creep into their heads, or for rules that would lead them to a secure and happy life. They had all expected too much. Far too much.

He was told he'd had a breakdown and there was a brief measure of sympathy. How to quantify that 'measure'? A cup, a litre, the width of an embrace? The gentle look in the principal's eyes when she told him to leave the premises suggested that had it been left to her... But after all he had tipped the desk over as he walked out and hit the two kids nearest the door on the head with his book.

But it was long ago. He could laugh now at the memory.

He'd said to the policeman this morning, My daughter's been missing for twenty-eight hours and what are you doing about it? The big cop, Benny Marak, had been in his class, friend of Jack's. Might have been one of the kids he'd whacked on the head. Not the time to mention it. The other was a girl assistant, eager, anxious to do right, straight short hair and scowl. Prepackaged lady cop.

Doing what they could, sir. Understaffed. Overextended. Procrustean excuses.

He no longer had faith in the guardians of society. You could stuff a uniform with straw, add on a pumpkin head, and it would be about as much use as some of them.

He wished he could stop questioning his own thoughts, but there was no one else to argue with and he loved a good argument. Gave up on SHE when she lost all sense of proportion and began to throw kitchen utensils at him.

Best thing he could do to show that an old man had his uses would be to make dinner for Jack. He looked in the freezer. The eyes looked back, the mouth grinning among the packages of caribou meat he'd brought back from Iqaluit three years ago. Should still be good. They'd liked him there and he kept in touch with a few of the teachers. Maybe next year.

He'd had his methods and the breakdown had been treated as a medical matter from which he'd been cured. He knew how to teach. There was an eagerness to learn among the older Inuit that had given him energy. Teaching teachers. He wished he'd asked them to teach him Inuktitut in return for his help. Never too late. After we've found Candace, after she's returned, I'll see if they'd like me back at the summer school. After Candace turns up.

After she's found.

"The ground doesn't open up and swallow people, does it?" he shouted.

Were there instances? In myth, yes. In real life there were sink-holes, storms, earthquakes and such-like freaks of nature. But here, the weather was usually moderate. Occasional tremors led people to talk about the "big one" that would happen some day – within the next thirty years they said. Tsunami escape routes were already marked out in some towns. Like Tofino. And his emergency kit was not ready.

But if she had simply gone? He considered all the ways of leaving. The road to Vancouver. The road to the North. The ferry to the Island. The sea itself. The now unfriendly border.

Food. Comforting food. His mother used to make a great fish pie with egg and parsley in it. He took the last piece of Arctic char from the freezer and put it in the microwave to thaw.

While it spun round and round, he turned on the laptop Simon had given him and looked for clues on the Internet.

●

Hi cyber-mates

Marguerite here.

This morning, H pushed me back into the house as if he wanted to push me out of his life. Can I get you anything, sweetheart? Just the use of my legs back, please. Anything but that, darling. If I could. And then that weary 'I'm not a magician' look.

He thinks I use this laptop to search for my photos and to check up on birds. I thought I saw I saw a cedar waxwing on the maple tree this morning, but with the mist off the lake and the leaves falling, it could've been a shadow. Like the ghostly person I called out to, who was there and then not there. As for those two women in the store with their mean faces looking down at me, if I'd had a knife, I would have cut right into their clothes and maybe punctured the skin. Just a wish, folks, not serious. I have my own ways of revenge. At school it was Erica who told the others that the first part of my name, my real name, means worm in French. So what do you think I got called for the next three years! Affectionately of course, they would say now. Liars! My name actually means pretty green flower.

What I want next, and he will give it to me, is a better digital camera. I've already figured out how to get the pictures onto a disc. So today, friends, and you especially Lauren, since you asked, yes they did set up a search for poor C. What a waste of time. HE thought I didn't know what was going on between them. Did J know? Was C pressing H to leave me, which he cannot and will not do? Did either of them have a hand in her disappearance? Not that I mean anything sinister. They're not bad men. They might though have gotten desperate. There was a book wasn't there? *When good men do bad things.* Something like that.

It's a sad day when a neighbour disappears. And creepy because you don't know where to look. Was it one of the men I pass in the street? Have I seen a killer when I've gone up the ramp into the library to check out the books they keep on hold for me? Last week I borrowed the latest Dan Brown. My book group turns up their collective smart nose at him. But, hell, he passes the time. And I do have time.

TNT M

After she'd signed off, Verlyn went into the kitchen and took another fig out of the fridge. She rubbed its soft skin with her finger and then cut it into quarters. Anyone would think she was pregnant. As if! They might have had another, a late child, if. It wasn't a matter of age, only of her ability to care for a baby who might have grown up with a better nature than his big sister.

Thirty-nine when her life had changed forever and the doctor, looking across her hospital bed at Hayden, had said in a low voice, man to man, "Some things will be, if not impossible, perhaps difficult. You'll have to..." They'd walked away then. And she knew that the physician had more sympathy for her husband than for her, the damaged victim.

She put the fig on a paper towel and took it into the living room. There was something historic and primeval about eating a fig. She sucked on the first piece and gave her daughter her due. There was no denying that the child had been devastated by her mother's accident and had tried her best to help at home. But then, in a storm of words, two years later, as soon as she'd finished grade twelve, she left. She called and visited but was remote as a distant relative and never stayed for long.

When the phone rang, Verlyn reached for it and checked the number on the little screen.

"Hello sweetheart," she said, and waited for the man to tell her she was beautiful.

•

Whose idea was this? Candace knew she'd slept and dreamt. Her leg hurt less. The idea had several parents. Like electricity. Like the telephone. Like DNA. Some of the inventors forgotten, left behind, while others took credit. Jack was in the kitchen now saying, I am committed to the project, to playing hockey on Saturdays, to finding my wife. Headlines: *Unknown celebrity disappears.* Wilfully or otherwise. And has other needs. Clean underwear. A glass of wine. That thought cleared her mind. She truly wanted a glass of wine. Would have drunk out of the bottle, broken the top off for want of a corkscrew and poured it down her throat.

When they came to measure the space, to chat, to provoke, she would make her demands. Bargaining chips. Where were they in this scenario? And who?

Family and friends must be looking. Frantic.

Erica had children and could not be totally focused. But their father? They had not abandoned him but lately considered him a boring old fart, a figure of fun. Lovable and respected but not taken seriously. He'd be the one most committed to finding his daughter.

"Dad," she shouted, but knew that her voice didn't reach the upper air.

Jack would reach for her in the night and then recall that she was missing and turn over and go back to sleep for a while, then wake up again and call out her name as if he could conjure her out of the darkness. He'd remember that he loved her and would regret that last argument. Love means looking for people.

Three maple leaves drifted down onto her. She chewed at the edge of one and then took a few more bites. No one had ever said they were poisonous.

She hugged herself to get warm, and rubbed her arms and legs. She knew that in this chilly hole she could die if no one came soon. But that was ridiculous. Searching, they would come upon this place. And they must be searching, fanning out, sending dogs to sniff their way along her footprints. Soon there would be flashlights, shouts, a crowd of searchers, one finally crying out, Found! She is here. She is alive. Thank God. Celebration. Life from now on had to contain more joy. *What is joy? Time spent hiking with Kathy and Martine and the others. Being Aunt Candy to Tannis. Certain nights with Jack.*

This was not a deliberate act. Jack had not pushed her into this hole because she was barren. A few years ago, she'd overheard him murmur to a neighbour they barely knew, "I thought we would have had kids by now," seeing himself perhaps owner of a giant contracting company: Wilson and Sons and Daughters.

"I thought we would have had kids by now but she..." Candace had walked away from the open window, wounded, not wanting to hear the rest. She had cried alone and the scar never quite healed.

"Jack. Help! I'm here. We'll adopt three Chinese babies. Please, somebody."

She heard a dog bark and called out again. But there was no reply and the bark grew fainter and fainter.

•

Simon said, Simon was always *saying,* "There's not much we can do now but wait."

Erica said, "So we wait, Simon."

"Look at this. I thought telegraph poles, you know. Bus stops," Marcus said.

"It's a very old photo, Dad."

"Please, think of it as an effort. I am trying to do something. Which is more than..."

"More than?"

"I made copies at the library. They let me put one up on the notice board."

They were passing the poster round. He'd printed the message in block letters and not added a phone number. Contact the police, he'd written, because old people living alone were vulnerable. Erica passed him a plate of cookies. Apparently they were to eat unnecessary sugar to help them cope.

"Yes, thanks." Marcus knew better than to ask if his daughter had made them. She paid Jenny of Jenny's Gourmet for stuff with a homemade look. A busy girl, Erica.

The kids were growling softly like two young tigers. Of course he loved them, he had to, they were his grandchildren. But they were mysterious. Tannis was eight now and had the look and occasionally the attitude of a young SHE.

As for BJ – Oh why this fad for calling people by two initials when the world was full of interesting, presidential, academic, biblical names! And now the eleven-year-old, consonant-laden boy said, "I'll help you put them up, Grandpa." Marcus wanted to hug him and buy him a magical gift.

Erica, and he knew she knew, was his second-favourite child and she now confirmed her status by repeating herself. "The photo's too much out of date, Dad. Look at her hair for one thing."

Simon said, "The information's right. It might help. It's not as though any of us is rushing around doing anything useful. Off you go before it gets too dark. Got tape, Marcus? Scissors?"

The boy wouldn't hold his hand, but they walked side by side and stopped to tape up posters of his lost child. BJ, handy with the roll of tape, held the end while Marcus cut and stuck. After they'd put up six, the boy was restless.

"That'll be enough," he said. "People will see and call the cops. And then you'll find where she is."

"A few more, please. And then we'll go to the game store."

"We have to get back."

"Tomorrow then."

"Doesn't open on Sundays."

"Next Saturday then."

"Thanks, Grandpa."

Marcus hadn't intended to go back into the house when he returned the good child. He wanted to get home in case, well just in case. But Erica pulled him in and hugged him and said, "She'll turn up, Dad. I know she will."

He could tell there'd been arguments while he'd been gone. Tannis was nowhere to be seen. Simon was fussing with a pile of vegetables on the counter. He asked Marcus to stay but there was no echoing invitation from Erica. BJ helped himself to a glass of juice and went off to his room.

"Thanks for helping," he called after the boy.

Erica by now had her hands in soapy water and was washing bowls and pans, then rinsing each one under the running tap. She appeared to be cleaning out a cupboard. He'd given up telling her that using a dishwasher, as long as you only turned it on when it was full, was more ecologically sound than doing dishes by hand. Less soap. Less water. He sighed and picked up the drying cloth, forbearing also to mention for the fiftieth time that this little piece of material was a great germ collector.

Sitting in the living room with coffee for her, green tea for

Simon, decaf for him, there was the sort of silence that brought all kinds of ghastliness into the air as if each of them had an appalling image of Candace injured, raped, dead, and had let it loose.

Finally Simon said, "I think it's important to keep our heads."

"'While all about are losing theirs.'"

"Okay Dad! Nobody is losing it. I mean we're all doing our best so why are we sitting here," Erica cried and ran from the room.

"It's a question of whether we are really. Doing our best, I mean. But what else can we do? I'd better go after her," Simon said.

Marcus got up and let himself out of the quiet house. For the first time since she'd died, he wished that Sheila were alive and here with him. He wanted to be counted as someone important to the situation. He wanted a co-worrier. He wanted to talk and to be heard. *I'm her father and I have rights. Rights to what?* Loneliness and fear enveloped him. He got in his car but had to sit there for ten minutes till he stopped shaking before he could drive on.

When he got home, he went to see if the message light was flashing. Nothing.

He picked up the phone and punched in Jack's number, then thought better of it and put the thing back on its rest. If there was news, he would be told. Best thing he could do was remain here in case she turned up.

He sat down in his comfortable recliner, Christmas gift from the family two years ago. Thoughtful but defining him as old. He reached for his pad and pen.

Candace has to be somewhere.

Complete disappearance is rare but happens.

Is she alive? If so, why no call, not even from kidnappers?

Has she been attacked? Murdered?

He shuddered and threw the pen down. Long since, he'd given up trying to protect his daughters from harshness, from heavy traffic, from the fury that had moved into the house in their last years at home. A Victorian father, a rich Victorian father, might have been able to say, "No, you cannot marry that artist fellow, no you cannot marry that ambitious man with a face like an uncooked steak." But power had flown out the window once they started high school.

He wanted to sleep awhile and then wake up and find Candace leaning down to kiss him. But enough! The matter called for action. Light in the window. That's what people did. What he would do. He drew back the drapes so that the lamp on the coffee table could shine out into the darkness and summon his girl home.

At once, there was a knock at the door, rat-a-tat.

He opened the door a little and it was pushed wide and arms embraced him so that for a moment he thought his light had wrought an instant miracle.

"It's not Thursday, Wendy," he said and pushed the woman back.

"I know how you must be feeling," she said, moving inside. "I knew you'd be waiting."

She began to unbutton his shirt.

"I am waiting. For her. But we can't do this now. Not now!" He tried to move her hands and push the buttons back into their shrunken holes.

"You need to relax, you old list-maker," she cried. She had caught sight of his pad. "Nothing you can do is going to help right now, in this house, at this moment. She will or won't return. We can but hope she's in some sunny place screwing her socks off and shouting for joy. And listen to me. Whatever's happened, it's not your fault."

Somewhere there was music. Somewhere people were normal.

"Come on, Peter Pan. Wendy's here. Neverland time."

He had never felt less like flying. The woman had made a

travesty of that book, another one the kids had loved when he read it to them, and he cursed himself for telling her about it. The story meant nothing to her. The words and names fell out of her mouth like stones.

"Go home," he said.

She sat down, her face crumpled into tiny folds. Marcus wanted to tell her she was too old and too big to play silly games, but he knew he'd regret it later. He'd always regretted those few times he'd talked back to SHE and had given up being anything except meek and mild long before the end. But Wendy now, sitting here, demure, with her ankles crossed and her hands drawn into the sleeves of her long blue sweater, was a different kind of woman entirely. Sharp words made her shrivel into a kind of obscurity. She became a shadow of herself, a reproachful shadow: He was the bully.

"It's just that at the moment —"

"I know, love. I'm sorry. I was too quick. You'd like to go slow today. When Harris had his accident, it was days before, and then... But, you know, she's probably perfectly fine. Somewhere she's fine. She'll turn up and wonder why you were all so worried. There's a message gone missing someplace. Why don't we have some music? Maybe that."

"I don't want to be distracted," he said again. "I just feel I have to keep concentrating, focussed. If I take my mind off her, something awful will happen. I have to keep thinking."

"That's Jack's job."

"I don't think he's up to it."

"Rats! Garbage! Unless you're thinking what one or two people in town are thinking. I mean it is usually the nearest. The last person to see the victim."

"Candace is not a victim!"

"Of course not, sweetie. All I'm saying is, Jack's the one who has to keep his mind on his wife."

She walked across the room and put their favourite CD in the player: The first act of *Madama Butterfly*. Slowly she began to take off her clothes. He tried not to watch but couldn't help wondering whether she was wearing the pale green underwear.

•

Jack took a step back and felt his shoe sink into mud. For Chrissake! For Chrissake! He'd come round to share a pizza with the old man, knowing that he must be worried and worried himself about Marcus's oddly enquiring mind and oddball behaviour, and there he was rutting like a caribou on the living room floor. The odd position was no doubt due to the old guy's sciatica. He turned away and went to sit on the front step. No wonder there'd been no answer when he knocked. He wished deeply that he'd gone straight home instead of stepping into the flower bed to look in the window. They'd even left the freaking drapes open and put a lamp there. A floor show!

He wished he'd agreed to have dinner with Erica, with Hayden, with anybody in the whole world. But there, with his daughter missing, out there, lost in a violent world, her father who should in all decency have given up sex long ago was enjoying himself like a frigging animal.

He went back to the pickup to think and began to chew on the pizza. It left a bad taste in his mouth as if the pepperoni was past its prime. I'd be laughing, he thought, if it were not for – if it were not for the huge fact that Candace is gone and we should all be waiting, watching.

When Gary, full of concern, had told him they could manage without him on Monday and he should stay home in view of what had happened or might happen, Jack had held up his cellphone to show that he was in touch with the world, cops, kidnappers, Candace herself. Then he had agreed he might take a day or two off because it was seemly. And there was old Marcus behaving in a way that was far, far on the wrong side of seemly.

But there was no instruction book. No *What-to-do-if-your-wife/sister/daughter-goes-missing For Dummies.* They were all in the dark place on their own. He began to eat another slice of pizza and, unbidden, worries about the work ahead came into his mind. He took out his pen and made a few calculations on the lid of the box while he ate. Then, still angry at the old man, he threw the box and the rest of the pie onto the lawn. Maybe the lovers would be hungry later.

He drove slowly home along the quiet streets. To settle his mind, he looked at the buildings as he drove past. On the left, the shuttered, three-storey bank building. Arguments were still going on about declaring it a damn antique to be preserved just because the nineteenth-century builder had put a fancy front on it. There it rotted, probably a haven to rats and roaches. He couldn't understand the men and women who were so violently against progress. Did they want this pleasant but decaying place to stagnate, remain as it was, a monument to twentieth-century dullness? And here they shopped. And here they worked like ants in these little dark offices. There's the movie house where they watched images of themselves killing and fucking and being dull. Conclusion by future historians: They were a self-regarding people. Offered a chance of new, bold designs, they cried out and the god they didn't believe in crumbled them to dust. Well, they were going to get Pine View and they would rejoice in it and point it out to visitors with pride. In a year or two the ugly strip mall too would disappear and be replaced...

He stopped the car in the driveway. He had felt joy just then, pride, anger too. And this was not the time for it. How could he so quickly forget Candace even for a moment? She was lost and here he was making plans. He understood those holy people who whipped themselves with chains. Then he had to shake his head to chase away the image of Marcus's naked bum. We are all dealing with this in our own way, he thought. But there were limits, surely.

Candace is lost. Diverging streams. Lost temporarily. Lost forever.

He walked up the path to the house hoping with all his might to find her there, knowing he would shout at her in relieved anger if she were. Where the hell have you been?

The door wasn't locked. He went inside the house warily. Lights were on.

"Candace! Love! Are you there?"

But it was Simon who appeared at the top of the steps.

"What the hell. How did you get in?"

"Erica has a key."

"Well you can't just barge in here like that."

Simon came downstairs.

"Sorry. Look. I just had this idea. The computer."

"You've been looking at my computer?"

"I couldn't get into the files."

"Explain before I throw you out. And I mean throw."

"I thought there might be something on her email."

"Do you think I haven't looked? Every five minutes. And the cops asked. They looked. What is this, Simon?"

"Can we sit down?"

Jack led the man into the kitchen. He wasn't going to have him taking root in the living room, settling in, putting forward mad theories.

"Beer?"

"No thanks."

Jack opened a can for himself and waited.

"Marak came to see us. To see me. Got us talking."

"What did you say?"

"The questions they ask. They're cunning. Before you know it, you've said things."

"What things?" Jack stared at his brother-in-law, dissecting the term. Not brother, not legal, and couldn't stop himself from yelling. "What things?"

"All right. All right. Well it didn't go back to the teddy bear. I mean I don't think they suspect Erica. But they wanted to know who Candace saw, I mean sees. Who she liked, likes. Whether you have arguments. And they picked on little things we'd mentioned. How she yelled at you the night of the fireworks. The week she stayed with Marcus."

"That was because we were decorating and the place smelled of paint!"

"It was as if they were trying to put bits of a puzzle together."

"And getting it wrong. You never, ever volunteer information to the cops. They twist words round, turn them inside out. They pick on someone and make the pieces fit, and before you know it they've locked some poor guy up and then ten years later it turns out he's innocent and it's, Sorry, here's a cheque to help you get on with your life after ten fucking years of being afraid to have a shower."

"These guys are looking for your wife, Jack. I think they're doing their best."

Jack closed his eyes and tried to think of a peaceful scene to calm himself; the beach at Island Harbour. But Marcus was lying on the sand naked.

Simon said, "This list."

He had the copy of Candace's shopping list in his hand. Marak had taken the original.

"She was planning to make ratatouille by the look of it."

"Oh." Jack hadn't considered the end product of the list, what was to be made out of all those vegetables including eggplant, which he despised. Did she sometimes go to another house and make a meal for a man who produced a bottle of wine and with whom she later had sex? "She usually went shopping Saturdays."

"Which means she hasn't run away, Jack."

Simon wondered how many times and to how many people he was going to have to make that simple statement. Jack hoped, Erica hoped, Marcus hoped, that Candace was alive and possibly happy, though he might leave the happy part out in Jack's case, shopping, travelling, and had left a message that had got lost. But in the space, images spilled out, imitations of a hundred newspaper articles: *Young woman abducted and raped. Skeleton found in field. Teeth used to identify corpse.*

"She hasn't run away."

"You didn't come to dinner. I brought this banana bread."

"Banana fucking bread!"

"You have to, you know, keep your strength up."

Simon had the sort of face people trusted. Clear eyes, like a glass brain looking out at you. One look at his paintings though and you knew the guy had another side to him, maybe several.

"And besides that, Jack. You have to watch out that you don't do anything suspicious."

"Go!"

The front door slammed. One day the glass panels would shatter.

Simon was right, damn him, about the shopping list. The fear he'd been trying to keep at bay gripped him again. Like an approaching monster, the prospect had to be considered: She had gone. Been taken against her will.

He opened the door again. Simon was only trying to help. He should call him back and be nice to him. Appreciate his concern. But he'd cycled off, forgetting his helmet that lay on the step like a huge black beetle.

Jack stood there looking up at the short curved street that he and Candace had chosen to inhabit. Garden Court, an offshoot of Garden Street, parallel to Garden Drive, as if the builder had run out of names. Pleasant people had planted themselves in these Gardens. They were mostly friendly but not nosy. Not till now.

On Saturdays, after the groceries were put away, Candace usually cleaned the kitchen. When she got back, she wouldn't want to start right in catching up with chores. He fetched the bucket from the basement and her rubber gloves and a brush. Candace used a mop. Standing, she swirled the thing over the tiles and then removed the dirty cover and put it in the garbage. He decided to get on his knees and scrub the floor with soap and water as his mother used to do. That way he could get into narrow spaces.

SIX

It had all come to nothing when Wendy yelled that there was a face at the window. Fool! He hadn't closed the drapes. Not intending to do anything that shouldn't be seen. He'd only wanted there to be a light for Candace. He felt ill. The woman was now in the kitchen making tea, rattling cups, opening the fridge. Suppose Candace herself had looked in and then disappeared again.

"I don't want tea," he shouted. "Go now. In case Jack comes."

"He might've seen us." She laughed horribly.

"Please go," Marcus said. "I need to think."

She put her coat on and stood in the hall. He realized what a small area it was: A tiny table, a few coat hooks, a worn-out welcome mat. Wendy filled the space and was expanding to suffocate him like a damn airbag.

"I only want to take your mind off things."

"I have to keep my mind on things."

"So maybe Thursday."

Why was she so persistent? What did she expect from him? Love?

"Look," he said and stopped because really her only wish was for kindness. "I'll call you, honey."

She softened, shrank.

"You'll let me know if I can help. In any way."

"I will."

He watched her go down the path and then fold herself into her Smart Car and drive off towards town.

There was a white object on the lawn. Kids passing by often threw beer cans and other junk out their car windows. Slobs. Badly brought up. Pick it up in the morning. He was about to go back inside but now everything had significance. He went to look. A pizza box. Did it contain an ear, a finger, a demand for a million bucks? He approached it with care. Walked round it. If it had been going to explode it would have done so on impact. He picked it up and took it into the house and wiped the dirt off the outside. The three remaining slices of pizza were jumbled now. Unappetising but smelled good, and he was hungry. He picked a piece up to eat and then noticed the writing on the lid.

So there had been a face at the window, a hostile face. A gangster's face.

The numbers written on the greasy cardboard were large. U.S. 50,000. Can. 30,000.

Who had sent the message and drawn a diagram that might be the secret sign of a gang or a torture device? It looked like a tilted guillotine.

He spat out the cheesy crust in case it was poisoned and made two slices of toast and spread them with jam. He poured himself a cup of tea and sat down at the table with the box in front of him.

Considering the message:

Why two currencies in unequal amounts?

Why had the messenger left the box where, if it had rained heavily, it might have lain unnoticed for days?

Had the shock of seeing him with Wendy, he shuddered, driven the perpetrator away?

Nothing, well hardly anything, happened without a reason.

His head was beginning to feel like one of the pumpkins in Joe Raven's patch.

He called the police.

No one could respond at the moment. He told the desk person that there was no hurry and he would talk to the sergeant in the morning. He leaned against the kitchen counter. What a day! Candace gone for only twenty-four hours and he'd behaved like a jerk and been discovered. *Be ye sure your sins will find you out.* Another rotten saying but true. The jails were full of found-outs. And Candace had been gone longer than that. Calculating from 8:25 Friday morning when she'd been seen outside the dentist's office and it being now 6:33, she'd been gone for thirty-four hours and eighteen minutes. That was a very, very long time.

He looked again at the pizza box and knew that it was Jack who had come round, Jack who'd looked in the window and SEEN. And then had thrown what was meant to be his dinner onto the lawn in disgust. But why had Jack come? Did he want to tell his father-in-law some self-justifying tale or seek comfort? Was there news?

Marcus took a beer from the fridge and went to sit in the recliner. At the back of his mind, like a wasp, hovered the mote of suspicion that Wendy had planted there. Jack wanted to convince him that he had nothing to do with his wife's disappearance. Jack had nothing to do with it!

The damn doorbell rang. He waited, not wanting to see Jack, whom he would never be able to look in the eye again; not wanting to see Wendy standing there with her overnight bag. But on the step stood one police officer in uniform. And what was he to say? That he'd called in haste, read too much into a pizza box probably thrown onto the lawn by kids?

"Come in," he said.

"You got something?" the cop asked.

"As a matter of fact," Marcus began, "not really." And then, hearing the man's disparaging tone, he said, "It's nothing, a mistake. My son-in-law must have thrown this onto the lawn.

When I called, I thought it might be some kind of message from kidnappers."

•

Hi, Cyberites,

They searched behind the townhouses this morning. They looked in garbage cans. They stared up at trees as if she might have taken to living in the branches like a bird. Their footprints were likely covering up any clues. But there were no clues. I could have told them that. It was of no help to C but people feel they have to be doing something. A lot of the trouble in the world is caused by people who feel they have to be doing something. There should be courses at university in minding your own business. Maybe there are. I just read that a professor at a fairly well-known university is doing research into why people hate each other. And getting paid while he does it. Ha!

I love this town. I used to love this town. People are kind in general. They stop and let me cross the road. I suppose that's faint praise! Some of them offer to help. I've lived here all my life. My dad came over from Hungary in the bad times when it was unsafe there not only for Jews but for anyone who cared about other human beings. He used to rant at mealtimes about racism, exclusion, nationalism. You could get indigestion before you'd even touched your food. He met my mother the week after he landed in Montreal. 'I found my love,' he used to say in that dark accent, 'in the laundromat. Music was playing. I led her out into the open space and we danced as our clothes also twirled round and round.' I've wondered since what he was wearing.

He exaggerated that as he exaggerated everything. But it was a sweet story and my mother and I loved it. After they got married they decided life would be better, at any rate warmer, out here on the edge of the Interior.

We had a great view from our apartment over the bakery. We could see up and down Granby Street, along Cray to the edge of the lake and the unknown universe beyond.

I went to school with half the population – so it seemed. A lot of them have moved away but if the developers, that is, Streicher and Wilson, get their way, there'll be an influx of strangers.

Ghills Lake will become a town that lives on its own flesh as it were. Industry has died. So there will be building supply stores, decorating boutiques, places where these new people can work and sell things to each other. A kind of self-perpetuating town with no real reason for existing. I looked at the map – H doesn't understand about me and maps. No. That's not quite true. He does but he doesn't want the truth to pierce his consciousness. He might bleed. And I marked the empty spaces.

Now J and his cohorts are after the strip mall. Althea took over our bakery for her café and that will go. 'Only the finest ingredients' was my dad's boast. Substitute 'cheapest' for 'finest.' I know what went into the mix.

If J is convicted of making away with his wife then the expansion plans will be on hold. And a good number of people in town will rejoice.

And in reply to you, Boris, I'm not one of those people who looks at the world and thinks we are a bunch of unimportant ants. Ghills Lake, for those of us who live here, is our universe. It's all the world we have.

And what we don't need, especially those of us on the Historical Society Board – or as scoffers call it, the Preservation of the Status Quo Ante Committee – is anything that spoils the style of the place. We do want our town to move on but we want to choose the time and the rhythm.

If you drive here from Vancouver, the first thing you'll see is the big sign that says, "Welcome to Ghills Lake. Pop. 78,532, home of Billy Rabinovich." People say who in hell was he? For one thing Billy was a woman. And a hero.

TNT *Marguerite*

•

They knocked as Jack was trying to dry the floor. Too much water for the small cloth to soak up. How did people get the right size cloth or sponge? It had taken him nearly an hour and there were still damp places and a puddle in the corner where the floor was uneven.

He went to open the door and his feet left wet marks on the hall parquet.

Marak came in looking brutal, followed by the young sergeant carrying a plastic bag.

"You're washing the floor?"

"It's what my wife did on Saturdays."

"I see."

They *saw* a guilty man wearing yellow rubber gloves removing bloodstains. Marak peered into the bucket but the water was only a grayish colour.

Jack took the gloves off and washed his hands and invited them into the living room.

"Sorry to bother you so late." This time four eyes looked closely at the sparse furniture, the three upholstered chairs and the shabby recliner.

"My wife likes space," Jack said, realizing that he had foolishly answered an unasked question. "And the couch is being re-covered."

They wanted to know where and he had no answer.

"Candace arranged it. There must be a slip somewhere. A receipt." He was digging himself in deep. By now they were imagining this non-existent sofa at the dump with her body in it, crushed. Let them hunt for it, then.

"You're smiling, Mr. Wilson." He was no longer Jack.

"Something she said."

"Can you share it with us?"

"I want to know what you're doing to find her."

"We're here."

"And she obviously isn't."

"Was there anything unusual in her behaviour yesterday?"

"Yes! She didn't come home or leave a message. That's unusual! She's an organized person. She wouldn't go off anywhere without telling me, and while you're sitting on your asses here, she could be in real trouble somewhere."

"Is this your writing?"

The sergeant put her hand into the bag and brought out a dirty pizza box. She opened it slowly like a conjuror to reveal traces of cheese and tomato and the figures on the lid.

"I was trying to figure out some of the costs. Materials. First phase. All that."

"And you threw it onto your father-in-law's lawn. For a joke?"

Here was a place for lies. A construct. And he was not quick in that way.

My father-in-law was screwing his brains out and...

"I knocked on my father-in-law's door and there was no answer."

"He was at home," Marak said.

"If you must know," Jack said and paused.

"Yes?"

"I suddenly couldn't face him. I knew we were both worried out of our minds and I didn't know what to say to him."

A crowd of unasked questions flew round the room like mosquitoes. He lied again to ward them off.

"So I left the box on the step."

"He found it over by the flower beds."

"That's weird. I left it on the step."

It seemed like hours before they went away, Marak and the woman, Berry.

They repeated their questions. He suggested raccoons might

have moved the box and then said, "How many slices were there?"

"Three," the sergeant said.

"Aha," Jack said. "I only ate three and there were eight. Somebody or something had the other two pieces and threw the rest away."

Disbelief, which he'd never thought could be palpable, descended. A curtain fell. The play was over for now. The sergeant put the box back in the bag and Marak said they would look for other prints or even, with sarcasm, paw marks.

He managed to drum up some righteous indignation and to shout at them, "Why not leave it to the Mounties?" as they walked to their car. He knew it would annoy them but couldn't help himself.

How could you do this to me, Candace? You aren't cruel. Except unknowingly. Please come home.

His mother! What if she read about it in the paper down there in Florida or one of her cronies sent her a text message? It was too late. She would be furious with love and anger and would get on the next plane.

•

What did the blind do for beauty? Candace put her hand on the rough wall. It returned nothing but a sense of dirt and hardness. She touched her own sweater. Soft. Her skin. Smooth. Perhaps rubbing a piece of velvet, say, would give a blind person a moment of sensuality. And after velvet, skin would be a disappointment. Why aren't you made of plush, beloved, like our old teddy bear? Then there was music, which was always better understood with your eyes closed. She liked blues but Jack...

"Jack!" she shouted. And yelled his name again. "Jack. Where are you?" Her voice had lost power.

And sitting here, thinking up dumb abstractions, wasn't going to get her rescued. Her leg was less painful. There might be a way to climb. A foothold here. A handhold there. Like the climbing wall Tannis and BJ had taken her to. You can do it, Aunt Candy, they'd said. But she was terrified a metre off the floor and backed out while the kids in their ignorant fearlessness pegged their way to the top.

Fear was a luxury in this situation. Getting out of here was a matter of life...

She took off her remaining boot and began to pick at the wall with the heel. It was only dirt and stones and came away easily, rubble falling down beside her. When she could get all her fingers into that hole, she raised her arm and began to scratch out another one above it.

She stretched further and the pain in her leg made her cry out. It wasn't broken, she knew that now, but there had to be a damaged ligament in her calf. She took her blouse off and put her coat back on. The blouse was hard to tear. One of Erica's bargains. Cheap material sewn as if it were going to be used for sandbags. Eventually it gave way and she wrapped it round her leg tightly to give it some support.

Her feet were cold and the ground was rough. She put her boot back on and rubbed her other foot. There was misery in this place.

She knew now that hunger does gnaw as if a small rodent is chewing at your insides. There'd been an article, morbid she'd thought at the time, about last meals. Well-known, though not to her, chefs had given the menus they'd choose if they were to be executed next day. Two of them had opted not for truffles and caviar but for simple roast beef dinners. So much for cordon bleu.

Her own final feast would begin with carrot and orange soup and end with a cheese souffle. It occurred to her then, in that moment, her hands covered in muck, that if someone didn't come for her soon, she might well have had her last meal: Chinese food picked up on her way home from work on Thursday and eaten half cold in front of the TV and without ceremony. Henceforth there would always be candles and flowers and they would eat at the table. When they bought a decent table. Had he cooked the lasagne?

Jack! Please. I am in despair.

Jack: How long before her past became his future? Marrying again. Someone in her twenties. Children. She imagined six of them following him like a row of ducks, their only toys building blocks. A slim blonde woman hanging onto his arm.

Maybe three times, they'd had THE CONVERSATION.

Do you mind?

Of course not.

We could adopt.

Not sure about that. Mystery package.

What are you doing, Jack? What are you doing right this minute? I can't stand this much longer. I am cold and wet and sitting in my own mess.

●

After he'd finally got the floor dry and put the wet towels into the dryer, Jack opened the front door and looked out. The street-light was shining on the ornamental cherry trees at the edge of the lot and on the evergreens near the house. He knew the neigh-bours laughed at him as he planted and replanted the shrubs, walked to the road to check the placings, trying to get the colours right in their seasons. Candace had encouraged him to spend time in the yard as if – well maybe as if she wanted him to be occupied at weekends and not bothering her. But Candace wasn't here and the rhododendrons and laurel no longer seemed impor-tant. He bent down to pluck out a couple of weeds and then heard the car. It had to be Erica. But when he turned, he saw that it was Simon. Simon again!

"Hi, Jack."

"Simon?"

"It's a bit late for gardening."

"It's a bit late for a visit."

"You have news?"

"No. Why have you come back?"

They sat down in the living room, Simon in the deep arm-chair and Jack on the old bucket chair which he turned, with dread, so that he could look at his brother-in-law.

"The cops came round again – to ask about the pizza box. Do you usually throw trash onto her dad's front lawn? Like it's a habit? You know."

"I was upset."

"That's what I told them. You can't expect a guy to be acting rationally when his wife has disappeared, been gone now for two days. I said he – that's you – probably suddenly thought of something and rushed off. Meaning originally to share the pizza with the old man, you changed your mind and hoped he'd find it there."

Simon looked at his brother-in-law, men connected through two sisters. It could be that Jack was now outside the law, facing him as he was and hissing, "I told you. You never, ever, volunteer information to cops. They twist words and turn them inside out and use them against you or against someone else. They've done it before. Picked on someone for a suspect and made up evidence and lied even to get their man locked up. Then they congratulate themselves. Victory for them: One innocent sucker's life ruined forever."

Simon recognized panic and the need to hit out. He repressed the urge to hiss back, *These guys are looking for your wife,* and said, "I didn't tell them anything they hadn't figured out already."

"Well you confirmed it for them."

He let the steam dissipate and then said, "What do you think? Would she have taken off for Vancouver or somewhere?"

"Not without saying."

"She was going to make ratatouille maybe. Will make rata-touille, I mean."

"I should buy the stuff for when she gets back?"

"To get a good eggplant," Simon said, "hold it. See how heavy it feels for its size. It should be kind of light."

Jack pictured himself at Grady's supermarket holding the ugly purple things, weighing them in his hand, and people watching him, thinking the poor guy's out of his mind or worse, thinking he doesn't care. He couldn't help smiling, almost laughing at the idea.

"I'll just get something ready-made for now."

"Right."

"So. You had a reason for coming?"

"Two really. I know I shouldn't even be thinking about this right now but there's a deadline. The art show a week from Saturday in Vancouver. I need to take some of my stuff there next week. It's getting to be a last chance for me. I'll need to borrow your pickup. I feel awful for asking, for even caring about it but..." He began to cry.

Jack shook his head. Eggplants. Weird paintings. Other people's tears. None of it made sense.

"Of course. Do you have a tarp or something? I've been going to get a cap put on it."

"Thanks, Jack. I won't talk to the cops again."

They were silent. Jack imagining the paintings in the back of the pickup. Simon seeing them on the walls of the gallery on Seymour.

After a minute when silence seemed to have cleared the air, Jack went to the kitchen and got two beers out of the fridge. When he went back into the living room, Simon was standing up and looking at his picture.

"Good that," Jack said in consolation.

"Thanks." Simon took the beer.

"Now listen, blabbermouth, and do not, not, repeat this, especially to Erica. I don't even know why I'm telling you except I can't get it out of my mind. What happened was when I went round there with the pizza and no one came to the door, I looked in the window and there was the old man bare-assed on the floor with a woman."

"God! Doing it?"

"Having sex, yes."

"Ah!"

At a time like this. Those words hung between them like letters on a birthday streamer and didn't need to be spoken. They didn't speak for a minute. Jack was trying to erase the awful image again and knew that the other man was probably doing likewise.

"Maybe she was a healthcare nurse."

"That's not funny. He's old. It was disgusting."

"He's entitled to do as he likes."

"Not to be obscene."

"He can't have expected anyone to look in the window."

"You know what I don't like about you, Simon. You're too goddam reasonable."

"I'll scream and tear my hair out if you like. But I'd rather try to find your wife."

The guy had a point. Jack sighed. He wanted suddenly to be on some remote island where there were no relations, no friends, and where he himself would be free from all this. A movie scene, perhaps, with Candace coming towards him holding out her arms. Only the two of them in the entire world. Music in the background. A grassy meadow. The sun coming up.

"Sorry, Simon," he said.

"So the figures on the lid?"

"Had to do with work. What did they think?"

"I think they thought that you might've had a ransom note and weren't telling them. Or that – well – possibly you were figuring out her insurance."

"That's ridiculous. Her insurance policy's only worth $100,000. Mine's worth five times as much."

"Maybe you shouldn't mention that."

"I'm sure they know by now. Look, Simon, I have not harmed Candace. Why would I?"

Simon only looked at him in that innocent way that threw the question right back into his face. They were quiet again. Then Jack said, "It's the not knowing."

Simon, thinking the knowing might be worse, said, "I don't think you should be on your own."

"I have to be here."

"You'd better come to dinner tomorrow. If you don't come she'll be upset. She'll blame me."

This was guilt of another kind. He was being blackmailed into accepting kindness. I want out of this, his senses shrieked. Please come home, honey.

"I'll be there. You said two questions."

On the step Simon said, "About money."

Jack waited. If the bastard had come round to go on in this sympathetic and roundabout way and then touch him for a loan he would throw him down the steps. He moved closer so as to be able to get a grip on him.

Simon reached out to pat Jack on the shoulder and said, "If there's a ransom demand, we could let you have ten – maybe fifteen – thousand."

Jack couldn't stop tears coming into his eyes. The guy had sandbagged him and he wanted even more to push him down onto the concrete but thanked him instead.

"Don't mention it," Simon replied as he walked down the path and then drove off in a cloud of virtue.

It wasn't fair when people acted out of character. Jack pulled a leaf off the azalea by the door. Candace. All this was her fault. Wherever the hell she was.

His cellphone rang. He grabbed it and said, hopefully, "Yes?"

"I think I might know where your wife is."

"Who are you? What's your name? What do you know?"

"You haven't looked hard enough," the voice said, and hung up. He tried to call up the number but it was "unavailable."

People were going to do things like this. Marak had warned him. Cruel and idle men and women would send disturbing messages.

He called the police station and the desk officer said he would pass it on. *You haven't looked hard enough!* The words stung as if his own conscience had spoken to him. He wasn't out there searching day and night, wailing and gnashing his teeth. He felt impotent and very tired but knew that sleep was impossible. He put the familiar symphony on the player and tried to make some sense of what he knew.

●

Darkness. Second night. Must be. Shadow of birds on the wall. Creatures. Angels?

Men and women moving. Searching. Sadness. No one looking. Have to make an effort.

Jack! Please! I am here.

SEVEN

Jack woke up shrieking. Couldn't believe it was his voice. Only kids and the insane cried out like that. Thank God he'd closed the window last night. The figures in the dream were only shapes, lumpish shadows, but they'd been closing in on him, threatening to drop on him, come crashing down. He got out of bed quickly as if the demons might pursue him.

He had a long shower to clear his mind, and while he was drying himself looked around the bathroom counter in case he'd missed some clue. Her hairbrush. Hairs. DNA. Heaven forbid they'd need that. The souvenir dish they'd brought back from Dominican Republic. Weird vacation. Some fear there. Awful poverty. Columbus monument. Artificial local dances set up for tourists. Next time, he'd said, we go to the Yukon, because what he wanted was reality. Rocks you could touch. Water that was clear and cold. And then had said, we'll have to wait till the building's complete.

There were real lumpish shadows on the street outside. Not stopping to pick up the newspaper, he walked quickly to the truck to avoid questions, let them make up stories as they would. He heard random words: News. Turned up. Your wife. Had the reporters stayed out there all night? What kind of a job was that? He drove fast as if he were being pursued by a convoy of vans, their cameras aimed at him like so many guns.

The town was quiet. It was too early for the football teams to be assembling in the schoolyard for practice. A few joggers were out in the drizzling rain. A woman in a blue jacket bent down to gather up her dog's shit from the sidewalk. Was it worth having a pet, especially a big one like that, if you had to pick up after it?

He parked the car and walked past Althea's café. He could smell muffins and coffee but no way was he going inside. While he was putting a dollar and a quarter into the slot for the *Sunday Echo,* Althea opened the door and said, "Come in, honey. I know what you need. Sit there."

He succumbed once again to the force of kindness and sat obediently on the banquette.

The front page of the paper showed the bright faces of three very young soldiers killed in Afghanistan. The price of oil was up again. In Vancouver a man had died in a road race accident. Would that kid's family have felt better if he'd gone to war with those other three and died a hero? He flicked through the pages and found her. He wished he'd given the cops a different picture. Candace Wilson. They'd put together a bio. Probably got the information from Alys, Kathy, Martine. Another description: a woman of medium height with brownish hair, wearing a short beige coat and high-heeled boots. Medium heel, Erica had said. He thought about the heels of boots. Who measured them? What did it feel like to run on them? But she walked in her Nikes and carried the boots to wear in the office. The other way about made more sense but she had to look smart at work, she said. Did the cops know she was likely wearing running shoes? He was connected to Marak now by the thread of mystery.

He glanced up at the TV in the corner. Last night's hockey game being replayed. Paretski bashed into the barrier. The goalie flat on the ice. Nobody taking advantage of the empty net. Two days ago, he might have cared.

He felt a hand on his shoulder and started. In the second before he turned to see who it was, a cop had handcuffed him and he was standing in the dock while the judge accused him of murder and demanded he go to jail. I am innocent. Sure, they all say that.

"Didn't mean to startle you," Marcia said. "Sorry. I guess you're on edge. I saw you looking though."

She sat down opposite him in the booth. Smart suit, some kind of brown check. Good makeup. Younger looking than her real age. She had to be fiftyish. Up early. Probably been checking out the markets and was off to count the money in the bank vault.

"Looking?" he said, afraid.

"Yesterday. At the mall. This ugly little strip mall we're in now. Thinking maybe, the next project."

"Far from my mind," Jack replied. "I just want to know where my wife is."

"But you have to keep on. Dan told me about the meeting. Like you said, there are men depending on you. And investors who could turn nasty pretty quickly. Not to mention the people who've already put a down payment on one of your fancy townhouses. It's important to look ahead. Beyond Pine View. These are hard times but there'll be opportunities for smart people."

"I've thought about it – the mall."

"And I think you're absolutely right. Those of us who truly care about Ghills Lake know that we have to clear and rebuild. Make way for the future. We want a progressive-looking town."

He wondered if she was running for office.

Althea the waitress came over as if she sensed that Marcia was bullying him.

"'Morning, Ms Radwanski. Coffee?"

"Please, Althea. To go. And a bran muffin."

"More coffee, Jack?"

"Thanks."

"She will turn up, honey. They always do."

Sympathy again. I'm an obvious whimpering jelly to one and all. Banana bread. Dinner. Feeding time at the zoo. Other men and women were coming into the café, early Sunday morning regulars. Only Marcia seemed to have this sharply practical idea of comfort, offering him a diversion.

He turned to her and said, "So the mall?"

"We could make a significant loan. Get an architect to design something along the lines of the one in North Van. It will be like your townhouses. New and not flashy."

"I have to think about Candace right now."

"That's the thing. You're starting work tomorrow. People – some – people are going to think it's strange. The thing is. They're not going to protest. And then, you know, should she not turn up, you could name the place after her."

"You are grotesque," he shouted.

Althea ran to the table with a tray and gave him an unrequested cinnamon bun with his fresh coffee. "You have to eat," she said.

Marcia said, "I'm practical. Only work keeps you going at these times. Why do I turn up at the bank at seven and come in on Sunday too? It's because. Well, you don't need to know my problems. Just so you know, I do have problems in my life, Jack. And work is a blessing. That's all. So keep on. And I'm sure Candace will be fine. You know."

He didn't know. He knew absolutely nothing. He wanted to get up and make a statement to all the customers, all the early passersby: I have no idea where my wife is. I only want her to come home safe. And for those of you who knew about her and Hayden Cosgrave, it was nothing, over, a mistake.

Instead he followed Marcia out into the street. She hugged him and left him there on the sidewalk. He turned and Althea was standing in front of him holding a small bag.

"You forgot your bun." She gave him a kiss on the cheek and ran back into the café.

●

I, Candace, am not, will not, be unconscious. Not consciously. Have to keep on breathing, sucking water. Losing weight. Hips. What matters? Never clean again. What is *again*? Time. Must be awake. They are getting close. Hi, honey.

●

Jack went to the office first to pick up the plans. On his desk was another picture of Candace, in Tuscany. She was saying to him, "Wait. My hair's a mess." And he'd answered, "You have lovely hair. Smile." Walking back from the beach, they'd hardly made it to their room before they stripped off, not caring if the door was locked or if they were seen. And afterwards, laughing, laughing. And now, the memory had given him an erection.

At this time! Now! He was horrified. He understood why women sometimes said *men!* in that disgusted tone.

Barb came into his office. Didn't anyone knock any more? Talking like a nurse, she said, "These are the other drawings you wanted." She was about to come round the desk to set the papers in front of him. He reached over and snatched them, said "Okay. Later." And stared at his computer screen as if it contained the answer to the mystery of the universe. He knew that any inconsiderate behaviour on his part would, in the circumstances, be forgiven. Forgiven or, in the minds of some, put down to guilt. "Thanks. I'll be off to the site in a minute. Bill?"

"Yes," she said. "He called in. The guys'll be there tomorrow."

"Good of you to come in today."

"I guess we all want to be up and doing and besides."

"Yes. Thanks."

"If there's anything?"

"I'm fine."

He concentrated on the wall plan, the grand design. Twenty-three fine townhouses and a golf course, ladies and gentlemen, laid out by one of the top pros. Add in a waterfall, a restaurant. Call it

The Weir. Get the famous golfer to open the course. All appliances included. You'll love the marble. Your choice of colour. He kept on repeating the sales pitch until his erection had subsided.

The phone rang. "I'm at the site," Bill said. "No sign of a protest. Maybe in view of."

"Right. I'll be there soon."

He went to see Hayden Cosgrave. The lawyer was back in his office, working on a Sunday morning like everybody in town, it seemed, peering at a document as if he was about to read the will to the family in an old murder movie.

"Ah Jack. Just a moment."

Had Candace left a will? How long did it take for a person to be presumed dead? Jack, horrified that those questions had come into his mind, glanced round at the certificates on the wall, the picture of Verlyn on horseback which anyone with taste would have removed, and the one of Hayden with the premier, both of them smug as owls. Hayden looked up finally. Probably had needed time to gather his thoughts. There was no question that he'd had the hots for Candy. It had been obvious at the golf club Christmas party that something was going on. At the town meeting he'd asked several people to move so he could sit next to her. Jack had witnessed that from the platform when he was waiting for the crowd to quiet down so that he and Gary could show the slides and explain the benefits of life at Pine View.

Hayden was still not speaking, only shuffling the papers on his desk. Jack wanted to lean over and slap him on the head. But he waited. Seven years of law school bought a smidgen of respect.

"How's the wife, Hayden?"

"Well, you know. Okay. How's –" He stopped himself in time then said, "Have you heard anything?"

Jack shook his head. There was something going on here. Given the circumstance, the man should have got to his feet when he came in, put a hand on his shoulder, offered sympathy. This sullen coolness could mean a couple of things. Either the rat lawyer thought Jack was guilty or he knew something.

So, slowly, Jack said, "You have any idea where she might be, Hayden? The cops are bound to ask you."

The man sat straight up, attentive now, and shook his head. "So what can I do for you, Jack?"

"Well, you know, I could be sitting at home, just waiting. Maybe that's what I should do. But I'd go crazy and it wouldn't help. A lot of people are looking to get to work or they'll have to move on, out of town. Machinery standing idle."

"I'm aware. You're starting tomorrow."

"So I'll need to change the dates on the contract, sort out the indemnity."

"I am kind of busy but I could see my way."

Which meant he was upping his fee while he was talking. On the wall behind him, among the certificates attesting to his worthiness as a lawyer, hung a picture of himself in his old football sweater, number thirty-five. What it told about the guy wasn't flattering. That had been his golden time, rushing about a field in pursuit of a ball with a bunch of other sweaty men. The best years of his life. Pathetic when you thought about it.

Jack thanked him and said he'd drop by on Friday with the papers. As he walked away he couldn't help wishing, in a dark way, that Candace had gone off with the rat. At least he would have known where she was, alive and maybe even having a good time, though he doubted that. It was a straw of awful hope; that she was with someone, safe. And the longer she stayed away, kept her secret, the more reluctant she would be to come back even though he, or someone else in town, might well be accused of murder. He shook his head as if to make that idea fall out of his brain and die on the floor. It would take hatred, deep and black, to pull a trick like that. And Candace was a person who made allowances, not a hater.

It was the presumption, a few people's presumption, that he might or could have killed his wife that was beginning to grind into his soul. What hint had he ever given in all his life that he was an evil man?

•

How many hours? Mom came and said pray. Prayed for her to be dead and was afraid. Said sorry to the bear. Wrote poems. Poems they wrote. In school book. Two halves once joined. Two lives. Cloth not blood. Tied apart. Rhymes with heart. Dark. Office now. More work. Women in Africa. Starving. Only rice. Rice is nice. Good. Leg stiff.

Little stones. No life left. After all. No life left. Cold water. She dipped her fingers in the little puddle again and sucked on them.

•

Simon knew now, was absolutely certain, that Candace was not far away. He felt her calling to him. Why to him and not to Jack? I can't/won't believe that Jack has harmed her. Yet even that thought coming into his head meant that there was suspicion. And if there was suspicion in *his* mind, then in how many other minds round town. There were so many possibilities.

Suppose Jack and Candace had fought and he'd accidentally killed her and buried her somewhere. She'd gone back home after she found the dentist closed and found him with another woman. Words had been said and she'd set out to the Arctic where she had once been with her father. She was fed up with them all and was deliberately letting them worry. How long would they worry? How many weeks or months before they accepted that most likely she would never return? Erica had woken up crying that morning and he'd comforted her in the usual way. Afterwards she told him she'd felt deserted in her dream, a blank kind of dream with space and no humans, not even a dog. It was an end-of-the-world wilderness.

"I'm beginning to think this is an awful place," she said, handing him a mug.

"When I sell more of my work, we'll get a house with a real studio for me and a proper office for you."

"I'm talking about the town, not the house. The way they talk and look at us. We're all suspects now. It's my mother's fault."

"Your mother's been dead for four years nearly, honey," he replied sipping at the green tea that always revived him after sex.

"She left a kind of scar."

He refrained from telling her that mothers usually do and that already, perhaps, BJ and Tannis were marked for life by her own loving behaviour.

"As we know now, she likely couldn't help behaving the way she did."

"Stop it, Simon. She wasn't sick then. Just – what's the word, fucking malign."

"Come for a walk with me."

"I can't. I'm doing the accounts. It takes my mind off – things. And the kids'll be up soon. Tannis has to get to her practice."

"A little walk. I have a hunch."

Simon took his hunch off to Verlyn's. It was her morning. On Sundays, Hayden always left coffee in a Thermos and spicy cookies that Verlyn said were made from an old Bulgarian recipe on a tray. They were similar to the ones his old Ontario grandmother had made and stuffed into his pockets on summer mornings before he went fishing in the stream. They were rock hard and even the ducks wouldn't touch them.

He took the tray into the living room.

"Simon, love," she said.

If she'd been able to move, he would have been afraid of her. He handed her the coffee.

"Tell me about the world," she said.

"You get out, Verlyn."

"Out but not exactly about."

"Of course we are all worried. I'm going crazy because I can't think of anything else to do right now. The greater world. That's what you're thinking. The wars, Zimbabwe. Endless trouble. You watch TV, read the papers. You know all this stuff. You're involved. So one missing woman might seem not to count against all that. But she's my sister-in-law."

"You have such a nice voice, Simon. *Mellifluent,* I think is the word. What shall we do today?"

"I have an idea about maps. It's not new. Nothing is new. Maps as an art form. Maps as a means of deduction. If we make a rough map of this area of town."

He took out his sketch pad and quickly drew the area around the dentist's office.

"Here's our house, your house. There's the lake. The picnic tables. A seagull for decoration."

There was a screech as if the seagull had materialized and flown in through the window.

Verlyn shouted, "Stop. I know what you're doing and it's not true."

Simon waited till she was calm, and then he said, "I don't know what you mean. I'm only –"

"I know what you're only doing," she replied. "Go away. Go home. I was looking forward to this morning. Your visits are one little bit of sunshine in my life and you have to spoil it. I thought we were going to work on shadows. But it's her, isn't it. And you don't like me really. I'm not a charity. I'm not some poor thing. I don't need you or anyone else."

"I'll come back tomorrow. I do like you, Verlyn, or I wouldn't be here. As it is there's something I have to do."

He kissed the top of her head, and when he looked back from the hall she was pulling the wheeled table with her laptop on it

112

towards her.

Gently, she called after him, "See you tomorrow."

He left her house and walked down Maple, crossed Dogwood and made for the dentist's at the corner of Cray and Pine. Dr. Chan had set up his office in his own house, very handy for the people in the Lake Point area. They had, they liked to think, smugly, everything they needed here without going downtown at all. So Candace was annoyed at finding the dentist's office closed, annoyed too that she'd built up courage to go for treatment and been thwarted. Last known fact: She had been seen kicking the door and walking away. He kicked the door himself and turned. In her place, which direction would he have taken? Water dripped from the guttering overhead. It was a sign. He headed towards the lake.

•

Marcus looked up at contrails marking the sky. There was too much travel. Too many people were rushing around as if their homes were alien to them. India. China. Thailand. And what did they find when they got there after they'd burnt gallons of fuel and polluted the atmosphere on the way?

He was too early for Tannis. Erica had sounded crazed when she called and asked him to pick the child up after this special Sunday rehearsal. Whining and scraping sounds came from inside the school. He took a stroll round the building. A teacher came out the door and looked at him.

"I'm waiting for my granddaughter," he said. But did they all say that, perverts and kidnappers, those who preyed on the young? The vile men who would surely end up, if there was a hell, in the last, most awful ring.

This, though, was a trusting young woman. She smiled and said, "They'll be out in ten minutes."

At least then, unless she'd gone inside to call the police, he didn't look to her like one of *them*. She'd accepted his word. And besides, he was old. And besides, stupid, he said to himself, she knows who you are. Was there a cut-off age for perverts? Did they get past it? He perched on the low wall not bothering about the damp cold stone. This was the third day. "On the third day, he rose again." Maybe they should have gone to church and prayed. At worst, it couldn't do any harm. And at best? He and Erica and Jack and Simon the Gentle Sloth were getting snappish with each other, and that surely was no help to Candace wherever she was. Assuming she needed help. Did he hope she did or not? The implications were huge either way. If she had just taken off to be alone or with a lover, it was very wrong of her not to let Jack know. Having the cops dragged into their lives was bad enough, but what if, tomorrow, they had to call the station and say, *She took off to Las Vegas and forgot to tell us. She's home now. Just a little holiday. Thanks for your help, everybody.*

He began to feel angry. The cops already had him pegged as an idiot. The pizza box! He could see Jack hurling it to the ground after he'd seen what he'd seen. It was indecent of him to look. Had he stood there and stared for minutes before Wendy caught sight of him? In his desperation, had he become a peeping Tom?

Chattering. Voices. People around him now to gather up Jeffie, Rosy, Samantha, Lisa. A rush of kids carrying instruments emerged from the doorway as if expelled from a compressor. Tannis saw him and first looked disappointed, then smiled and shouted, "Hi, Grandpa." When she was close to him she asked quietly, "Have they found Aunt Candy?"

The question in different forms seemed to be coming at him from all directions. Parents were not moving away as quickly as usual. Slow motion. Waiting for a word.

"Not yet," he whispered to the girl. And then he said, "It must be too cold for ice cream."

"Oh, Grandpa!"

She got into the car beside him chattering about heat and cold and pumpkins and her cello teacher and a girl in her class who had cried and run out of the room for no reason.

Some flavours these days were beyond pleasant, but at Betsy's counter in the mall Tannis chose a conservative strawberry cone. She was one of the lickers, running her tongue over the creamy ball and reducing it slowly, round and round. He bit into his spicy ginger and his back teeth ached.

A fit of envy came over him. This child would live long after he was dead and would come to know the answers to all kinds of political, historical, geographical questions that were unresolved and likely to be for some time.

He decided to make a list of them in a letter that she might open when she was, say, sixty.

Glynis Judd crossed the road to murmur, "Is there any news of Candace?"

"Not yet," he replied. "The police have leads."

"So hard for you all, and for Jack."

She walked on and a trail of sympathy oozed after her as if she were a snail.

"When I'm bigger, I can get my clothes from Mom's store and they'll be free," Tannis said.

At home, Marcus began to write to the elderly girl, the woman his granddaughter would become. He decided to write it by hand because it was a formal thing, not something to be opened by just anyone. Hackers these days read everything on the Internet. Fools paid their bills online unaware of the villains lurking in space, waiting to empty their bank accounts overnight or, as the speaker at the last CARP lunch had warned, taking a few dollars at a time so the victim didn't notice. Though those chickens deserved to be plucked if they weren't keeping an eye on every single withdrawal whether it was five dollars or five hundred dollars. And anyway it was cheering going into the bank and chatting to gorgeous Sharon if he was lucky enough to end up at her counter.

But the letter. Why was he writing it to Tannis and not to her brother? She had more curiosity, was more in tune with the world even at her age. That's why she seemed sad some days. The boy was here and now and himself.

Dear Tannis, When you open this, I, your loving grandfather Marcus Brandt, will have been dead for decades. Whenever I died, whatever year, I mean, there will be any number of events, wars, political struggles, scandals, still going on. I will die with a mind full of unanswered questions. (I want you to know that I'm not writing this just because your Aunt Candace has disappeared and I'm feeling uncertain.) And by the way, too, I'm not out of my mind. I do realize that you are unlikely, unless strides have been made in the way of time machines and so on, to be able to pass these answers on to me. I have tried to believe in life after death but it simply doesn't compute. Lack of imagination on my part maybe. But the idea that trillions of souls or reconstituted bodies hang around in some ethereal no-place sounds like overcrowding to me. Here is here. Dead is dead.

It will just please me to know, as I lay dying, that some time, someone, that is you and your generation, will have some of the answers.

He read that over and it did sound as though he was mad, but it couldn't be helped.

He started on the list. He could revise the order later or, to use the appalling word, *prioritize* the questions.

Has the North Pole melted?
Have the Brits and Americans rebuilt Iraq and Afghanistan?
Did the President of the US start World War III? (Not a good question. It could happen next week, next month. If that happened

in his lifetime, and some said it had already, see above, he would erase the question.)

Did we stop using plastic bags?

Have the Chinese bought up America?

Did Alberta run out of oil? Did the Americans or Chinese move in and take over our natural gas, water and anything else they fancied? But that too was happening now.

Did the military take over Pakistan again? Also possibly happening 'as we speak.'

Under the Alps between Switzerland and Italy, there is a gigantic tunnel (can a tunnel be 'gigantic?'). Scientists are trying to discover how the world began. Will they manage to do that before the world ends? Dumb question but he decided to leave it there for now.

What happened to Aunt Candace?

He erased that one because she must be found soon, before... Before?

The clock on the mantel had stopped. It often seemed to at this time of day. The hands had hardly moved for the last half hour. It was only 12:15. And then the minute hand came out from behind its thicker brother and moved on a second towards the six. It was the beginning of afternoon. He'd decided in a Lenten way not to have a drink till Candace was found. But beer hardly counted. He opened two bottles and took them into the living room. Someone would likely turn up to drink the other, and if not, that was okay too.

He almost decided not to answer the phone but jumped up at the fifth ring.

"For God's sake," he said. "I thought you were her."

●

Rattling of the earth. Earthquake. Voice, mine, saying, I am here beloved. Poem read once. When reading poems was. Mind into their mind. Mined. Missile. Arrow. Can make them hear. Prize for finder. Water all round her now. No clean water. Light gone. Drink tears. Prison. Days scratched out with fingernails. The earth. Persephone and pomegranate. All things beginning with P. Piss. Stink of it not unPleasant. Drink it to survive. How to get it to mouth. Dribble of wetness down side of cell. Kind captors. She dipped her finger in it and put it on her tongue. If toxic at least wet.

•

Hi Cyberites,

H went out early to his office this morning. Something to do with the case in Abbotsford, so he said. Then he goes to church. God knows what he prays for. I guess that's a kind of pun.

Here's more about my town. She flew planes in the war, did Billy Rabinovich who changed her name to Robinson. You see her picture as you come in from the south. H thinks the sign's pathetic and we should take it down. Visitors ask if 'he' was an athlete, a skier maybe. She was a hero. That's what she was. Anyway it's better than having the world's biggest hockey stick outside your town or a giant artichoke. H talks about the future as if it's going to be good, but for all we know it might only be a big black void. We do not know. I overheard J talking to him and listened to see if I could pick up signs of guilt. Did he think H had done away with her or hidden her in a motel somewhere so that he can, anytime, do with her what he thinks he can no longer do with me?

But C isn't the seraglio type. Now me – before – I would've liked nothing better. Bathed, scented, waiting. Great sex all the time. For a few months anyway. Like that rhyme about sitting on a cushion eating strawberries and cream.

But I was telling you about the town, right. There are a few movers and shakers. Take the mayor, a corrupt little asshole or the best thing since sliced salami depending who you talk to. He was in our class at school. You'd've thought he'd never get beyond pumping gas, but he moved on to serving drinks and then cleverly jumped into a power vacuum.

Empty spaces are dangerous things.

To find out who has done away with C, we need to find out who had secrets to hide. It could be she was killed because she knew too much. If we could discover who she knew too much about, and there are at least three close to her I could name, then we'd know who did it.

Say what you like, Boris, but truth is best.

TNT M

•

It was Marcus's idea to get them all together after lunch but Simon had taken the meeting over.

"Green," the boy said.

Jack looked at him. He liked the boy better than the little girl, who seemed whiny and detached, but made an effort to love both. It was required.

"What about you, Tannis?" Marcus asked.

"I'm not allowed to think."

"Tannis!" her mother said sharply and then looked round at the others. "Why don't we leave this till dinnertime. It's 1:30 now. I have loads to do. You and Jack'll be back here at 5:30, Dad."

"I don't think we should be wasting any time, that's all."

Simon said, "It's about what we know. Maybe collectively we know more than we think. If we put our heads together there could be details, like a jigsaw puzzle. Pieces that fit together and add up to something."

"That's exactly why I asked Jack to come here to your place now, Simon," Marcus said. "It maybe isn't convenient but we're all worrying. So Tannis?"

"Mrs. Cosgrave gave me a cookie and patted my hand. She

thinks I'm still in kindergarten."

"Where did you see her?"

"Yesterday. She was wheeling her chair up the ramp into the library. She said she was sorry for me, and that Aunt Candy must be in a dark place and that someone is to blame. I bit on the cookie. It nearly broke my tooth."

"She's a spiteful woman," Erica said. "She'd no business to say that to you. I know she's damaged but she could behave decently at a time like this. Behind all this sympathy, there's a kind of nastiness, people making up stories and pointing fingers."

"Honey," Simon said. "Maybe she meant well."

BJ put in, "Look. I think she meant Aunt Candy has fallen into a hole. Disappeared. Not been taken away or anything."

Marcus brought out his list. "After likely places, we have to go for unlikely places such as Beatty Park, the ravine, the marina and then Vancouver. I know the police have asked in the city but it's a huge place. I think we'd know if she'd crossed the border to the States."

"She didn't have her passport with her," Jack said.

"I watched this TV program," the girl said, "where this bad guy took this woman and kept her in a storage place. One of these big, huge spaces. She died."

"I told you not to watch those shows, Tannis."

"Well it might help."

Silence.

"My parents," Simon began to say. But Erica shook her head.

BJ began to talk about his new game as if he had to fill in the gap.

Jack wondered what Donny and Bertie Belchuk had to do with anything right now that couldn't be spoken of in front of the kids.

Marcus said, "I'm not saying life mustn't go on, but I think we have to remain, as it were, engaged."

"Engaged, Dad?"

BJ and Tannis slipped away from the table, carrying their lunch dishes, and could be heard moving about the kitchen.

Simon whispered, "My parents have offered to take the kids away somewhere, Disneyland maybe, till this is over."

"Over," Jack said. "What do they mean, 'over'?"

"Just trying to be helpful."

"Just trying to do a bit of brainwashing. I don't mind them going there every other Friday but a whole week no way," Erica said.

"They're trying to be helpful, Errie," Simon repeated.

"The kids come home from there covered in plaster dust and full of weird ideas about –" She stopped to say "thank you," as BJ came and took away more dirty plates.

Marcus said, "Walters Storage. The warehouse. We should have them searched."

"No way the cops can go in there and open up every locker," Jack said.

"Can with a warrant."

"That's unrealistic, Dad."

"What's fucking – sorry – unrealistic is that my daughter has vanished off the face of the earth. And we're sitting here." He looked at his watch. "For heaven's sake. I nearly forgot. I have to pick your Aunt Rose up at the bus station."

He tried to kiss Erica who turned her head away and then said, "You'll bring her here for dinner, Dad."

"Right. Thanks."

"I can't see any sense to this. The questions have all been asked and the answers add up to one big fucking zero. The truth is we have no idea," Jack said. "I'm going mad. I'm going round in circles."

"I walked the route from the dentist's to the office and took a few detours." Simon said. "I didn't see anything new but sometimes you miss something. It's like looking at a painting. Keep looking and you see details, figures in the background. You see people in a gallery and they'll stand in front of some great work of art for maybe five minutes. Five minutes. And think they know it. When they've missed – well – everything."

"This is awful," Erica said. "We're sitting here. Talking as if it's a dog we've lost. I can't bear it."

She ran up the stairs and Simon went after her. They sat on the bed and held hands.

"I don't know if I really loved Candace," Erica said. "And I feel awful about that. But she had that way of seeming to care about you and then would come out with some little negative words. I usually came away mad. Like when she said, 'What a pity about Tannis.' 'My kids may not be perfect but they don't need your pity, thank you,' I said. And then she said, 'Only that she's got his looks not yours.' What was that about?"

"Just a backhanded compliment, honey."

"I've wanted to hit her sometimes. I know I won out in the gene stakes but she knows how to make the best of herself, as our mother would have said. And why did she have to marry Jack? It wasn't as if – like me – she had to. And I shouldn't be feeling these things now.

"And don't say anything reasonable, Simon. I've had it with reasonable. I want to scream. She had no business to disappear like this. And he'll get away with putting up that awful development because of sympathy. Say something."

"I can only think of reasonable things. I'm sorry."

"For God's sake don't apologize."

He held her close and stroked her shoulders and her neck. They lay back on the bed.

"They'll hear."

"They're deaf. They'll be plugged into their iPods or whatever."

Jack called out, "Goodbye," from the hall below.

"When mother became ill, you know, she kind of mellowed

in those last days as if the iron in her heart had melted – if iron
could melt."

"I'd better see how the kids are. You just lie there. I can put
the roast in when it's time."

"Thanks, love."

She can't have got far in those boots, ran through Erica's mind
like the refrain from a blues song. And Simon had said yesterday
that they must search while the trail was fresh as if she'd gone hiking off somewhere and would have left a line of little spiky holes.
He seemed overly disturbed but was that measurable in these circumstances and was she herself anxious enough? Was she showing
enough emotion, shedding useless tears, uttering sad, hesitant
words? *My sister is missing.* When there are children, it's hard to
walk away. But life, my life. Is there anything more ordinary? I
work at the boutique, selling overpriced clothes to oversized
women. Well not all of them are big, some are thin as twigs. I
look after my kids and have sex with Simon three or four times
a week. People tell me sometimes that I look tired but I don't
always sleep well. I seem to spend my life in a box and other times
in a forest. There are days when I think all the people in town
are looking out their windows, spying, talking about me or about
Simon. Probably saying to each other why does she put up with
him? My most fun lately has been at the protests, standing with
the others and shouting. We had a common cause. And they were
my comrades.

The police have asked me if I have any idea where she might
be. And I have several.

Jack has never seemed like a violent man and if he'd found
out about her and Hayden surely he would have gone after him,
not her. But then might have held back for the sake of Verlyn.
He could have killed her so that people wouldn't protest and he
could get on with the work on the development.

She sat up and pushed that thought out of her mind. It was

time to get on with the rest of the day. There should have been a protest walk to the site this morning but no one had called, no one would go out. But Jack was not a murderer. She would stake her life – or would she?

You could absolutely say that about Simon. Simple Simon. Simple sexy Simon.

But Jack?

Or did Candace decide to leave them all, had she finally cut herself off from the family?

Where was she? She had accepted a lift from a stranger and been...? No!

She had run away with a lover and didn't care that her family might be worried.

She was trying to tell them something. I'm making lists like the old man. Had Jack, finally fed up with Candace, killed her unintentionally. Manslaughter. Man's laughter, she'd thought it meant when she was at school. Five years in jail.

The door opened. Tannis came and stood beside her.

"Don't cry, Mom."

"I'm not."

"Aunt Candace will be okay. She'll come back soon."

Erica held her daughter close and said, "Sure she will."

EIGHT

Marcus hadn't expected his sister Rose to come all the way from Camrose. But she's your daughter, my niece, she'd said on the phone as if she had loved Candace and was necessary to the family in their time of desperation. To be fair, she did love the girls, in her way, a slightly envious way.

So now they were walking on the path to the lake, the two of them, and he was trying to be companionable and even grateful, though he'd had to fix a bed up for her and clean the bathroom and get in food and talk when he'd rather have been thinking on his own.

"This is where Jack's company is building. There'll be all kinds of fancy things, underground parking, and a golf course over there."

Birds were flying round as if they knew the trees were going to be cut down. The police had searched around the safety fence that enclosed the site as if Candace might have burrowed underneath it. They'd walked over this whole area with their great clomping shoes, probably crushing all kinds of clues, and found nothing.

Rose stared at the pictures on the board, drawings of what the houses would look like. Straight roofs, overhanging balconies.

"Architect must fancy himself as Frank Lloyd Wright."

"Better than Gehry," he said, feeling himself clever, imagining too much glass geometry. "And at least he had an architect. Isn't just throwing something up he's drawn on the back of an envelope."

"I thought protests had stopped all this. Erica wrote me. She seemed very upset at Candace."

"Ah well."

"Ah well what, Marcus? Don't be cryptic. I hate it when you're cryptic."

He didn't feel in the least cryptic. Didn't think he had ever been cryptic. And felt more like a blathering old man a lot of the time. "It goes back."

"You're doing it again."

"Anyway, she's married to Jack. She loves him, I guess. Stands by him. And they could get rich. Where she works, they're keen on progress. They call it progress. More people coming into the town."

"And he's going to start building with her out there missing."

She stopped and looked at the machines poised over the foundation. The piledriver had been moved onto the site beside the crane.

"Why won't he wait? It seems as if he didn't care."

"There are workmen involved. Money. Tons of money. He's been waiting for two months. It was getting expensive. And of course he cares."

"I see."

It was a very significant "I see" and Marcus turned to look at his sister. She was a small woman, roundish now, face burnt by the Alberta sun. Nice hair, thick hair, still had bits of brown in it. She looked like a motherly sort but there was always a chance of danger with her. Unpredictable. When they were kids, she led and he followed and no prizes for guessing who got the blame when clothes were torn and skin grazed. Up trees or into the slough, anywhere that was forbidden. Later, she'd introduced him to her friend Sheila and then abandoned him to his fate. For a time he'd been grateful. The coaster years had been mainly good.

"Now that she's missing, the protesters are staying home?" Rose asked.

"We won't talk about this tonight. The kids will be there for one thing." *And for another I wish you would just shut up.*

"I wish we could stay at your place and order a pizza."

"Tomorrow, maybe."

"Tomorrow I have to go to Vancouver."

He didn't ask why she had to go to Vancouver or whether a trip there was her real reason for flying out.

"Erica must be frantic so why is she cooking?"

"She has the kids. And Simon. In fact Simon is the one who seems really anxious."

"Anything going on there?"

Marcus decided not to answer any more of her questions. They led along difficult paths and he wanted nothing to do with them. He also didn't want to prance down memory lane with his sister and talk about their, according to her, idyllic childhood. She had thrown a Rose-coloured blanket over Father's late nights and Mother's sorrow and recalled only those few happy outings to Lake Louise or Drumheller. She was a woman more for the exotic moments in life than the every day. Which was why she'd turned up now. To deflect her enquiries, he pointed to the fence round the site and said, "The townhouses will cost about seven hundred thousand each. All appliances. Exercise room. Golf course. Choice of decoration. Marble in bathrooms extra."

"He send you out as a salesman?"

"I've read the ads."

"It doesn't say 'built over my wife's dead body.' Not yet anyway."

"Rose!" He walked on ahead of her, hating her, wanting her to go away and leave him be.

She was making a horrible story out of Candace's disappearance and she had no right to do that. He just hoped she wouldn't start all over again at Erica's. He turned to warn her and she'd gone. He could only have been a few strides ahead of her surely. Christ! He saw himself on Erica's doorstep and Erica asking, Where's Aunt Rose? And him answering, She was right behind me and then...

He walked back and saw her standing looking at the site, at the machines, and the great hole in the earth, and knew exactly what she was thinking. And wished he didn't.

•

Simon had suggested Erica should go for a run. She hoped no one would see her. She was wearing his rain jacket with the hood and kept her head down.

It makes you feel guilty not to like your nearest relations but it's often mutual, she thought as she trotted past the cemetery. And yet when they're threatened, the family tie becomes a clamp and love has nothing to do with it. Simon had whispered in bed last night that in the market people were saying Candace had gone off with David Altrow, the professor who'd bought the Grange house. It couldn't be true but was better than having them say that Jack had murdered her. Altrow, the most recent man to move into town, was a stranger, a man living on his own and therefore suspect. But why did it have to be him? And there was a class thing going on which she hadn't considered before. Why was it not thought possible that Candace had run off with a janitor, a garbage man, a window cleaner? Because the family would have felt let down? Was that it? And if she'd run off with a woman would it have mattered whether that woman was a teacher or a maid?

But by now if she'd simply gone away with the least desirable person in the world, that would be better than...than what they were all beginning to sense was true.

Erica looked around. There was the lake, the island, the shore. There the place the new sewage system would go. Another cause of strife in the town: One group thought the sewage system was way overdue and the only healthy route. Those who'd fought against it because it would bring more development to the area had been proved right but at the same time were wrong. Clean water, Pine View or not, was a necessity.

The underground parking would go there below the trees. Beyond, the rough terrain would be made smooth and punctured with small holes. Sand was easily available for the traps or whatever they called them. Before long, electric carts would carry golfers from green to green.

Canada geese flying overhead were squawking crossly. Access will be limited. Candace was blind to all this. But then she was married to the problem: A man who grew up here and couldn't understand the horror of what he was about to do. A man who blithely set about spoiling a lovely place, adding more traffic to the town, more pollution.

State of mind, the police asked. What was your sister's state of mind lately? How could I answer when we hadn't really talked for months? Her own anger had silenced Candace and fear of attack, verbal only, had reduced their exchanges to below commonplace if there was any ground there at all. And what about my state of mind! I've fought against the damn project from day one, organized groups, talked to politicians, and it will still go ahead. Why did money have to win every damn time!

The town had grown first of all as a way station for the miners who went further north to search for gold. Now it was a place for loggers to stop by as they hauled their loads east; and for short-stay tourists. But the surrounding forests were almost logged out. In her sleep, she could hear the slogans of the pro-development people, the uncaring. Okay so owls don't turn everyone on. What about space, Candace, unclaimed, free space? Does everything have to be owned? The houses Jack's going to build are pretentious homes for the near-wealthy. Pillars in front. Visions of Tara. Tacky. A blight.

Erica laughed grimly and said to the seagull standing on a picnic table, "I've been arguing with my sister who might by lying dead somewhere. If it wasn't for my kids I'd get on a bus and go to some remote place and scream and go crazy. This is beyond the teddy bear, Candace. Return at once. All our lives are in limbo. And yours?"

Switch channels, Erica! Think dinner?

She saw two elderly people walking a little apart as if they'd quarrelled. It was her dad and his sister Rose, the sharp-eyed aunt who'd let her and Candace ride horses before they knew how, without lessons, "just learn as you go along," throwing her brother's kids into harm's way without a thought. And then they spent hours working as cheap stable help. Two weeks on a ranch in Alberta. What did you do on your summer vacation? They knew more about horseshit than horses. Even now the smell of it made her feel sick. She'd resisted all her parents' attempts to get her interested in the local horse scene here in town. Candace had tried it for a while but found the lessons tame and the other kids snobby. As for the gymkhana. As for Verlyn Cosgrave who was the smartest, fastest rider between here and Calgary...

The beef was in the oven. Rose liked meat. Erica recalled the routine Sunday meal when they were kids: Ham and scalloped potatoes and sprouts. Next day, cold ham with that terrible salad that included jello and marshmallows and grapes. Tonight there'd be potatoes and carrots baked round the meat. Green salad. Pie to follow.

She jogged back along Havers Lane where she'd first really kissed a boy. Party, second house on the right. Candace was a wild dancer in the crowd. Pills. The first drug experience: A sensation like being thrown about on one of Rose's ponies. Candace had held her head while she threw up onto the host's bathroom floor and then said, "Let's get out of here."

They'd run home as if they'd committed a crime. Only fifteen and sixteen but able to recognize danger.

●

If I dig down? I have claws. If I dig down, will I fall into China? Or Australia? Land on a kangaroo? She rode the kangaroo along the Great Wall until an army clad in long skirts and silver breast-plates surrounded her and she began to feel warm again and licked the tears off her face. Someone had cried.

●

Simon fought against it. It wasn't appropriate. He'd said himself that they should fix their minds on Candace but the image was too strong. He put the colander back in the sink and grabbed a piece of paper from the message pad by the phone. He drew the curved lines quickly and knew exactly the shade of skin, the sug-gestion of light, the blurred movement he could put in with paint.

Erica looked at him and then at the drawing. "It looks like two whales coming up side by side," she said.

"What it is," he answered. And then the words came out of his mouth like a story told against the narrator's will.

"He was what!" Erica shouted. "Who the fuck with?"

"Jack didn't know. She was well – underneath."

"I don't believe it. I just don't believe it."

"Maybe he's in love," Simon said.

"And maybe pigs can fly."

"It happens."

"But now. Now. When his daughter's missing and maybe – well who knows what's happened to her. And did you have to tell me this minute when dinner's just about ready and where are the kids? They should be back by now. You shouldn't have told me. How'm I going to get it out of my mind!" She banged her fist on the table and her sleeve caught the platter of food so that it fell to the floor. "And Rose is coming and I'm doing my best to stay calm."

●

When Jack arrived, Simon was trying to clean up. Jack was sorry about the dinner. It was clearly the remains of roast beef with vegetables and rich brown gravy. And then he felt sorry for even thinking of food. He took a few paper towels from the roll and bent down to help, hiding his face. He'd begun to fear that all his thoughts were floating into the air for everyone to read.

"So you had to tell her."

"I shouldn't have said anything."

"Better if I hadn't told you. It was the shock of it."

"Would you have been shocked, Jack, if it had been, say, last week?"

Difficult question. Jack thought about it. No, it would've been more surprise, amusement. The old man can still do it. There's hope for us all. That kind of thing. So that Candace, by disappearing, had changed how he saw things. Dangerously, it would change many people's take on every single daily event. He shivered.

"D'you think we could kind of scrape the beef and veggies and put this back together? You could make some more gravy."

"I'll call for pizza," Simon said.

"Make it Chinese," Erica said as she came back into the kitchen. "Dad will be here soon and we will pretend nothing has happened. Although to tell you the truth, I – well I don't know how I'll be able to look at him."

"If you tell me what you want, I'll go pick it up," Jack said.

●

Marcus knew he shouldn't, but instead of going to the door he stepped into the flower bed among the brown-leaved azaleas, and looked in Erica's window. She was holding a bread knife and began to tap herself on the chest with it as though she was counting. Tap, tap, tap. If she was planning to cut her throat with the serrated blade, it would take time. She caught sight of him, dropped the knife and gave a silent scream. He went to the door.

"What the hell, Dad?" she shouted. "When we're all on edge!"

"I wondered, that's all, why people look in windows."

"Because they're nosy or stupid or want to break in. Come in."

"No news?"

"You?"

"No, but I've had a thought. Rose stopped at the store, by the way. Wants a sweater or something. She'll be along soon. What were you doing with the knife?"

"Cutting bread." She sat down. "So you've thought."

He brought the crumpled map out of his pocket and spread it on the table.

"She set off to the dentist's here and was seen banging on the door."

"She's usually so efficient. How come she got the date wrong?"

"Consider the dentist. Anyway look. She retraces her steps and moves towards work. The hairdresser sees her go by. Suppose she'd changed her mind about going to the office. Maybe she was going to look for Jack at the site. She had an hour to spare. After that, no one saw her. Nothing. That means the area of disappearance is here." He drew a circle on the map with his finger.

"It could be the whole wide world, Dad."

"No, it couldn't. The lake, see. She would've had to come back. According to Jack, he wasn't at the site. That's what he says."

"Don't talk as if you suspect him."

"I don't. Others do. The police say it's always someone close."

"But we're not talking murder here! She has disappeared or perhaps left town for reasons of her own. Just don't go there. Okay? Or it was some stranger. Something we can't imagine. Don't want to imagine. Go talk to Simon. I've got to set the table."

He looked into the garage but it was dark except for a couple of candles. Simon was sitting on a stool staring at a canvas. Marcus crept away and sat on the couch in the living room feeling like a discarded sock. He planned an article in his head for the retired people's magazine: The old and the useless. Why we prefer to stay home. In his own house, there were things to do, ways of surviving while here, now, he had no occupation, was surplus to requirements. Not wanted on this voyage.

Simon put his head round the door and said, "Ah" and backed out again.

He returned a moment later with two glasses of red wine.

"I saw you sitting in the dark there. Didn't want to disturb you," Marcus said.

"Sometimes you get a better perspective without light."

The kids came in with their great aunt.

"We found her on the doorstep."

"I'm a foundling," Rose said and laughed.

"So it's going ahead," Marcus said to Jack and then realized that he sounded aggressive. Maybe Jack expected blushes and cast down eyes. Tough! He'd tried hard to feel ashamed but the fact that he'd been spied on made him mad. What was the use of having your own home if anybody could look in the windows, like jailers peering through little squares in cell doors. And now he bet they all knew and were not going to mention it. He daren't ask but wondered why, when there was such a great smell of roast beef, they were eating black bean chicken and egg foo yong. Across the table, Erica looked as if her lips would disappear altogether. The kids were quiet though the boy gave his grandfather a look that suggested "Don't expect much joy round here today." Simon was fussing. Have some more of this, more of that. This is really good. Jack, stone-faced, was picking at the food with his chopsticks and letting it dribble back onto his plate. Marcus glanced at him. What had Wendy said about it always being the nearest? And dearest? Though if he had done anything to Candace, he was putting on a good act. And anyway he couldn't and wouldn't. He was reliable, decent Jack Wilson. Had behaved decently when he found out about Hayden. But then there was a motive in that. Jealousy had killed many.

"Nothing from the police?" Erica asked in a voice so false it would have cracked him up if it hadn't been such an important question.

"She hasn't used her credit card."

"There've been no charges on it?"

"No."

"I think," Simon said, "that we might talk about this later."

Not in front of the children!

"Perhaps you could play your piece on the cello after dinner," Marcus said to the girl.

"Diversion tactic," BJ said. "Who wants to hear that noise?"

"She plays very well," Simon said.

"I need to practise. The concert's next week."

Erica opened her lips and said, "So. In spite of this, in spite of your wife being missing now for three days, and who knows what's become of her, you're going ahead, Jack?"

Simon the peacemaker said, "Not right now, Erica."

"There are so many things we can't talk about right now, eh Dad? So I'll just be quiet."

"Some native people," BJ threw in, "have a talking stick and only the person holding it is allowed to say anything."

Tannis laughed. "You don't need a stick," she said. "You talk all the time anyway."

Her brother thumped her on the shoulder and she slapped his head.

"Cut that out," Erica said. "If you want dessert, try to behave like human beings."

The kids, allies again, made monkey faces and grunting sounds.

Marcus echoed, "Human beings."

Erica stared at him.

"I have to get home," Jack said. "Thanks for dinner."

"You've hardly eaten anything."

"I'm fine."

"Don't forget your fortune cookie," Tannis called after him.

There was a silence after the front door closed, and then Simon asked, "How long are you staying, Aunt Rose?"

Erica had taken the empty dishes out to the kitchen and returned with the salad.

"A couple of days. I can't leave the farm for long." She looked accusingly at her brother as if daring him to say that the remaining stock, one horse, a couple of goats and a hen or two, does not make a farm. Animals were animals and needed attention. "We always used to have ham on Sundays," she said. "I've wondered about keeping a pig. I know they can be trouble but they sure taste good."

A moment later she was eyeing BJ like the witch in Hansel and Gretel as if checking his weight and fat content. "You should come and visit me in summer," she said to him while Tannis jiggled up and down to make her existence clear. "Would you like that?"

"We were thinking of driving out to Banff next year," Simon said, building a protective shield. "We could stop by."

"My goats have kids and you could collect eggs."

"Goat eggs," Marcus said. He wouldn't trust his grandchildren with this erratic woman who might well forget about them and leave them out in the field overnight with the beasts.

Rose said, "I'm sorry about Candace. I feel it in my heart. And yet we're sitting here eating and digesting this food and she might be starving someplace. In the dark. Desperate."

"Please don't go there, Aunt Rose. We're all in different ways doing our best."

"I'd be out there scouring this place from top to bottom, knocking on doors."

"We've done that. The police are doing that."

Marcus watched as Rose realized she wasn't raising any hell with her comments and decided to become the family comedian.

"Do you know," she said to Tannis, "why bears sleep in the winter?"

"No."

"Because they can't *bear* the cold."

Tannis smiled politely.

The boy stifled a groan.

Simon tried to persuade Tannis to get her cello.

BJ edged away from the table.

Rose picked two rolls from the basket and began to juggle with them.

The boy watched and then said, "Anybody can do that with two."

"Throw me another."

She held her audience, juggling three rolls deftly, never dropping one. Simon smiled.

The kids applauded. Marcus wished he was at home – alone. And Erica in the doorway, holding a pumpkin pie, began to laugh hysterically.

●

Peace. Nothing. Emptiness. Keep moving feet. Legs.

●

Awareness. Jack had failed awareness. He had no idea what was going on in his wife's mind. He looked round and sank back into the booth. He should have gone further afield. This café with its hockey photos and shabby chairs and TV always on low was too familiar. He knew most of the customers. But he wanted coffee. He wanted a kind of comfort. He was hungry too. If he kept his head down, no one would see him and he could think. It was better here than in the quiet house.

Candace was a calm woman mostly. She was considerate

mostly. Truthful up to a point.

Had lied only to save his feelings. He had never asked her what she would most like in the whole world, probably in case she wanted something not in his power to give.

He felt a hand on his shoulder and started. A cop, prosecutor, jail. I am innocent. That's what they all say, sir. Just come along with us.

Brian Hampson appeared in front of him. "I'm sorry. I guess you're on edge."

"The not knowing is hard," Jack answered. It was his prepared response now.

"But we have to keep on, eh. Let me get you a coffee."

"I've ordered already. But thanks." There had to be gratitude. For sympathy, for banana bread. Althea came and set down two large coffees and two cinnamon buns covered in sticky icing. "The buns are from me," she said, smiling, kind.

I'm not a man now, Jack thought. I'm an obvious whimpering jelly. Everybody can see this, and this woman is offering me food for my grief, starchy comfort. In another moment he might have cried but Brian said, "The cops wanted to talk to me."

"You?"

"They went on about the development, the opposition. You know. After all I'm a major investor."

"Surely they don't think..." Jack felt as though the ceiling was about to fall on his head.

"But listen. Never mind all that. I think you're right about the mall. Marcia told me you and Gary are going to press on with it."

"Wait a minute."

"You have the advantage. People are caught up with – with other things and not exactly paying attention. You get the lakeside property looking like something, say in six months or so, and then talk about taking out that mall and putting in something attractive, modern, supermodern. I know this architect. A smaller, classier version of West Edmonton. I showed you that picture of the place in Milan. Open cafés, smart stores."

"My wife is missing," Jack heard himself say in a voice louder than normal.

"And I have thought about that, Jack. If, God forbid, she doesn't return. I'm not being insensitive here, just looking ahead. We have to do that because life goes on. You could see the new building as a memorial."

Jack began to laugh. He was laughing. He heard hyena sounds coming from his own throat and then a kind of choking noise. Brian was holding his hand. Althea was offering him water. He pushed them away and ran out of the café.

●

Marcus just wanted to walk the route by himself. It was going to rain later. Rose said she was going to watch the eight o'clock news and then go to bed, Alberta time. He took his raincoat and walked down Cray to the dentist's surgery. Dr. Chan had explained to the cops that he was suddenly called away on Friday morning, but he was more likely having sex with the hygienist in the storeroom, though that could have been awkward if the receptionist had been at her desk. But she wasn't. She'd called in sick or, in the view of those with devious minds, had been told to stay home. And the dentist, in love with Candace for decades, had gone out the back way, pursued her and killed her on the old "If I can't have you, no one can" rationale.

Too many people in town watched mysteries on TV or read awful books about murders because their lives were too damn dull.

Weird kind of work, dentistry, always having your hands in people's mouths. There'd be satisfaction in keeping people eating well, having nice smiles. His own lower teeth were shifting and beginning to look like leaning tombstones. No doubt he could, at great expense, have them straightened.

He turned along Harris Street to the three-storey building where Candace worked. Glenn, Barden and Tyler, promotion, advertising, a mixed kind of business he'd never really understood. Were they quite legal? Had Candace discovered some trade secret and been killed because of it? False advertising wasn't exactly rare. They had a contract with the solar energy people. Not likely to be anything sinister there. But where there was money there was envy, there was greed. Where there was greed, there was desperation. He turned to the lake, the direction she'd apparently taken, and wished he was wearing high-heeled boots so that he could sense her feeling as she moved towards the water.

He looked up at the giant billboard with its coloured picture of the structure and an architect's plan of the layout. Fifty-five percent sold. Sixty splendid townhouses. Great views. Sure, if you had a front unit, otherwise you were looking across the park to the strip mall. "State of the art." To what art exactly did that refer? If it was architecture, they'd missed the target. He was halfway to the on-site office trailer and then thought he'd better go all the way and not look – though who could be watching in the semi-darkness – like an indecisive old fool who'd lost his bearings. Though he had. My bearings are long gone. Worn down.

"Hi, Marcus."

Jack was locking the trailer door.

"I was just walking the route, that's all. Trying to figure where she went."

"I'll drive you home."

"How's it going?"

"Should be ready to go tomorrow. I tried for today but couldn't get on to them at the weekend."

"People are wondering."

"I know."

"You know what you're doing, I guess."

Marcus didn't want a lift. He wanted to keep on walking in the rain, coming down heavily now. He'd seen a movie where someone kept walking in a downpour because they were in love. And I love my daughter. That's the truth. He wanted to get soaked through because it was the only thing he could think of to do in reparation for her disappearance. Somebody should suffer and pneumonia was a slight martyrdom.

"Come on, Dad. It's dark. You're getting wet."

Jack didn't often call him anything but Marcus. He savoured the 'Dad' and got into the passenger seat.

"How's Rose?"

"Fine. She's going to Vancouver to see a friend tomorrow. Getting the Greyhound. I offered to drive her. Some mystery about it. Wants to go on her own."

He looked at Jack's strong hands on the wheel and imagined them gripping his daughter's neck. And said aloud "No!"

"What?"

"Nothing. A thought, that's all. I guess we all have our nightmares right now."

Jack put his hand on Marcus shoulder as he brought the car to a stop, and said, "Right, Dad. We just have to keep on, that's all."

"I don't think we've asked the right people yet."

He leaned over and gave Jack a half hug and stepped onto the sidewalk.

NINE

Marcus wasn't pleased to see Wendy's Smart Car parked outside his house and wondered if Jack had noticed it the other night and would make a connection. Since then, he'd wanted more than anything to sever relations with the woman. But he opened the door for her and she followed him into the house. Before he'd had time to close the drapes, she began.

"Your daughter went shopping in Vancouver. She was attacked and her purse was stolen. The blow to her head made her lose her memory. She's in hospital, unidentified, languishing. I bet you anything you like that's what happened. She's all right."

"I never saw you as a detective," Marcus said. "And it's late."

He had almost, without thinking, led her upstairs to the bedroom. He wasn't going to risk that face at the window again. Every time they had sex, it was always going to be the last time, but when he saw her, he wanted her. And really she wasn't all that attractive. Comfortable, yes. A face to smile at. Thick hair that wasn't dyed and fried. Shapely body. Kind eyes. Maybe it was that look of acceptance. And then he remembered that Rose was in the spare room.

"My sister's here," he said and then for no reason at all, "I had my children young."

"Children are always young when you have them," she replied, knowing full well what he meant but tired of him saying it as if he had to tell her exactly how old he was every time she saw him.

These people, Marcus and his family, were oddly calm. Jack had been going to work. She'd seen Erica ambling around near the lake. If someone of hers had been missing, she would have been, not frantic – she didn't think frantic – but out there looking, turning over every stone, peering into every crevice.

"You seem away," Marcus said.

"I have my psychic moments."

They were sitting in the living room and she was holding his hand.

"Would you like tea?"

"Sure," he said and got up to chip another coaster off the wall.

"What," Wendy said to herself as she went to the kitchen and plugged the kettle in, "is in this relationship for me?"

Maybe she should make a list. He was always making lists. But after a few minutes she could think of nothing to mark down beside a, or b, or c. Did she need the diversion? To feel wanted? *I am not without love. I get by.* Don't need money. But would like it. In any case this was never a transaction. But she was kidding herself. Independence was important. Right! Fine but here was a decent man offering her affection and a kind of sex. He treated her body as if she were one of those celebrity women who show just about everything they've got when they're supposedly dressed. He liked to see her in underwear. And she felt, now, as if she did want to be with him. She felt pity for Marky. There was a deep loneliness in the man, a need for good times. And sometimes the sex was fine. The amazing leaping passion, the lovemaking she'd had with Harry had gone on into their fifties. No good expecting that again in one lifetime.

A cold breeze had blown into the room although the window was closed. She felt the chill round her head, behind her eyes. The air she breathed in chilled her nostrils. Sitting down, she ignored the steaming kettle and waited.

What the hell was she doing? She'd had time to bake a cake let alone make a mug of tea. Marcus called out to her. There was no reply. Had she walked out without a word because they couldn't have sex? It was, she said, the one bit of excitement in her week. But maybe she only said that to please him.

She was sitting in the kitchen like a statue, her face frozen.

"Are you okay?" he asked very softly, afraid. "Try standing on one leg, honey."

She said nothing. He went to the shelf to get the *BC Health Guide* to look for the chapter on signs of a stroke. He knew that balance mattered. "Come over here. Lean on the counter and lift one foot," he said.

She didn't move. He had to call 411. 911. Rose.

"Your daughter is in a very dark place," she said, intoning like a priest or a magician.

"You all right?"

"A very dark place. I need a cup of tea."

He made the tea and poured some into two mugs. He felt that it was important not to interrupt her thoughts but couldn't help asking the dread question, "But is she alive?"

"How could she have gotten through to me if she was dead?" Wendy snapped, and then more gently said, "But the signal was very weak."

Rose appeared like a ghost when he was turning out the lights.

"You've had a woman here," she said and sniffed.

"Neighbours are being very kind," he replied. "You can't sleep?"

She sniffed again.

"Marcus," she said, and he heard significance. "I haven't come out here just because of Candace. Though you know it's a time to be with the family. Where's Jack's mother, by the way? I'd've thought she'd want to be with her boy right now."

Marcus waited.

"Truth is, I'm having a hard time with the farm. I'm thinking of selling up. It's impossible to get anyone to come in and work for a few hours now and then. They're all out in the oil patch

earning tons of money. Someone took one of the goats. Stole it."
She began to cry. "I was going to make cheese and sell it."

He wanted to cry himself. His feelings had become a mass of
jangled wires again. There was Candace out there in the dark.
Here was his own sister wanting to sell the family home, which
she should have done long ago, and maybe wanting to move in
on him. And crying on account of a damn goat.

"And besides," she went on, "I'm not all that well."

And wanting to be nursed!

"Go sit in the living room," he said. "I'll heat up some milk
for you. I could make toast if you want."

"The living room," she said, "is uninhabitable. That mess
you've made on the wall. What were you thinking!"

It would be like that. For years it would be like that while he
nursed her and she cried and Candace never returned to cheer
him up. It was a dark, dark place indeed. And his sister sitting
on the stool at the counter like a bird of prey reached for the
cookie jar.

●

Hi Cyber-pals.

How are you all out there? Craziness rules here in Ghills Lake. This
is the third night. It's dark. Fear has taken over the streets. People
don't look one another in the eye. They whisper and creep.

I've watched them all going about as if something holy has happened. Quiet they are, and sly. Candace, sleek, smart, pussycat
Candace is gone and somebody knows where she is. Hands up those
who think she's dead. I'll feel really sorry if she is, if something
horrible has happened to her. It's not a matter of whether you like
somebody or not, it's knowing them since you were at school
together. Time. So they're part of your life story, characters in it.

Erica and Candace. Sisters though you'd never have thought so
to look at them. Erica smaller, a genuine blonde. Candace tall, reddish

brown hair. And on most days, they walked to school separately, avoiding each other. I liked their mother. She sometimes looked at me as though she would've preferred me to those two little demons who were always quarrelling. They gave her a hard time, I think. Especially after their dad began to make long trips up North.

Erica absolutely does not deserve sweet Simon. He is the only person in town aside from Maj Harim who understands what I go through every single day of my life. Once a week Simon comes to sit with me and we create imagery together. He starts with, say, a blue tower and I add three trees and we end up with a magic place. Reality, he thinks, is for dull people. One day, he says, I might have a show. But I know that what I add to his drawings is like the sparkle on a Christmas tree. Glitter. Dust. Ash if you like. But I don't care. Dear 'Dr. Dread,' as I call him, once suggested that a sudden shock might bring life back to my lower extremities. If that happens, if it happens soon, my lower extremities and I will be after Simon full steam ahead.

Erica is only against the development to aggravate her sister. No principles really. She was for sewage treatment and against building but they're opposites. No one's ever died here of cholera or whatever you get from raw sewage. (Tchaikovsky drank infected water on purpose. Listen to some of his music and you can picture him reaching for the glass.)

Thank you. Just set it down there. I'm fine.

Sixteen times a day I lie and tell somebody or other that I'm *fine*. Maj arrives at 9:30 on weekdays, except Friday when he comes early to take me to physio. He brings me coffee and then asks what I want to make for dinner. He sets everything I need within reach on the kitchen table and then leaves.

Today he called to say he'd be late tomorrow, then he asked me what I thought about the rumours. Would Jack Wilson be arrested soon? I told him sharply that it was wrong to assume guilt. He echoed, 'As yume gild.' He goes to ESL classes and needs practice. Like I said, the town is oddly silent but there is noise in the air. The hum of communication; a cat's cradle of rapid messages going to and fro faster than light. It's an infiltration of words that undermines the place, like gas in pipes or rats in sewers.

When I've put together whatever it is we're going to eat at night, pasta sauce or chili, I set it on the stove to cook. I can do that.

When Hayden returns and says, "How are you, love?" it's my chance to say something like, "I want to go to Budapest." And one of these days, he'll have to say yes. "It's my roots, dear," I'll say for the fiftieth time.

He's fallen asleep in front of the TV, worn out from putting together another coffee table. He's always going to Vancouver, to IKEA, as if, by adding another damn piece of furniture, a Scandinavian bookcase or a lamp, he can make me whole. And then he spends hours swearing, losing small parts, shouting at the wood. He beat this coffee table into submission but it wobbles and isn't much use. It releases a lot of frustration, I suppose. His, not mine.

TNT M

As she signed off, Verlyn wondered whether the cops checked into chat rooms or looked at YouTube. The small group she communicated with were, like her, confined in some way. Only the man who signed himself Boris seemed to get around. He had, he said, just sailed his yacht back from Mexico to Aruba.

•

Marcus knew he wasn't going out of his mind. He was almost sure of it anyway. But when you're over seventy, sure is an uncertain word. Jack had been seen laughing apparently. In public. Laughing as though he'd just heard the best joke in the entire world. Yet he would have sworn that Jack was not a bad man.

Was it something to mention to the police? Though by now, in this town, they likely already knew.

Memory of a cold summer day years ago. Opportunity. Barbecuing. Setting it up. Light. A small explosion and Sheila said, "You could have killed me."

"Could I?" he'd replied as if it were an option. And had laughed. Then had to apologize for the burnt burgers. And one of the girls had said "Maybe you should give up trying to barbecue, Dad. We could go to McDonalds."

He never went there with them because the smell and the buns reminded him of that one moment when the devil's hand had touched him. Had Jack been given a chance and taken it?

The real question was, Can people disappear off the earth? A brief earthquake unnoticed by everyone else had opened up a small crack in the ground and Candace had fallen into it? He was beginning to sense in his bones that she might never come back. He daren't allow himself to think of what had happened to her. That was a deep, dark place.

And yet Jack had laughed.

●

Jack heard a sound outside again. He left the house lights off and took his flashlight from the hall table. Garbage was scattered about. Crows! Crows? The lid on the container fitted tightly. Specified by the council so raccoons and bears couldn't open them, they were standard issue. This part of town was to be kept clean. Crows could not have pried the lid open. Besides, crows slept at night, didn't they? A dog on its hind legs wouldn't have enough leverage to open it. So it had begun. They were desperate now. In their office the cops would construct an edifice from scraps of paper. Old bills, demands from charities, a copy of the *Builders' Digest* from which he'd torn a page about cement. The letter from his mother, the plan he'd drawn of a house he and

Candace might build one day. He could see their gloved fingers, sorting, putting grubby fragments into piles, making walls. Their building was likely already one storey high. They would add colour, lights, sound and erect a cathedral of accusation.

He felt like a cornered rat with only one option: To bite someone.

He made a cup of tea and a slice of toast and sat in the rocker and thought about Candace.

Her absence was his absence. Neither of them was here. She had taken his life with her, wherever she was. He imagined her on a beach in California, lying on her stomach while a blond beach bum oiled her back for her. Did beach bums still exist or were they all surfers now? Surfing. A life riding waves. Sea washing over their heads. Tumbling into the frothy water.

The judge was saying, "We don't know what you've done, or if you did it, but the fact is your wife has disappeared to your advantage. Sixty years plus a day. Develop that!"

Jack tried to shout "advantage!" but no sound came out of his mouth.

When a hand touched his shoulder, he cried out, "I am innocent."

"Sorry to wake you, sweetheart."

A hologram of his mother was standing in front of him.

He knew it was a nightmare and tried to see through her.

Then she said, "I didn't want to trouble you so I decided to walk from Vancouver. A young woman I talked to on the plane was coming this way."

He looked at the clock. It was 8:15. Night, or morning? He looked out the window and saw a few stars. It was evening. He'd been asleep for half an hour. Ghosts had moved into the house and he had to get out of it.

•

Erica did not, although she hated what he'd stirred up in this previously peaceful place, want to think that Jack could have been responsible for Candace's disappearance. If rumours were true, he had motive and he had all kinds of opportunity.

The kids' voices rose above the sound of the TV. At that pitch, the dialogue was well into the sixth retort.

"My name means princess."

"It means the kind of acid that turns your teeth and insides brown so they rot."

"Shut up."

"Acid."

"Mom!!!!"

Erica poured two glasses of milk and took them into the living room. Both children were disturbed right now. BJ, feeling useless, had become more aggressive. Tannis kept trying to help, hating the mystery, afraid, wanting normalcy, in the shape of Candace, returned. Erica handed her a glass of milk and the girl took it and sat back on the couch. Her computer had become a hostile thing. Questions from friends about her aunt, sympathy, creepy suggestions had destroyed her pleasure in the magic box.

"BJ," Erica said.

The boy looked at her with his uncle's hard stare and shook his head. "She'll have to learn," he replied.

"Don't watch that for too long. It's nearly bedtime."

On the screen, a red car drove down a winding road and disappeared. She went back to the kitchen to consider what was needed from the supermarket for the coming week but the image of that shiny new car stuck with her.

"Picked up," that was the dreadful phrase. Candace might have been picked up. Two simple words that contained a variety of vehicles, a number of different monsters and nothing at all good. *Young woman found...*

She tried to stop thinking and began to chop walnuts. Found, young woman. Found by a monstrous man with a kind smile.

The Dreaded Enticer, the Villain who waited behind every dark corner.

She shrieked, "Get your hands off me." But it was Simon who had come up to her and put his hands on her shoulders. She turned and put her head on his chest and began to sob as blood dripped onto his shirt.

●

Hi Cyberites,

I have to consider this:

I knew about Candace and Hayden, just hadn't made up my mind what to do about it. It's not easy for me to do anything the way I am. Hayde feels guilty enough as it is, although it really wasn't his fault. Not altogether. But guilt is good for a man.

He was seen to be laughing. Jack was. And then he was seen to go into the police station.

It could have been anyone walking near the bridge on Friday. I was looking for the waxwing. Maj stays in the car when he drops me off there. He tries to read the newspaper while he waits for me.

I almost got stuck in the dirt and had to move back and around onto the paved path, and when I looked again, the person had gone. Probably hid behind the big maple so as to avoid me. If I really thought it was Candace, I'd've said something.

Unless she was lifted up and carried off by a spaceship or simply evaporated, Candace has to be somewhere. You all know that. But is she somewhere alive?

Thanks for suggesting aliens, Boris. Sometimes the absolutely impossible is the only answer. Sherlock Holmes said that, I think.

I'm sure the police will check on H again. They've already asked what he was doing that morning. When he said he was 'out,' they weren't impressed.

Is this really the time to tell him I want to go to Budapest?
TNT M

•

Another foothold. Pile of pebbles. Little Inukshuk. Twenty. Twenty-two. All fall down.

Dead. They think I'm dead. I am not dead. Could now, if not in hole, disappear. A new life. Dye hair blonde. Good times, blondes have. It is written. What did I do wrong. Beauty. Have seen. Art. Child. No child. Jack cares. Has not found me. "Jesus loves me, that I know." Anyone there? Is anyone there? Last person left in universe. All destroyed. All others, ghosts. Unworthy. Mother. The hollow halves. White stuffing fell out. And suddenly. The bear was dead.

•

The steak should have turned to ashes in his mouth and the wine to vinegar, but both were good and Jack realized this was the first real meal he'd had since Friday. He also realized that the bottle was nearly empty. His mind, though, was clear. He knew now what tack to take with Simon and with the whole town. First he would post a reward for any information regarding his wife's disappearance. He would put a notice in the paper thanking all those who had helped search for her. In the morning, before he went over to the site, he would go to Marak and talk with him man to man.

He asked for apple pie and ice cream. It would soak up the wine before he drove home.

Candace never let him eat pie except at Thanksgiving, Christmas, birthdays. Candace, he thought, and saw her for a moment sitting opposite him, raising her glass to him, smiling, loving him, as she had and probably still did. He had promised himself but hadn't mentioned it to her that, once the building was up and running, he would take her for a vacation. It would have to be short but could be somewhere like Vegas or Mexico. She talked about Mayan ruins. Or was it Aztec? Was there anything on her mind? That was what they'd asked him. All of them. Especially Marak, the smartass kid from grade eight, grown up and turned policeman, leaning forward, showing teeth: Anything on her mind? Jack had almost shouted, "How should I know?"

But he was her husband, he was meant to know. He'd heard talk, perhaps from Candace, about ideal relationships where every thought and murmur was exchanged and chewed over. Perfect knowing, knowing the other inside out. Can that be? He was unsure. As she hurried through the kitchen that morning, checking to see what was in the fridge, scribbling her list, was she protesting inside, thinking why didn't he get off his ass and do the shopping himself?

What had she mentioned lately? She had enthusiasms. Like those places in South America left by people whose lives were ruined by invading Spaniards. Chichen Itza. Tulum. Maybe not the Spaniards' fault. Some said the people of those cities had become extinct from disease or famine.

He'd only said to Marak, "She was interested in history." But people didn't leave home secretly to check out ancient sites. They went on tours.

"The two of you getting on okay?"

Marak was still single, different women in his life now and then but nothing serious, or he would have found better questions. Should've left the interrogation to his sidekick.

Candace's mind? He thought of it as a pie chart. Food, twenty percent, work, fifty percent, clothes and purchase thereof, twenty percent, family, twenty percent. And at least fifteen percent for hair given the number of times she mentioned it. But that was well over a hundred percent and nothing left for him. It couldn't be right. There had to be a sizable slice for *husband*. As for his own head-pie, for months it had been ninety-nine percent Pine

View with only the thinnest of slices left over for everything else and there, very likely, lay the problem.

"I'm sorry, I'm sorry," he said aloud, looking round, then noticing the place was empty. He was the last customer.

"You okay?" the waitress asked.

"No. I'm not. I shouldn't be here. My wife's gone missing. I don't know what I'm saying."

"You're that guy. You poor man." She poured the rest of the wine into his glass and sat beside him offering him comfort.

Comfort was wrong. He was not entitled to it.

"Bring me the cheque, please," he said sharply and then regretted his tone. The moment he left she would call the cops and tell them everything he'd said.

•

"The thing is, sir, you're well over the limit."

"I have every right to be."

"Sure you have."

•

Keeping an eye on the screen above the bar, Marak said, "I should've got tougher. Trouble is, I've known the guy since he was eight and can't imagine."

"I'm surprised you're going to say what you're going to say. I mean we know, in this job, that nine times out of ten, it's the husband, the lover, wife, uncle, son, auntie, granny that did it. The nearest. They have the reasons. They have the opportunity."

"Where d'you get all this? How many murder cases have you been involved in? This isn't Chicago."

"Okay. I read. I watch *Law and Order*. And it's true. There are statistics."

Marak sighed. He'd sighed so often in bed last night that Jess had accused him of having sex in his dreams. "I just don't want,"

he said, looking at his young colleague, "to accuse the wrong guy."
Berry was bright, eager, ready for excitement and likely waiting
for a chance to use her gun. She drank beer because she liked it,
not just to seem like one of the guys. But she was, after all, one
of the guys.

"Right," she said.

"Right," he echoed. "It does too much damage to a person,
an innocent person, even to call them in to help police with their
enquiries. Look what happened in Portugal a few years ago. These
parents immediately became suspects. The press hounded them.
It marks people forever."

"Maybe you should be in another line of work."

If she hadn't been a woman, if she hadn't been smiling at him,
he might have reacted to that. But then he saw her eyes harden, her
mouth tighten. It was absolutely the wrong place to be discussing
the case but he had to make things clear, to himself as well as to her.

"Okay. Let's go through what we know, what we've heard."

"It'll take all night." All the same she was keen. "You start."

"Setting Jack aside for the moment. I said, for the moment!
Who next? Hayden's wife was very happy to let us know about
his feelings for Candace."

"Everybody in town knew."

"Wife an invalid. Can't have sex. A likely suspect then."

"Verlyn Cosgrave!" Berry said.

Marak made signs to her to keep her voice down.

"That'd be something. There are a few people who'd like to
see her in jail. But she can't walk. Then there's the sneaky kind.
No one suspects them. There's sweet, simple Simon Belchuk.
What about him?"

"He'd be my second choice."

"Why, Catherine?"

"Because his paintings are violent and no one is that sweet."

"A cynic at your age?"

"I watched Simon when we were searching behind the school. He skirted one particular area. I went back later to check it out and he was there again, with a stick, looking, crouched down, rubbing over the grass with his hand."

"Did you speak to him?"

"I kept out of sight and then, as if he knew I was watching, he walked off quickly."

"You could've told me this. So was he screwing his sister-in-law? It doesn't seem likely. But what do I know." Marak sighed again. "Let's start again at the beginning."

"Don't you have a home to go to?"

"Kind of. What do we really know? Candace went to the dentist's office on Friday morning intending to go to work after she'd had a small filling replaced. The doctor was not there."

"Why did the dentist not let her know he wouldn't be there?"

"The receptionist said she'd cancelled his appointments but forgot Candace. Could've been deliberate."

"Right. If all else fails, we can blame Dr. Chan. So, to continue. She angrily walks away. Walks towards the lake. End of Candace. The gate to the site was locked. She kept on walking and got on the bus to Vancouver? If so, she was not seen. It was her habit when in the city to have lunch in the bar at the Fairmont. Not seen there either. Did she get into a car with a person known or unknown to her? For me that's the only scenario."

"In that case, we're looking for a body."

Marak knew she was right and wished she wasn't. He'd gone out with Candace himself for a year and would have married her if Jack hadn't enchanted her and beaten him to it. He could only think it was some magic spell or drug. Jack was not good-looking, was obsessive, at school he had compiled football statistics and made a chart out of them, and at that time appeared to have no glittering future prospects. That she was unhappy and might now have left Jack made him regret that he hadn't been more persistent. One of life's appalling ironies.

"No results from the pictures we sent out?"

"Nothing of any use."

Various sightings had placed her in Abbotsford, Campbell River, on the ferry, at the airport. The black shoe found by the boy and his dog had been a great clue until they found that Candace had been wearing sneakers and carrying high-heeled boots when she left home that morning.

"So where do we go from here?"

"More questions. Map out the movements of all the suspects."

"We're getting ahead of ourselves," Marak said. "We don't know she's been killed. We can't accuse anyone of a crime till we know there's a crime. And before you say it, I know it happens but I'd like it not to, not here in my town."

"There is another thought. People protesting this Pine View development could have kidnapped her and are holding her hostage."

"That would involve her sister and there's been no ransom note. Go home before you start telling me she's been beamed up to Planet Wingnut."

•

Kim Selwyn had taken a lot of notes too quickly. She'd have to sort them out later. She'd gleaned enough in her first few hours in the town to know that Candace Wilson had been murdered by her husband or her brother-in-law or her lover.

Sometimes it's just dumb luck. That's what her first editor had told her. Hard work and sweat and persistence were the givens in journalism. But now and then if you were in the right place at the right time, you also got a break. That she should be sitting now in the adjacent booth to these two cops almost made her go to the store next door to buy six lottery tickets. She'd come to Ghills Lake searching for "colour" and hoping for gossip or even for the clue to the mystery of the missing woman. Even maybe actually finding Ms Wilson herself. Heroine and writer. Two prizes at once. But at school and in life so far, at the age of twenty-eight, prizes had not been given to her. Tired of prowling around, she'd come into the bar for a glass of wine and found gold.

The cops were leaving. Male, mid-forties, tired-looking, no extra weight, handsome in a sad sort of way. The kind of man that made soft women want to comfort him. Kim had lost time along that route once and knew that it was a trap. His companion, a young woman with a deep voice, about five six, small for a cop, had a happier look, an eager person, pleased with herself, probably having regular sex. She had the kind of loose-lipped mouth that could mean generosity or, as in Professor Grimes's case in Journalism 201, downright sleaze.

They'd spoken quickly and sometimes lowered their voices, so Kim's notes were patchy.

She didn't use her laptop on these occasions because it was conspicuous. In her small moleskin she could be making shopping lists or plans for her next vacation.

From Cathy and Marak she'd learnt that Candace Wilson had likely been murdered. They weren't calling it murder yet but there was every indication. The victim was not known to be suicidal but had obviously slept with several men in town and perhaps the woman in the wheelchair too. Not happy at home therefore with Jack the Developer.

Kim had gone about unnoticed as if she were someone's relative come to stay. It wasn't a village so no one enquired about the newcomer. The locus of the investigation though was limited to this end of town, wide streets, some old wooden houses left over from when the place was rich and miners came and went. But most of the buildings were dreary wartime or fifties ranch-style houses built when electricity was cheap and oil would last forever. The few newer ones, too big and sprawling to fit in with their neighbours, had the look of belonging to people who'd acquired money in illicit ways. The Wilson house was one of thirteen in a cul-de-sac not far from the lake and just off the highway that led to Vancouver going south and to Prince George going north. It was, to put it politely, unpretentious. Jack the builder needed to fix up his own place before he embarked on new stuff. Like that old saying of Granny's about the shoemaker. The front porch looked as if it could be pulled away from the walls by a sturdy child. She'd knocked at the front door after she'd seen him leave with three reporters sticking to him like burrs. It gave her a chance to look through the window into the sparsely furnished living room. Perhaps the Wilsons were planning to move on. Maybe they were, what was the word, *ascetic*. Didn't spend their cash on comfort but gave to charity.

The picture she'd put together of Candace had led her to expect a little luxury. A woman who might lie on a couch in the evening watching *Desperate Housewives*, perhaps for hints. A woman who liked a glass of wine, chocolates, cashmere.

Tomorrow she'd go to the office and find out more about the woman.

Beside the lake were the foundations of the building that was a source of contention in the town. Never mind an article in the *Sun*, she was beginning to feel a book-length manuscript taking root in her mind.

The waiter brought her another carafe of white wine.

"Here about the murder?" he asked.

"Murder?"

"We all know," he said, walking away trailing omniscience.

Of course he knew what she was about. Unnoticed? Like hell. She sat up and straightened her shoulders and felt a surge of excitement. *I am a writer.* This was it. Her story. She was surrounded by characters and words and they were hers to shape as she would.

What tone to take in the book? There was the grandiose approach: Here in this lovely town two hours' drive from Vancouver, situated on a lake and known till recently only for its tourist attractions and forestry, speculation is driving the citizens to suspect their friends and neighbours of the vilest of crimes.

Well, that was one way. Then there was Raymond Chandler: It was a wet night when I approached the house of the missing woman. A light in the window suggested that the man inside was unable to sleep. I knocked.

I will investigate further, she thought, closing her notebook and picking up her wine. Some of it spilled down her shirt. She noticed that she was drinking from the carafe.

Tomorrow she'd look for the sad woman on the bench again. She'd been a great source, glad of someone to talk to. Youngish, wearing boots and a heavy coat and a woolly tuque, as if she were going to a cold place, she hadn't waited to be asked but had started right in to talk about the mystery. Candace Wilson, a woman, she'd said, who'd walked too quickly for her own good, an ambitious woman, had been murdered by a person known. "Go see the father," she'd advised. "That will explain a lot." And then, looking round first to see if anyone was near, she had gone on, "No question it's about the building. This town is at war. The townhouses will block the view of those homes near the lake. There will be fences. There will be awful people moving in who think they've bought the lakefront. I believe it's a revenge killing or –" But she never finished that tantalizing sentence because a man came over to the bench and the woman walked away with him.

"A sandwich, please," Kim said to the waiter. "Tuna if you've got it."

"The day we run out of tuna, lady, will be the day the seas run dry."

After the man had gone to the kitchen, Kim wrote his words down in her book because they seemed profound.

•

Marcus felt as though the world had tectonically shifted. Three
days had gone by. And the air, the whole atmosphere in the town
was full of words and thoughts and suspicion. Besides that there
was a girl wandering round taking notes. He'd seen her standing
outside his house and again in the park. Whose spy was she? No
one, surely, could suspect him of making away with his beloved
child. And yet, he sensed looks like arrows aimed at his back. A
father's job was to keep his children safe but that contract expired
surely when they were mature and had moved out. Especially
when they had been handed over to the care of others. In this
case to Simon and to Jack. So his responsibilities in that regard
were over. But that didn't mean he could slothfully decline to
shoulder the various burdens of life. First and most important,
he must keep himself healthy so that he was not dependent on
someone else for care. Regular meals and regular sex and a bit of
exercise took care of that. Second: As a grandfather he had to give
those two kids a sense of continuity, a feeling of love stretching
back over time. And that didn't just mean giving them toys. It
meant... He wasn't sure right now what it meant. He'd work that
one out tomorrow. The third matter was taking up much
thought. In unexpected events: Be calm. Be a rock. Do what you
can to find your missing daughter. Try not to mislead the police.

He'd tried to recall the couch when Marak asked but had to
fall back on the old man's excuse: Memory isn't what it was. But
who could forget a large piece of furniture?

Now it was clear. SHE used to complain about the lack of
comfort in Candace's home. It was as if the two of them, Candace
and Jack, didn't want visitors to settle for very long: Have your
tea, your coffee, and get out. Natural in the honeymoon period
but they'd been married for twelve years, or was it ten, maybe
nine. They were still paying down a hefty mortgage. Jack had

borrowed against the property to help with the project but that had to be a drop in the bucket. Likely they had little left for extras like comfortable chairs. And yet Jack had said there was a couch.

"Stop!" he shouted. That was to his own imagination which had slid a body under the cushions too fast. There was no couch. Therefore there was no body. QED.

Sleep wasn't going to happen. He wouldn't take one of the blue pills tonight. Unconsciousness was not an option right now. The sound of Rose snoring pierced the wall. He crept quietly downstairs and woke up the computer.

TEN

Hello Cyberites,

Monday, 7am. Still no Candace. I've been awake for hours because I can't help wondering if she really was the woman I saw on Friday. No, I didn't go over the ground. It's stony and my scooter doesn't run on stony ground. What are you, Boris, some kind of detective? I suppose I could have asked Hayden to look. But they have looked. They have all looked everywhere. C disappeared into thin air and one day they'll find her body in some remote place. One of those mysteries that never gets solved. And I'm sad about that because although I didn't care for her much she was a human being and, in her way, a good one.

Verlyn signed off. She was getting fed up with these demanding people. It was none of their business. By telling them the story, she'd poked a stick into an anthill and now regretted it. All these twitterers and bloggers with no lives had nothing whatever to do but read what others wrote and then comment on it. There must be, she figured, a large group of unemployed/unemployable people who did nothing but google and chat 24/7, and put videos of themselves out on YouTube. The vanity of that last was mind-boggling.

Hayden was being peculiar too. He wouldn't be drawn. Since Candace had been wiped off the landscape, abducted, beamed up, he'd become resistant. She wasn't sure how to react. Usually, the guilt switch worked. Could you get me another coffee, angel? My legs are cold. I'm in a lot of pain today, Hayde. Oh yes, he brought the coffee, the blanket, the pills but not with the same softness, without real attention.

Surely he didn't think she was responsible. Or was he heart-broken? Had he truly loved that woman? She wanted very much to cry and howl but she'd done enough of that in the months after the accident. She closed the laptop and considered her next move.

●

Erica admitted to herself that she loved Jack. When Simon had brought him back from the police station last night, she'd seen the vulnerable man. The man who had, really, only gone for this development in order to climb out of the ordinariness of his life and now was in despair, perhaps seeing Candace's disappearance as punishment for overreaching. They'd persuaded him to spend the night and when she'd given him a duvet and helped him fold out the couch in the living room, she desperately wanted to hold him close. And later, in the night, not sleeping, she'd had to stop herself from running downstairs and climbing into bed with him. She put it down to stress.

There was no path to a future that saw Jack as a loving step-father to BJ and Tannis while Simon went on a never-ending tour of art galleries and spent his life painting in a studio in New York: One of those "best thing for everybody" solutions that the win-ners invent to soften the blows they're about to inflict on their victims. But perhaps when he needed consolation, she might offer him more comfort than he expected. Horrified, she realized she'd wiped Candace from the picture.

She was sitting at the kitchen table with him holding his hand and both of them had tears in their eyes. It was dark outside, wouldn't get light for another hour.

"I want her back," he said.

"We all do."

"I wasn't running away."

"It was understandable. You had to get out of here."

"Not everyone will see it like that."

He looked at the clock on the wall.

"I have to go home and change and get over to the site soon. Once the work gets going, I'm kind of unnecessary there. I'll be in the office all the time. But I have to be there at the start. I meant to stay home but I can't stand it there."

His hand was strong, reddish hairs on the back of it, sinews prominent.

"Meanwhile," he said.

She looked at him, startled. Had he read her thoughts?

"Meanwhile," he went on, "what about you?"

"I'm coping."

"Still thinking of going back to school?"

He remembered. In the midst of his agony, he remembered her ambition.

She stroked his gingery paw.

"I really used to enjoy working in the store but now it's driving me nuts. I like handling the clothes but I'm starting to hate the customers. I could get my MA in a year, maybe eighteen months, and by then the kids'll be more mature. With that I could go back to teaching and teach high school. There's a little problem of money though."

His eyes narrowed as if he was trying to calculate just how much income she and Simon had per month. Whether they could keep up the mortgage payments, put things aside for the kids' education.

"Simon's last grant came in very useful," she said so he wouldn't think she was asking for anything.

And he was clearly trying to look as though grants for Simon's work were a fine use of the taxpayer's hard-earned money.

•

Simon was glad to see Erica talking to Jack. He didn't disturb them but went quietly by to the garage. Jack was about to need all the help he could get and the poor guy didn't even seem aware of it yet. Though surely since the discovery of the couch as well as last night's flight, he must have figured that they'd pick him up before long.

He stood and stared at *Confounded Glory*. He'd begun it days before Candace disappeared. Two weeks ago Friday to be exact, and by now it should have been finished, ready to go to the show. The blue was right, and the distorted faces and the ruined building. But he was not aiming for a picture that would provoke people to quote "Ozymandias." He didn't want those few who saw it to look into the distance and blame governments and tyrants, but to examine the world they themselves had created. And it still wasn't right. It lacked a detail.

He picked up a brush and closed his eyes. The brush found the palette and then, a moment later, the canvas. Another force guided his hand in small movements.

When he opened his eyes, he saw that in the corner of the painting now there was a car, a grey Ford sedan. He knew that car.

He sat down, afraid. I've never been one for signs and portents, he would have said if there'd been anyone there to hear him. He had never in his life painted anything with his eyes closed despite what critics suggested. Something, some spirit, had been within him at that moment. Candace had been taken by someone in a grey sedan. He wanted to pick up the brush and close his eyes again to see what else appeared but he knew that the spirit wouldn't strike again now that he was aware of it.

How to tell anyone what he suspected without being thought utterly mad? He felt chilled and at the same time glad he'd been chosen, if that was the word, as a conduit for this message. Message it absolutely was.

He went into the house. Jack was gone. The kids were in the kitchen eating cereal. He could hear Erica walking up the stairs. He took a clean J-Cloth from the drawer but the holes might make it a poor filter. Instead he chose a worn tea towel. He covered the phone with the cloth and spoke quickly to whom it might concern.

•

When your certainties are shaken, the world changes around you and you change with it.

Jack left the house not quite able to believe what had happened. "He's in his studio," she said, "and won't be out for hours, and the kids are asleep." All he'd done was offer to help put the couch back together. He'd tried to fill his mind with fear, fear of BJ and Tannis running into the room or of Simon returning but he couldn't help himself, she was already pressed against him and her thin bathrobe was no protection. Afterwards they stepped back from each other and looked away. *I have been having sex with my wife's sister while my wife could be suffering the torments of hell. Oh God!*

He hung his head as he walked down the path, hating himself, hating Erica. He had only that one other time been unfaithful to Candace though he knew that his was one-sided fidelity. And now, when she needed him most, whoever she'd fucked in the past didn't matter, he had let her down.

He got in the cab and looked back at the house. A figure was dancing about, waving at him to return. He didn't ask the driver to stop. If Simon had seen them, if he knew, then the whole construction of his life, family, kids, sympathy, missing wife, love, her father, was destroyed. Destroyed in less time than it takes to hard-boil an egg. Already there were too many questions, too many stares, too much whispering. Half the town had decided he was guilty of causing his wife to disappear. He felt outraged and hurt that people he knew might think him a murderer. To be called names and abused because people thought he was destroying the landscape was one thing. But this accusing finger pointing at him wherever he went had turned him into a stranger in his own town and even, in a way, in his own mind. Those who'd seen him as a monster before now had their opinion justified, so they thought. But there were others who had till now thought him innocent.

Last week his great desire was to be able to get back to work on Pine View. Yesterday all he wanted was for Candace to return whole, safe, fine, with some simple explanation of where she'd been. He would be angry. She'd explain about the message he'd missed. He wouldn't believe her but they'd carry on as they always had and the evil air of suspicion would dissipate. Those who had suspected him would be sorry. But right now his great wish was to erase the last half hour.

"Thanks," he said to the driver when they got to the house. He handed over a huge tip which the guy would put down to the wrong source of guilt.

•

Simon said. "I went after him to make him stay for breakfast. Funny, I came into the kitchen and he wasn't there. I made a phone call. Then I saw him in the taxi. I would have driven him. He only had to ask. I waved but he didn't see me. I guess the poor guy doesn't know which end is up."

Erica looked at her husband. Was he capable of putting on an act? He wasn't a dissembler. She was the deceitful one, the sinner. *I comforted him. And once we'd begun. And anyway, he was nowhere near as good as you, honey.*

"You okay?"

"Yes," she replied.

"Something strange happened to me, Errie."

You're not the only one.

"I went to look at *Confounded Glory* and of its own accord, my hand painted in a grey car."

"Of its own accord?"

Candace, with her disappearing act, had driven them all out of their minds.

"Like automatic writing," he went on. "A lot of people believed in that years ago. Maybe they still do."

She took hold of his hand. Normally his hand would have moved towards her breast. Now, as if he knew what she'd done, his hand remained in hers, unresponsive.

"I have never..." she began, and then said, "Let's go look."

Over the past couple of years she'd been not exactly dismissive about his work but not exactly sympathetic either. I'm not the best judge, she would say, and give him no decent, thoughtful response. Now, she owed him every bit of attention.

Still holding his hand, she went with him out to the garage. It was the usual chaotic mess. Pictures stacked against the walls. His attempts at sculpture from two years ago lay in the corner like abandoned pets. The new canvas was easily twelve by fourteen. The last time she'd seen it, it had been a tangle of lines and vague shapes. She stood still and stared at it. What did it mean? What did it mean to him? What did he want it to mean to her? There was violence without the colour red. A wrecked skyscraper in shades of brown lay on its side as if it had fallen down whole. Blue bodies lay in the streets, some already skeletons. And there in the corner was a tiny toy car, way out of proportion to the rest.

"My eyes were closed when I drew it in," he said.

She took more comfort from those words than he could know.

"It's quite," she said, "stunning. I think that little car gives the whole picture a sense of what we have done to the world and what we have to take responsibility for."

Any other man would have looked at her with suspicion but Simon simply said, "Thank you, love. That's kind of what I'm aiming for. Not everyone will be able to see it that way. But the car, you see. Why is it there?"

"You could just paint over it."

"No. No! It's a sign. I'm sure."

He hugged her and she leaned against him. And then he said, "It has to do with Candace."

"Every damn thing has to do with Candace!"

•

"A guilty man," Marak said to Catherine, "would not have driven down the highway and got drunk. He just wanted to get away for a while. Can you imagine what it's like for him in this town right now?"

"An innocent man would stay home waiting for his loved one to return. Unless he knows she won't."

"What are you doing here so early anyway?"

"Couldn't sleep for thinking about her. There are so many ways, so many places. And when they start building they could be burying her. He says no one could get inside that fence but he could. And that foreman."

"If you find me a shred of evidence, a sizable shred, we'll go and arrest him right away. I hate to think he's guilty but Jackson and Defrane think so."

"Why are Mounties so tall?"

"It's the boots. Go over there now. They're bound to be up and it's good to catch people first thing. I'm going to the Belchuks. I think the guy's weird but it's a lead of a sort."

"I think he's kind of cute, that dreamy artist look."

"I'll tell him to move into the twenty-first century. We know how to trace phone calls. I'll meet you at the site."

•

Verlyn couldn't understand why the woman was asking about the car. Had anyone borrowed it recently? Was her husband using it on Friday?

"Would you like coffee?"

"Thank you. I'll get it, shall I?"

"I'm perfectly capable," she replied.

First Hayden behaving with a kind of defiant thoughtfulness, and now this suspicious woman was following her into the kitchen and asking about their car.

For anyone else she would have ground fresh beans and used the French press but the stale coffee in the carafe would do for a cop.

"I've had my ration of coffee for the day," she said. "I'll just heat this up for you."

She felt the girl looking at the arrangements. The microwave on the edge of the counter. Pots and pans all on view. Ingredients in their labelled jars in easy reach.

"I remember you now. You were at school with Denver. You won the English prize she should've had."

"Not exactly my fault, Ms Cosgrave. I didn't bribe the teachers or anything."

Thinking like a cop.

"There was a lot of talk."

"It's all neatly set out in here," Sergeant Berry said.

"Accessible is the word."

When they were back in the living room, Verlyn asked, "So what's this with the car? Why are you interested in it?"

"We have to follow every lead however wild it seems."

"And you have a wild lead?"

Hayden came in carrying three bags of groceries and a bunch of roses. He didn't look at all pleased to see the visitor.

"Hayden. You remember Catherine Berry. She won that English prize in grade nine. She's Detective Sergeant Berry now."

"Hi, Sergeant."

"He gets to the store when it opens at seven Mondays, and shops for the week. She wants to know where you were on Friday with the car."

"No. That wasn't what I was asking, Mr. Cosgrave."

"It was, Sergeant. Really it was. I mean, I can't drive at the moment though we're hoping to get a specially adapted car soon. Aren't we dear?"

Hayden, set on his heels by this two-pronged attack, stumbled backwards and knocked the new coffee table over, dropping the bag and the flowers.

After the policewoman had gone and Hayden had cleared up the mess and rubbed fruitlessly at the spot on the rug with a soapy cloth and put the table back together, he brought in two glasses of juice and sat down.

"I've got the rest of the stuff in and put it away."

"Thank you, love. You're so good."

He drank his juice slowly and then said, "He was running away, Jack. They caught him driving out of town, drunk, as fast as he could."

"I guess they'll have to take him in."

"No choice."

"You were behaving a little suspiciously yourself just now. So where were you with the car on Friday?"

"Like always, I was at the office."

"Of course, my sweet. Now you just sit there and read the paper. I'll get breakfast."

She caught his look of suspicion and smiled.

"And thank you for the roses." She would have liked to shove them up his ass thorns first but patted him on the arm as she wheeled herself past him.

"Call me if you need me," he said, a tinge of fear in his voice.

She stopped the chair at the door and turned back. He'd picked up the paper. His head, grey hairs at the back showing now, was bent forward. He needed glasses or contacts. She had loved him. Had loved him wildly. And it was time to love him now, she thought, as she went to the kitchen.

•

Marcus was bewildered because:

It appeared that Jack had tried to run away.

Candace had not turned up but seemed to have really and truly disappeared.

Wendy wanted to move in with him.

BJ had asked for a rifle for his birthday.

He considered the four items. Last one first. The boy needs skates, his mother said. So he'd promised to take the boy to the mall on Saturday and had been told by the boy that he wanted to have a hunting rifle like his friend. Was he planning to go hunting? No, he just wanted a rifle. He would keep it safe. He'd seen how to do that on TV.

The kid had made it clear that any real grandfather would take him to Prince George or wherever it was easy to buy a gun.

I'm a pacifist, BJ.

Self-defence, Grandpa.

He didn't like it. He knew that BJ was a good boy, sensitive. But the games kids played on the Net were corrupt and violent. They had access to a terrifying and dreadful world where people went into schools and killed the innocent.

Jack had said he wasn't running away but returning. Was that before or after he'd been stopped DUI ? Good question. That he was angry was clear. That he was at work on the site now, also clear. He is my son-in-law, therefore entitled to the same from me as if he were my son. Was that true? Only if you happen to like the in-law in question. And he did like him. There was that drive in him, that wanting to get on. Not a satisfied man, Jack. But not dull and not a killer either. They said that though, didn't they? People interviewed after a criminal was apprehended.

Funny word to use that. Apprehend meaning to understand as well as to stop. *He was always nice to the cat. A quiet man. Wouldn't hurt a fly.* You could imagine Jack hurting a fly but not harming his wife.

Candace. Even thinking her name filled him with fear now. Images, words, whole scenes surrounded him. Nothing was good. There was only horrible black uncertainty. Dear Candace. When the girls had been dependent, young, he'd tried his best. Sitting either side of him while he read to them, believing what he said, they'd had faith in him. Then he'd taken it into his head to spend months in the far North, leaving them with their unreliable mother.

He prised three more coasters off the wall. What had possessed him to stick them there! He knew it was retrospective spite and was sorry now. Too late. Crumbs of paint were dripping onto the floor. There was going to be one hell of a cleanup job.

He hadn't even tried to explain the mess to the nice clergyman, friend of Jack's, who'd come round last night to offer comfort and to say it was all in God's hands. *The Lord giveth and the Lord taketh away.* How often had his mother said that after his dad had left and their lives spiralled down towards welfare? As a boy he'd thought the Lord a mean-spirited divinity who took much more than he gave. Anyway, the Reverend Reaver, on his way out, had made some cryptic statement about confessing one's crimes. And it was only after he'd driven off that Marcus wondered who in hell the guy was talking about. He shook his head and got on with his thinking.

Wendy had made her statement yesterday evening when she came round with turkey sandwiches and a Thermos of soup. Think of the savings. Think of the company.

"Think of my daughters," he'd replied before he shouted, "NO! I have got used to my aloneness and I like it." Nonetheless, here he was chipping the coasters off the wall and considering paint colours.

She would shift things around, mend the hole in his sweater, do the shopping, the laundry, the cooking. And, and this was big, she would literally lay Sheila's ghost for good. There would not be room for three in the bed. He continued to hack at the wall with the chisel while he went on weighing the pros and cons.

If he decided against Wendy and there was no other way to get away from her, supposing she got mad or was persistent, he could move out to Alberta to spend the rest of his life looking after chickens and vegetables and his sister Rose. That would be the noble thing to do. But Rose? Alberta? Back to shovelling snow? The picture loomed large. Endless fields. Beautiful sometimes but often just plain hard.

Wendy won hands down when it came to climate. As long as she wouldn't move the dictionary, it might work. The page was still open at "breviate; *noun, a short note or a lawyer's brief.*" Thank god they hadn't got round yet to needing Hayden Cosgrave or any other lawyer.

And it all had to wait. Nothing could be settled till Candace was found. Candace, our daughter, he murmured with a compliant nod to the shade in the corner.

•

It had taken such a short time for the cruelty to take over. Jack knew it was partly his own fault, but it was also the natural way of things. He'd read of cases in the paper where people began to throw accusations about only hours after something awful happened. When kids disappeared, vicious things were often said right away about the parents, the guy next door. *It's always the nearest.* Haunting words. It isn't always the nearest but sometimes it's the nearest disguised as a stranger.

The voice on the phone had only said, "We know what you've done." A harsh, croaky, smoker's voice. The note pushed under the door spelt out in letters cut from a magazine, *Be ye sure your SINS will find you out.* Who had taken the trouble to glue that threat onto the paper? Who in this age talked Bible-speak?

The capital letters provoked him. What sins had he committed? Was it a sin to disturb the ground? Were ancient bones lying deep beneath the foundations? He'd never believed in that kind of thing, in spirits. But for the natives, the Sto:lo, who after all had been here for thousands of years before their numbers were decimated by disease and intruders, ancestors were important. And therefore – he tried to take the next logical step but couldn't quite make it. One day he'd ask Joe Raven to explain it all to him. He and Gary had sat down with the chief to make quite sure that they were in the clear. In any case, right now, the band was too busy negotiating the forest deal with the province to bother about this little bit of property by the lake.

Should he go to the reserve and ask if there was someone who could, in some mystical way, discover where Candace was? But that could be insulting to the natives, implying that they held to old beliefs.

It was time to get with the practical. The note must be shown to Marak. If he came round, he could listen to the voice mail too. They said Marak was sleeping with Gary's niece now. No settled married life for him. Maybe there was less to be feared that way.

He looked out the window into the dim morning light. The reporters had moved off for the moment. They'd worked the ground and gathered all they could, twisted the information, chewed it up and spat it out in deformed lumps.

He called a cab and had it drop him at the Mall. At the café counter, Althea handed him a bagel and a cup of coffee to go without a word. He glanced round at the early morning customers, unsure whether to smile and nod or to look withdrawn. He chose the latter and walked out quickly. He knew that every single person was aware of his trip to Chuck's Steak Place. The cops might have accused him of making for the border except that he'd been on his way home when they stopped him.

Alys was waiting for him. "Jack," she said.

He tried to get away before fury drove him to shout at her there on the sidewalk.

"Let me speak," she said. "Listen. I'm sorry. I'm sorry. I should've called. I shouldn't have come to the trailer. I'm not like that. Everything fell in on top of me that night. I hadn't slept. I shouldn't even be talking about myself right now with what you're going through. I want you to know I'm not crazy. I want Candace back. I want the world to be all right again. I'm not going to bother you, but please let me know if I can help. All of us at the office are thinking about you. And I truly believe she will be back. She will be back."

She hurried away without giving him a chance to reply. Jack held on to the echo of her words as he watched her go. But Alys was not a messenger from the gods. There was no firm promise in her "she will be back" but it had given him a momentary feeling of hope.

●

Earthquake. All disappeared. End of the world. Bleak. Sad. Newness. Dark. Dry. Stone. In the forest now. Wet moss dripping from branches. Dad. Are you there?

●

"Jack!"

Bill was pointing to the edge of the foundation.

"What's wrong?"

"Ground's fallen in a bit here. Looks as though it's been pushed in."

"The machines haven't been near it."

"Could've been a strong person with a shovel."

"That's ridiculous. Nobody could get through the fence." He guessed what the man, his "friend," was thinking. On Friday he'd come and disposed of Candace, got rid of her body conveniently where it would never, ever be found. "Let's get on with it. We've lost enough time already."

The din around him covered his thoughts for a while. He went to sit in the trailer and rethink his situation.

You might want to talk to a lawyer, Marak had said, implying a courtroom, a judge and jury, a life sentence. Might as well have poured a load of dirt over his head. But it would all become clear. She would be found. If Candace had wanted revenge for some perceived slight, she'd succeeded. He couldn't think like that. She wasn't evil. He could blame fate for this: On the day when he should have been jumping up and down for joy because the men were back at work and his dream was on its way to becoming reality, he was being accused of murder. The police hadn't come right out and said so because there was no evidence, but they could make some. The couch that had never existed. His stupid drive last night. Every bite of steak and mouthful of wine would be held against him. Was probably being held against him. It had looked like celebration instead of what it was: desperation. And all round town he saw the looks on their faces, people he'd known for years, some of them since kindergarten; their thoughts might as well have been printed on their foreheads.

I had no idea, he said to himself, that a time like this, with Candace missing and possibly, possibly, dead, could be made worse.

"Hey." He jumped.

Yuri Beslov's face appeared round the door. Without waiting to be asked, he came in and sat down on the other chair. There was menace in the way he did that.

"So you've begun, Jack. I could've halted it. Could now."

"Right, Yuri. The guys are glad to be back at work. You want something?"

"I want you to know I understand."

His words sounded like major menace.

"Understand what?"

"Why you had to take off. Happened to me once. Dumb thing to do but you go with an impulse. Wasn't smart to get drunk. What I did was after we'd moved here, you maybe know the story. And I wanted to buy the Greenville place. But I was a foreigner. A foreigner! I've lived in this country since I was seven. So they turned me down. They didn't like my name, which I could have changed to George Best but I like to live with the truth. And there was my so-called accent. You remember George Best, the soccer player?"

"Before my time."

"So. I was in a rage when I got home. My wife said, 'What's wrong, honey' in that dumb way they have and I hit her. Never before, never since, God rest her soul. Then I took off in the car fast, driving for the hell of it. Irina called her sister, her sister called the cops and they stopped me just outside Hope. Would've been fine except for the open bottle of rye. That and I hit one of them."

Jack said the only thing he could think of, wondering where this was going to end, "Not real smart, Yuri."

"That's what I'm saying. I know what you were doing. I also know you might need a lawyer and in this case you don't want to be employing snotty, and without being professionally jealous here, useless Hayden Cosgrave."

The guy had him in a cleft stick. If he said he needed a lawyer, he would appear to admit some kind of guilt. There was a quid pro quo demand about to be made. He waited.

"My son's just out of law school, working for Kelly and Brant. Just give me a call. He'd be cheaper than Hayden."

Jack said, "Congratulations. Great to have another lawyer in the family. Hayden deals with my business affairs and such."

"And your wife?"

There was a shout from the site. Jack almost knocked the other man down in his hurry to get out the door. They'd found Candace, she was in all that dirt and rock and she was dead and they would say he'd put her there. It was almost a relief to see that the BobCat had slid halfway into the foundation and was balancing on the edge. The driver was new, Jack didn't remember seeing him around even last week when he'd talked to the whole gang. He wanted to ask but Bill had taken charge and was telling the driver, who looked about twelve, to back up real slow, to turn the wheels a little to the right, to wedge them in if he couldn't move.

"Slowly. Gently there." Twenty tons of machinery and man were all poised to topple into the hole.

"Tell him to jump out," Jack shouted.

"He can do it," Bill replied.

"Jeez!" Yuri said.

They watched as the man in the cab moved the levers and the wheels turned left and then right. They gripped the soft earth and the Cat inched painfully back to level ground.

The driver put the brake on and hopped down from his seat. The four men around him applauded.

"I need a drink," he said.

"What's your name?" Jack asked.

"He's okay," Bill said.

"Has he driven heavy machinery before?"

The driver turned truculent and said, "Look, asshole, I just saved that thing from going down there."

"You drove it too close to the edge in the first place, shithead!"

"Now everybody. Jack, this is my nephew, Graeme. He's going for his licence soon. So he's getting some practice in. Graeme, this is the boss."

Jack felt a volcano rise inside him about to spew fire and rocks.

He looked around and saw men standing by, indecisive, ready maybe to walk out if he said the wrong thing. A vision of the foundation as a perpetual swimming pool, his gift to the town, came into his mind. He took three very deep breaths.

"Okay Bill. I'll leave it with you. But don't let him on that thing again by himself."

As he walked away he thought he heard the kid say, "That the guy who's murdered his wife?" and stopped himself from going back and throwing him down the hole.

"Maybe there's a curse on the project," Yuri said.

For the second time in minutes, Jack restrained himself and did not knock the man down.

"We have a good foreman. Thanks for your advice, Yuri. I'll see you around."

"You sure will. The council has asked me to keep an eye on progress and so on. And listen, Jack. Don't pay any attention to what people are saying."

A few minutes later, he saw Marak coming to the site alone and felt relieved. He dreaded every hour the heavy footsteps of two cops coming to arrest him, jangling handcuffs, Marak saying, There's no need for those, reluctant to arrest his old friend but seeing the necessity for it. He pretended to be absorbed in the plans for a moment and then looked up and smiled.

"We found your couch," Marak said.

Jack knew he'd turned red. "I have to explain."

"It's this thing of people dumping their old sofas in the woods on the slope. How do they get them up there? Can't be easy. Yours was this plaid-covered three-seater, right?"

"No," Jack said. "There was no couch, Marak. Candace and I like space. We don't like that cluttered feeling where you have to walk round chairs and tables like in a maze."

"You said there was a couch. You said she'd sent it to be re-covered."

"I don't know why I said that. You have to understand I was rattled. I guess I didn't want you to think we couldn't afford to buy furniture."

"What you have to understand," Marak said very slowly, "is that we found what looks like some of your wife's hair on that couch."

The Cat roared into action. It was a sound Jack had been waiting for these past two months. Three days ago he would have felt delight, relief, and maybe even done a victory dance. Now he felt like jumping into the excavated hole and waiting to be built into the foundation.

"She got around," was all he could think of to say. "It could be anyone's."

"I shouldn't be advising you, shouldn't even be talking to you on my own. But really I think it's time you got yourself a lawyer, Jack. It will be out of my hands soon."

"I have truly done nothing. I have no idea where she is. And I want her back." He felt himself near to tears and wasn't about to let Marak see him cry. "Thanks anyway. I'll talk to, well, not Hayden. Somebody."

"And Jack, I should have got to you last night but I didn't know."

Jack saw the other cops then. Saw them talking to Bill. Saw the other men moving away, picking up their lunch boxes, their jackets. The morning was unwinding in front of him like the yellow tape two cops were unrolling from a spool.

"It's a possible crime scene so we have to do this. They're sending special equipment from Vancouver. It'll be here tomorrow. Then we can, kind of, get to the bottom of this. We're getting shit for not covering this area sooner."

Jack knew he was going mad. His head was spinning. They thought, then, that she was down there, in the foundation.

"No one could have got inside the fence," he said. *Except me, and Bill the foreman, and Gary.* "This is stupid. You can't do this."

"We can, Mr. Wilson," a guy in plain clothes said, coming

up behind Marak.

And Jack knew they could do anything they wanted.

"We'd like you to vacate the site."

Bill came and touched him on the shoulder. "Jack."

"It's okay. I'm fine."

A word of sympathy at that moment would have reduced him to rubble. He walked away.

A lawyer! Helping the damn police with their enquiries? He set off towards town. He was confined. A man without wheels for the first time since high school. And every window had a pair of binoculars in it. Every street light had a listening device attached. All CCTV cameras were trained on him. Somewhere, in a central room, a policeman could see where he was at every moment. By now his house was bugged and there was no privacy.

Voices too. Chattering. Phones. Emails. All the information concerned him: We know what you've done. If he'd reached his hand into the air, he felt that he could have grasped words that were flying round town like a flock of evil birds.

"I've done nothing," he yelled. "Nothing!"

He noticed a young woman in a parked blue Toyota staring at him, waiting.

He pretended to be singing and then realized that would mark him as uncaring and possibly triumphant. He walked back to the trailer to get his coat and bag.

•

M here, Cyberites.

You are wrong, Boris. There is a God but not in the way of those pictures you see or like a voice coming down from heaven or the guys who talk on TV and tell you that Jesus wants your money. Jesus does not want your money. Trust me. Even when He was on earth, He didn't ask for money. In fact He despised it.

Does He see everything? That's impossible too. And it's absolute egotism to think He is keeping tabs on totally insignificant You – or Me. Perhaps where you are, in the sunshine, by the sea, you should take time to think about spiritual matters and discover what the word 'god' really means instead of spending your time screwing young women on your thirty-foot yacht.

Here in my town, the earth is being shaken. J. W. is back at work. I can see the top of the great crane from my bedroom window. There's something exciting about it. I'd go down and watch but that place gives me the creeps now. Was it Candace there, the day she disappeared? She's vanished, that's all there is to it. I still think she left town. And I'm not going to say any more.

TNT M

•

Erica said, "He should have waited. That's all. It's disrespectful. It's hateful."

Simon didn't like it when she came into his studio uninvited. Her presence took away some of his imagination because she trailed garments of motherhood, businesswoman, and now worried sister, into the room and draped them around him too.

"It was bound to happen," he said. "It's about money. You can't have land like that sitting idle in these days. And there are many others involved. Guys who need work."

"Stop being so goddam reasonable," she shrieked.

And the painting, the idea, the colours, his moment of wild inspiration drained away. He had never wanted to hit her before. She stepped back.

There was no way of explaining the loss to her or to anyone except another artist or a writer, a musician. There was no way of reaching into his mind to retrieve the image that had been in his grasp a minute before. In anger he drew her to him and lifted up her shirt and undid her bra, slipping the straps over her shoulders and pulling off her shirt at the same time so that he had in his hand a beige-coloured rope he could have used to strangle her.

"Simon," she said.

"Get out," he said and put her bra and shirt into her hand.

"Simon!"

Crying, she pulled her shirt round her and left the garage.

I've become a monster.

He set aside the big picture and picked up his sketch pad. The face looked back at him with the sad eyes of his sister-in-law. He took his ink brush from the table and etched in a rocky incline beneath the body. She had been gone now for three whole days and his only consolation was in depicting places where she might possibly be. Number four, the clearest, set her in a forest where birds and animals lovingly flew and hopped around her as in *Snow White*. It was a happy scene except for the humanoid wolf in the corner who appeared to be waiting for a chance to pounce.

"I am not mad," he said to the Candace on the paper. "Trust me. I am just out of my mind because I can't solve this. I want to know where you are. And I want to be the one who finds you. I want to show them that I can be useful."

But he had been out twice now at night, wandering round town, trying to get some sense of where a woman might go or be taken. He had only come back tired and disappointed.

He cleaned his brushes and went into the house.

Erica was sitting at the kitchen table still naked from the waist up, apparently making a list.

"Hello," she said.

After they'd tried to make love and were lying quietly side by side like stone figures on a tomb in an old English church, often a dog there too he recalled, Simon said, "It's no use. It's as if we're offending God."

"We don't exactly believe in him."

"I think," he went on, "that we won't find her till we all absolutely concentrate on that, give our minds to it, stop doing other things."

"You make it sound like that kids' game."

"And maybe that's what it is."

Erica turned to look at him. He had gone from this narrow carnal world to reality in a matter of minutes, the way she hated. She wanted him to go on admiring her body, her hair. If they ever went to a counsellor she would mention her need for "after-play." But now he was speaking the truth again. And he was damn well right again!

"You mean like prayer."

"I mean that we won't keep on having sex like this as if it's some kind of consolation. We'll go over what might have happened and walk around, talk to people. We must be missing something. As for Jack. As for Jack. He can't help himself."

"Do you think he...?"

"No, I don't. Not for a moment. Unless..."

He got dressed quickly and ran down the stairs as if escaping.

So he knew. He knew. And was running away from her, the adulterer. Erica had no tears left.

●

Three whole days and into the fourth. There was now no question of Candace simply taking off voluntarily. Dread and sorrow and fear hung around him, around the family, the town. Marcus drew out his list of murder suspects from behind the microwave. They numbered four and against each name he'd written a motive and an opportunity. Because he disliked Hayden Cosgrave, he made him number one. The motive there was obvious. To keep his wife from finding out about him and Candace as if she didn't already know. Opportunity, you bet! From his office window he could have seen Candace kicking at the dentist's fancy door and then followed her. But what could he have done with her? Somebody, because if ever a town had a thousand eyes this one did, would have seen him.

Two: Though hardly likely, Verlyn Cosgrave. Motive obvious. Opportunity, she was around "bird-watching" and saw "a woman" near the lake. That was hardly a reason to suspect her. And unless she'd hired a hitman or, and Marcus had for a while suspected this, she was not as crippled as she let on, she couldn't have gone after Candace. Verlyn was paying the world around her back for her accident, blaming them all. Doctors were said to be mystified by her slow recovery. One of these days she would get out of that chair and walk. Maybe Hayden should yell FIRE. That was how they got fakers to move in films.

Three: Simon. Motive, hard to figure. Opportunity? Loads as he has no job, no structure to his day, could be anywhere anytime. And his paintings show a sinister side you don't get when he talks about colour and texture in that soft enticing voice of his. Why people bought them – they bought them because they under-scored the weird world we all live in now: The randomness of violence and attacks and insane rantings by politicians and cruel deeds done by children and the vileness of pedophiles and traders in human flesh. All the killing in Iraq and Afghanistan. There was no innocence. So Simon had it right and people had given up on soft pictures of flowers and dogs and even nice sunsets. Maybe when he'd taken all the coasters off, if he ever did, he'd get Simon to paint a mural for him, a fall prairie scene with fields of ripe wheat going on forever. But that was assuming – assuming that the world would return to normal.

Jack, poor Jack, had to be on the list. If they'd taken a poll of citizens right now, eighty-five percent of people in town would have considered him to be probably guilty. Motive: Jealousy. Opportunity, absolutely. It was always or nearly always a close relative. And there was that foundation at the site. What a neat place to hide a body. He shuddered. No!

If he kept on down that trail, he'd be able to build the case against Jack himself without the need for a prosecutor.

But there was a fifth person not marked down, and that was an evil unknown whose motive might be simply to blight Jack's scheme for the new development and his life at the same time. Someone interested in keeping the world green even if it meant killing a few people along the way. That person, male or female, would, though, have a reason for keeping Candace alive as a bargaining chip. He hoped. There was that shred of hope to cling to.

If the police had anyone in mind as being "of interest" other than Jack, they were being damn quiet about it. The newspapers, local and provincial, would keep the story going for a week or two: Woman disappears in BC town. Then it would slip off the radar like the mystery of the six or seven detached feet that had washed up around the strait. In a way, the media were giving Jack free advertising. But would anyone want to move to a place where a woman could simply vanish, as BJ said, as if she'd fallen into a hole? There was a slick-looking woman reporter staying at Maia's, and others were hanging around no doubt making it all up as they went along.

Last night, sitting up in bed in the dark, he'd felt a great tug at his heart as if Candace were calling to him, pleading with him. We're looking for you, sweetheart, he'd said out loud. But were they?

He decided to go out and look near the lake himself. He put on his old shoes and a jacket and took an umbrella, a poor substitute for a diviner's wand but it might work, might pick up vibrations. He knew in his bones that she wasn't far from the water.

•

Dan Bright said, "If it were my wife."

"What?" Jack asked.

"Sorry. Nobody knows what they'd do in a case like this. And

I can see you're desperate to get on here. Makes sense. Life goes on, eh?"

Jack could only grip his coffee mug and try to understand why the entire world felt impelled to come and visit him at the site today.

"So they've had to stop," Dan said.

"You noticed," Jack replied, regretting his sarcasm. Calm! Be calm. "Good of you to come out, Dan. I've appreciated your stand on this. The cops have to do what they do, I guess."

"Right. You know. I know it's hard but Erica really upset my wife on Saturday in the store. I guess it's nerves. Bound to be. But they don't want to be losing customers."

The guy wanted him to apologize for something his sister-in-law had done! Jack put the mug down and put his head on his hands. It was all getting to be like a crazy movie. Or like that play Candace had made him see where everybody talked and nobody listened.

"We're all on edge," he said. "I don't know whether I'm on my feet or my ass, Dan. The not knowing is killing me. I'm here because I can't stand being in the house. But I can't do anything. If there was anything I could do, I'd be out there doing it. Two Mounties talked to me for hours last night. The cops are all over the place. She hasn't used her credit cards, but then no one else has either so she wasn't robbed, you see. If she'd been driving it would have been a whole other thing. She might be down a ravine somewhere. But she doesn't seem to have left town in any of the possible ways unless she was taken. She is a good, lovely woman. No one who knew her could've wanted to harm her, could they, Dan? I mean she helped out at the shelter and went to meetings in Vancouver about how to improve things for abused women. Nobody doesn't like Candace. I love her. She's my wife. We've been married ten years in January. I like it. Like being married. It's a nice thing, isn't it? Having someone there to talk to. And I haven't talked to her enough. That's why she talked to Hayden for a while there. That's over now. Where is she? Is she okay? That's what I want to know and I don't give a fuck what Erica said to your wife."

•

Marcus walked along holding his umbrella in front of him. Bill McGraw in whom, years ago, he had tried to instill a few rules of grammar, came towards him, said hello and suggested politely that he leave the site. It was a crime scene now, a place for people wearing hard hats and not for old men. And he himself would be going home soon.

Marcus moved away. A cop waved at him. He waved back.

In a hundred years, if not sooner, this whole place would be dust and rot. When the lake dried up, the dirt would reveal the sins of this generation and the last and the one before that. And reveal... No! He couldn't think that. It was too soon.

He wanted to go for his morning coffee at Burgo's and sit down with the other guys who gathered there on Mondays to chat. But there would be looks, hints, silences, and the coffee would turn to acid in his mouth because he had nothing to tell them. There is no news. No one has seen my daughter. The police are doing what they can.

He couldn't sit down at the picnic table because that would look as though he was enjoying himself and he wasn't. He did, though, lean on the edge of it for a moment, losing himself in the slow rhythm of the water as it sloshed onto the pebbles. A truck rumbled by on the road, the earth seemed to shake and his umbrella fell down. He bent to pick it up.

At least the ground wasn't muddy. A piece of paper lay in the dirt. He picked it up. It looked like her handwriting. The big straight *L* of *Life*, the curly-tailed *f*s he'd teased her about. He wished he'd brought a plastic bag. A smart man would always carry a plastic bag with him.

When he got home he took the paper out of his pocket, holding it by the corner though by now he'd ruined it as far as fingerprints went. Marak the cop would tell him it could have been there for weeks and he would reply that it couldn't because last Thursday it had rained all day and the ink would have washed out. He stared at the few words looking for a message. Had she written *Life* because she wanted no more to do with it? But why *couch*? There was no one whose advice he could ask. Plenty of people would be happy to offer it though.

His heart was thumping. Fear returned. Where was she? Where are you, Candace? He put the paper in the cookie jar for safety while he figured out what to do, and then lay down on the floor to breathe deeply.

•

Hello people. *Marguerite* here again.

There we have it. Who knew? Who could've guessed? A burly man, J, walks like a bear on hind legs, is having a relationship with our mayor. Mayor equals Motive. And which of them is the most likely suspect? Mr. Mayor looks to greater things. A seat in the provincial Legislature and maybe then moving on to Ottawa. He looks in the mirror his maid says – she also cleans for me on Fridays – and sees a prime minister. Not that his being homosexual matters except to his wife and two children, but it could be a big drawback to his ambitions. I'm not prejudiced in that way myself but a lot of people are and there is always the threat of blackmail.

It was B M who saw them *in flagrante* when he went to the trailer-office to check on something with J before they had to leave the site this morning. Arms round each other. Clinging, he said. It made him feel ill, he told his wife when he got home and swore her to secrecy. But this is something that should be known.

TNT M.

She signed off as a flicker of conscience told her that maybe it should not be known to the whole world and beyond, just in case. In case what? In case it wasn't true? Too late.

After she'd chopped ginger and garlic, and stirred in white wine and soy sauce, she poured the mixture over the salmon and put it back in the fridge to marinate. It took her awhile to find the carrots and potatoes in the wrong part of the veggie rack. Had H hidden them out of malice or bewilderment? She peeled three carrots and four potatoes and put them in water. Then she peeled one more of each in case Jack came for dinner.

"I don't usually feel tired," she said. The habit of writing to her group led her to talk aloud sometimes as if they were there, all around her: Lauren and Jim and Irene and Boris and Georges One and Two. People she'd never seen and never would see but who knew more about her than even H or Denver, especially Denver. But it was time now to concentrate.

She made a cup of tea and put it on her tray and wheeled herself into the living room. The Michael Bublé CD was still in the player. She pressed the *on* button then closed her eyes and pictured the woman in her boots and coat standing as she was on Friday morning beside the tree, not far from the lake but outside the fenced-in building site. She was there and then seconds later she was not there. Probably she'd dodged out of sight so as not to have to talk to her, to Verlyn. People did that if you were the least bit handicapped, as if you were infectious. Besides, in the beginning people were convinced, and she herself had hoped, that Candace had simply left Jack and gone off somewhere, anywhere, away from Hayden. It was too late to speak out now. Too much time had gone by and the chorus of "why didn't you tell us before" would be loud and accusatory.

Guilt overwhelmed her. A new, awful feeling descended over

her like a fisherman's net. Suppose Candace had died and it was her fault? "Mea culpa," she said aloud. "Mea maxima culpa." And, in that moment, she sensed a power, an intense and irresistible call to action. "Yes, I can," she responded to it. "Yes, I will." There was a chance of redemption here. *My body is useless but my mind is strong.* She conjured up the image again; the tree, the bird and the shape of a woman.

"Candace," she said. "Candace. Come to me." That was how mediums did it. They sent names out into the beyond and waited for a reply. "Candace Wilson. Candace Brandt." She moved her hands as if she had a crystal ball in front of her. "Candace, I command you, come to me."

Verlyn was sure that the drapes were moving: A spirit had entered the room and was floating around. "Where are you? Tell me where you are. Why are you hiding from us, dear?" She wasn't sure where that affection came from except that it was time to play nice. If she got a response, she would be the one to tell them where the missing woman could be found. She would be the hero. She waited. And then she felt a waft of air on her neck.

●

Jack had come home because there was no place else for him to go. Gary had said Wayne was capable of coping at the office. The men were sticking around on call and hopefully by Thursday... So the cops said. Thursday! The beer tasted sour. Even with the weight of guilt on him, he was relieved that the man sitting in the kitchen chair had not apparently come to assault him. If he was working round to it, it was a slow process.

Simon said, "Yes, I will have another, please, Jack. It's a bit early though."

"In Toronto it's 7:15," Jack replied. He got two bottles out of the fridge and passed one to his brother-in-law.

"Hayden came to me because he didn't know who else. I

mean, you know, the cops might think he was a serial killer or something though of course she's not dead – Verlyn. And I'm sure Candace isn't either," he added quickly.

"So what exactly happened?" Jack had found Simon on the doorstep when he got home from the police station and the man had been close to incoherent. "Tell me slowly, please. I've had a day. The cops are doing what cops do, I guess, casting suspicion round in every direction. They're going to come with handcuffs any minute now and a whole flock of media people will be out there, and half the people in this damn town will say I told you so. And I only want her back, Simon, you know that. Anyway. About Hayden. You were saying."

Simon took two mouthfuls of beer and said, "So Hayden called and asked if he could come over. He was kind of whispering as if there were spies about or something. So he came and he looked very – well, very un-suave. Very unlike himself. Rumpled. He got home just after twelve, he said. The caregiver had called in sick so he wanted to see if she needed anything and he found her, Verlyn, on the floor on her back, the wheelchair tipped so she was like a turtle lying there, couldn't right herself. She'd been like that awhile."

"Somebody attack her?"

"That's the thing. Everything was locked the way it usually is so no one can come in when she's there alone without her knowing. She kept saying, 'Candace. Candace.' And something about a conjuror. They've taken her to hospital to check her over. But Hayden, and you know what he's like, always so sure of himself, he turned into a quivering jelly. I told him if they keep Verlyn in overnight, and he's afraid, to bring his toothbrush to our place and he can sleep on the couch."

The world seemed to be closing in on itself, folding like a fan made of rock, and they would all be crushed. Insanity had taken over. Hayden the stolid. Verlyn the vengeful. Who next?

"She probably took too much of her medication and hallu-cinated."

Simon shook his head. He knew that at base he was a sensible man. But any sensate person could tune in to waves, feelings, thoughts, unspoken words, and the images that float around in the air. They were there to be grasped. He took a deep breath. Suddenly he knew that Candace was here, close by. In the house. He was aware of her. There was pressure on his chest as if he might have a heart attack: Jack had killed her by accident and then, desperate, had put her in the basement freezer.

"What's the matter, Simon?"

"I've just remembered something," he said, and got up and left.

It made no sense. Very little did these days. This was Monday. A whole century had passed since Friday. Jack looked in the mirror and saw that though there were purple patches below his eyes and furrows on his forehead, his face hadn't changed. His hair was still dark brown. *They'll put me in jail and I'll never get out.* Then his hair would go grey and his face too.

"I'm innocent," he shouted at the mirror. "Don't do this to me."

As if in answer, the land line rang. Another anonymous caller most likely, but just in case he picked up the receiver and listened.

"Hey, Jack. You there?"

"Stefan!"

"Listen, I just heard about Candace. Simon called me. If there's anything I can do, if you need any help whatever, I'm only a couple of hours away by plane. I can be there by noon tomorrow. I've checked the flight times."

Jack couldn't speak. For several seconds he held back sobs, then managed to say, "Thank you," before his friend's kindness overwhelmed him.

ELEVEN

Denver rubbed at the woman's lousy nails and told her in a gentle voice to put her other hand in the soapy water. She paid no attention to the vibrating cellphone in her pocket. It could shake itself stupid. He wasn't going to get another word out of her. It was entirely over along with her chance of a vacation in Europe next spring.

"Yes," the woman was saying. "It must be a nice place to work."

It's a frigging airport. People going in all directions, never the same customer twice, no loyalty. Always the same comment on her name. If her parents had to combine their names to make hers, they could've gone with Haylyn. "Yes," she told the woman, "it's great." *And I'm getting out of here next year. I was out of my mind when I decided to go to beauty school. It was all my dad's fault.* Hayley had a nice sound to it.

"When I get to Rome," the customer was saying now, "I always go first to the Church of Santa Maria Maggiore. Have you been there? It's amazing."

Fortunately right then, before Denver dug a file into the woman's cuticle, Jess called her over to the desk.

"There's some kind of emergency," she said, handing her the phone.

"Is it him?"

"No. I don't think so."

Denver listened. She went back to the passenger who would be in Italy by morning and handed her the buffer. "Do your own nails," she said, refraining from insults. "My mom's had some kind of accident."

At the bus depot she sat staring around. Just when she'd decided to make a change in her life, her life had changed. First thing was to find out what had happened at home. She didn't get on all that well with her mom but had felt sorry for her since the accident. Nobody likes to be a cripple. Not all handicapped people play it for all they're worth either. There was the resigned option and the cheerful helping others who are worse off option. Her mother had chosen subtly to undermine all those around her. For instance, if I had a car, I wouldn't be standing in this dim tacky place that looks like the waiting room to hell. People half asleep on benches, their stuff around their feet, maybe waiting to be transported to the other end of the continent.

On the wall beside the ticket counter, a poster read Education Speaks. Listen. And I will, she thought as she stared at the words. I will. And my dad will pay.

Three hours later, she found her father fearfully prowling round the outside of the house in the dark.

"You couldn't come to meet me at the depot?" she said.

"I'm sorry," he replied. "I'm kind of out of my mind."

"How is she?"

"Still in hospital."

He hugged her and said, "Oh, Denver."

"Hayley. My name's Hayley as of right now, Dad. Okay? So tell me what happened."

He sat down on the step and she sat beside him. The stone was cold and it was starting to rain but he just stayed there as if he was glued down.

"Can't we go inside, Dad?"

Reluctantly he got up and put his key in the lock and opened the door. He looked round the hall. She followed his look. Nothing had changed in six months. You could bet there was dust behind the hallstand, the old wooden piece with a shelf and mirror and hooks for coats, light summer coats. The Turkish rug looked as though it hadn't been vacuumed properly in an age. And there was a smell of meat gone bad. Her parents, her dad the respected lawyer and her handicapped mother, appeared to have been living in near-squalor, though that was perhaps too strong. At any rate, in dirt.

"Does Hetty Jones still come to clean?"

"She got sick. In fact, Den– Hayley, she died. Maj dusts around a little and then a woman called Rina comes every two weeks or so to do the bathrooms and floors. Your mother wheels herself around with a duster on a stick and I do what I can at the weekends – when I have a weekend. I've got a couple of cases on the go and I've had to go to Abbotsford a fair bit."

"Got a woman there?"

"Of course not."

"Mom told me you'd been running around."

"Well she shouldn't have. It was nothing. There are things children don't have to know."

"I'm not a child."

He was looking at her through the mirror and she was trying to get him to move on into the living room. His eyes were red-rimmed and his hair looked greyer. He was still handsome though. Her school friends had compared him to George Clooney but she couldn't see it. She propelled him forward and made him sit in the easy chair.

"Things have been weird. Candace Wilson has disappeared."

"I read about it. She's not back?"

"Gone since Friday. Nobody's seen hide nor hair of her."

"Do they think it was you?"

"No, Denver."

"Hayley!"

"No, Hayley, they do not. The thing is that something or somebody got into the house when it was locked and tipped your mother's chair over and she thinks it was a spirit."

"Dad! I don't believe this. She could've tipped. Leaned back too far. Anything. It doesn't have to've been a ghost. I bet Ms Wilson going off like that has driven you all nuts."

"She keeps saying 'Candace.'"

"Maybe she hit her head. Is there anything to eat?"

"We'll go for pizza, then to the hospital. I'm glad you've come, honey."

"I was planning on coming soon anyway. There's something I want to talk to you about."

Her father looked afraid again. He really did seem to be losing his mind. She'd read about times like this. Times when the child has to take over. It seemed in this family to have come a couple of decades early.

Her mother was sitting up in bed and burst into tears when she saw them.

"You're here, Denver," she said from behind a Kleenex.

"How are you, Mom?"

"Fine, really. Well, not fine. I'll be here for weeks. Hayden, you've got cheese on your face. How long can you stay, sweetheart?"

Sweetheart! I don't think so. Hayley put up a barrier.

"I'll have to get back to the job. They're a girl short. But I can have a few days." Best to lower expectations right away. "So what happened?"

"There was this force. Like a strong wind. I could almost feel a breath. And then, a voice."

"You didn't tell me a voice," Hayden said.

"I'm telling you now."

"What did it say?"

"It didn't actually speak. There was just breathing and grunting."

"Well then, Mom?" But Verlyn had lain back and closed her

eyes. She plucked at the sheet for a moment and then let her hand slip to the side of the bed.

When they got home, Denver/Hayley persuaded her father to come upstairs with her. Nothing in the closets, see, Dad. Nothing under the beds.

She couldn't believe she was doing this. In her childhood he'd dismissed all goblins and spirits as fantasies and here they were looking for them. Her old room hadn't changed. The same small bed, dresser, mirror, first makeup box. Curling poster of Heath Ledger, now dead, poor guy. Brad Pitt had become boring. Overexposure. If she stayed she'd get one of Xavier Bardem. That haircut in *No Country for Old Men*. Yum! But she had no intention of staying for more than a couple of weeks.

Her father came and sat beside her on the bed.

"It's okay, Dad," she said. "Mom will be fine. The doctor said she'll be home tomorrow."

He shook his head and looked round the room, bewildered, as if it was some strange place. "She's afraid to come back here," he said.

When the doorbell rang, the old man nearly jumped out of his skin. Hayley ran downstairs. Two cops were standing on the step.

"Hi, Raspie."

"Hi Denve. This is Detective Sergeant Marak. Can we come in for a minute?"

Two years ahead of her in school, only two, and here was Raspie Berry in uniform, a small policewoman with a gun yet. Who'd've thought?

"Sure. My dad's out of his mind right now, but sure."

She led the way into the living room and pushed her mother's wheelchair to one side.

"Don't," the man said. "Fingerprints."

"It appears to have been a kind of spirit that pushed my mom over and wrecked the coffee table. Do ghosts leave prints?"

"We have to check. Every possibility."

"I'm thinking she just tipped. She'll be home tomorrow and you can ask her. Not that you'll get much sense. She seems to think she saw Ms Wilson."

"There, you see," Detective Marak said. "Nothing can be ignored. It's been four whole days and maybe, just maybe, there's a murderer on the loose."

"We can't rule that out," Raspie repeated as if being his echo was part of her job.

Hayden came downstairs and joined them. He appeared to have gathered himself together. "Of course it can't have been a ghost but the doors were locked and the windows were shut," he said.

"Did you check every entry?"

"The basement, Dad?"

Hayley went down the steps to the cellar where, before the accident, her mother had kept jars of preserved fruit and pickles. She felt a strange shiver of fear and told herself not to be stupid. The footsteps behind her were Raspie's. Legs of the law.

"Weird," Raspie said.

The basement was divided in two. In the front half were her dad's papers, briefs and old books packed in boxes and raised off the floor on planks in case of flood. The second half was a dump. Her old bike, a box of toys, two garden chairs that needed mending and a pile of old clothes. A project for her if she did stick around for a while.

Raspie was already at the broken window over the sink beside the washing machine.

"How long has it been like this?"

"I've only just got here. I live in Vancouver now."

They examined the broken glass and called the two men to come and check it out.

"Dammit," Hayden said. "I thought Bill had fixed that weeks ago. I never bothered to check."

"Only a very small person could get through without hurting himself."

Dwarves? Monkeys?

It was Marak who drew their attention to the door, the door to the steps up into the backyard. "Never mind the window," he said. "Look at this."

●

"Can you believe it?" Erica said. "Glynis says people think Candace is around, doing odd things."

"It's nonsense." Simon tried to sound certain. He felt sick. And knew he should not have left another message for the police. He tried to put the call from his mind and concentrate on his family. He drank a cup of coffee quickly.

"What'll I wear for Halloween?" Tannis asked.

"Halloween!"

"It's only ten days."

"It's just that it might seem a bit strange to go trick-or-treating."

"She'd get extra candy for sympathy," BJ said. "Anyway if she's in costume, who'll know. She could wear one of those things Muslims wear."

"She absolutely could not," Simon said. "If your aunt isn't found, then no one will be out on the street. But in case she is and she will be, why don't the two of you go put some ideas together. I need to talk to your mother."

Erica heard BJ say, "Sex again" as they went out of the room.

"Sit down, love" Simon said. "We have to think about this. Consider Verlyn Cosgrave. Would you say she was entirely sane?"

"I've never thought she wasn't. Bitter, yes. But so would I be probably in her situation. Mean, sure. She always had a mean streak, even before. At school she told tales. But not crazy."

"Then what are the odds she saw Candace?"

"She can't have."

Simon said, "Remember the grey car. This may be part of the same thing. There's something going on that maybe we don't understand. Something that's beyond us. We live on this planet but we don't know the half of what's around us. We haven't been given the eyes, the intelligence, to understand."

"If – and I'm only saying if – Candace is around, why would she go there? Why not go home. She'd know Jack's worried. We're all worried. And now Jack's in real trouble."

"Only because he ran off."

"And the couch."

"They didn't have a couch."

"You know that. I know that. But the cops don't. And he lied."

"We've all lied," Erica said and stopped.

Simon was talking but she wasn't listening and then she heard him say, "I had this real strong sense of her when I was at Jack's."

"That's because it's where she lived. Where she lives, Simon. I didn't want to tell you this but I got a voice mail today, sounded like someone I knew. The woman said she was going to reveal the truth and we were all to blame. What did she mean?"

He took hold of her hand. "People behave in strange ways at a time like this. And afterwards, they'll be sorry. Or they'll just put it down to stress."

He was forgiving her for something she hoped he didn't know she'd done.

"My love," she whispered. And then as she looked into his ear, she remembered what day it was.

"For heaven's sake. I should be in Vancouver. It's the big Christmas show."

"Glynis will've gone."

"No she won't. She never does. She's afraid of the city. Thinks some druggie will stick a needle in her and rape her. I'll be back Wednesday."

As she ran upstairs to get her clothes, she heard Simon say, "Don't go, darling. Please. You're not thinking straight. We're not in our right minds. "

On the road, driving past the store and the school, past the path to the building site, Erica felt liberated and knew that was a bad thing. Yes, her heart was still full of fear for her sister. More dread, really. But she was driving to another world. The ballroom of the hotel would be filled with displays of soft and lovely clothes for spring and summer. There would be swaths of fabric, of hats, gloves. There would be sprays of flowers and glasses of wine. The year would turn. Does life go on? Yes it does, she said to herself. Tall pines either side made a green valley of the highway and guilt washed away in her wake as she put her foot down and headed towards the bright lights.

The colours for next year, they said, were soft blues, light greys, floral designs, swishy skirts, lots of white too.

At Abbotsford, she turned round. What was she thinking, running off like that when her mind wouldn't let go of the words she'd used only an hour before? *Some druggie will stick a needle in her and rape her.* All the way back home, she shuddered for Candace and tried not to weep. She had to be able to see the road ahead.

Simon welcomed her with a kiss. "There's no escape," he said. "We can only wait. Watch and wait. Sit down, love, and I'll bring you a glass of red."

•

Jack looked at the windows. Not Halloween for ten days yet and the glass was covered with soapy scrawls. He didn't bother to try to read the words. From inside it was mirror writing. Accusations were coming at him from all sides now. Phone calls. Email. Even a cryptic text message on his cell: U'll get wts cmng 2 U, from a sender called "dragonhead." Was his number written on a wall somewhere?

Two hours he'd been at the police station last night, not with Marak but with two hard-looking Mounties pressing him, pushing him, till he'd been almost ready to fall into their trap. That was how they did it, just keeping on and on, never letting up. And how many poor suckers were in jail because they didn't know when to keep their mouths shut? As he closed the drapes to hide the writing, he saw a figure on the path.

He went to the door and yelled, "You! You touch my windows again..."

But it was Hayden looking beyond hangdog. The man had collapsed like a damn balloon since Verlyn's fall as if it was his wife who'd gone missing.

"You'd better come in. Sorry I shouted."

"I guess there are vandals around. Idiots."

"If they took a poll, I wouldn't like to guess how many in this town would put me down as innocent. Only a few."

Hayden tried to switch over to some kind of sympathetic mode but he didn't manage it.

"So Jack. You know Verl thinks she was there this afternoon. Candace, I mean."

"I've an idea that's why they haven't taken me in yet. They half believe it."

"Do you?"

"No. Candace," he kept his voice from breaking, "would come straight here if she was okay. And if she was okay, I'd have heard from her by now."

"You knew about her and me."

"Yes."

"It was over. It was nothing. We only talked. Mainly just talked."

"I don't want to hear about it, Hayden. Beer?"

"Thanks."

"Look, Jack. You don't have to be reasonable."

"You've come here to ask me to beat you up?"

"Not exactly."

"So?"

After the man had gone, Jack went upstairs and lay on the bed again. He was too tired to think about dinner, too tired to make a cup of coffee. What Hayden had said disturbed him. He knew that the man was performing some kind of act of contrition in coming to the house like that in the first place. In the second place, he was giving him a heads-up in case of problems down the road. Investors looking ahead, worried about the new delay. Buyers considering asking for a return of their deposits, spooked by the fact that possibly, possibly, Candace was in that pit. Was Hayden throwing up alarm signals as a diversion to give him something else to worry about? The guy didn't have that kind of mind. Did he? Maybe the fear that he might have caused Candace to disappear and that now someone appeared to have invaded his house and possibly tried to kill his wife had driven the guy a little off-centre.

And Denver was back in town. Some mothers would be locking their precious boys up at night.

The poor Cosgraves. As if Verlyn's accident wasn't enough, now this. Surprised that he could even think about them right now and sympathize with them, Jack shut that family out of his head and allowed his own fear to return. Every hour that went by meant that there was less likelihood of Candace being found, being found unharmed. He had even, unwillingly, begun to think of the music she'd like to have at her service. Why did there always have to be music anyway? His head rang with the noise of heavily beaten drums and brass. A vengeful, shrieking sound. Let go of me, he shouted.

And now the cops, since they thought he had murdered Candace, would accuse him of trying to kill Verlyn too? Any moment Marak would knock on the door. *We can do this quietly or the other way, Mr. Wilson.*

Where is my wife, you bastards! What has happened to my wife?

To calm himself he thought about the project. There was nothing so solid and soothing as concrete, steel girders, wooden posts, slabs of marble. Centre island with double sink. You're going to love this place Mr. and Mrs. Newcomer. Key in the lock. Ribbon maybe. Dan the Mayor wearing his chain. I now pronounce this kitchen open. I now pronounce thee, Jack, and thee, Candace. *You* a, more modern word now. Nicer. You Tarzan. Me Jane. Shimmering images of costumed figures danced around him: A wolf, Red Riding Hood, a pirate, an ape, a giant bumblebee, a figure in black with a scythe. And the bee was stinging his thigh.

It was his cellphone.

"Jack!" All the way from Florida rang his mother's accusing voice.

"Mom."

"Why didn't you call me. I'd've been there in a heartbeat. I'll get the next flight out. You must be in hell."

"Mom," he said.

"I can't believe I had to find out this way. By email from Chrissie. I am your mother. I know we had our differences, me and Candace. She's one reason I come down here in the winter to be out of your way, but this is an emergency and I'll bet you're not eating."

"I'd love to see you, Mom. You know that. Just give it another day or two. And then. I have a feeling she'll turn up soon."

"You have no such thing. I'll get my things together. I'll let you know the flights. I'll try to get one from Vancouver to Abbotsford and you can pick me up there."

"Mom!"

"You're getting all kinds of sympathy from people, I bet. Don't believe they all wish you well."

She hung up and he collapsed, wishing for a return of the costumed figures in his dream who had all, even death, seemed to be friendly.

When his cell rang again he almost threw it across the room, but it was Marcus asking him to come over with an urgency that stopped him from saying no.

•

The older policeman, Marak, had given her a suspicious look. Or was he just checking her out the way most older guys did? He surely couldn't suspect her of coming back to haunt her mother and then trying to kill her.

Hayley walked into the bar expecting to see boys she'd known at school but, like herself, they'd no doubt all gone away. Gone away hoping not to come back to this little, boring, dump of a town. Big Jack Wilson was trying to give the place back some life and they hated him for it. Otherwise it might just as well fall into the lake, all of it. Like that drowned village in China. A couple at the bar gave her a glance and looked away again. Then a voice said, "You Mrs. Cosgrave's daughter?"

"And Mr. Cosgrave's too. S'far as I know." She bit her tongue. It was answers like that that had got her in trouble at school. But she was not in school now.

"Rum and coke," she said to the barman, who turned out to be Freddy O'Farrell from grade ten.

"Sure, Denver. Good to see you."

The voice called to her again and said, "Could you join me for a minute?"

"She's a reporter," Freddy whispered. "Watch out what you say."

Hayley picked up her drink, paid for it and went to sit with the woman who she could now see was thirtyish and sharp-faced and needed a better haircut and a manicure. "What do you want to know?"

"My name's Kim. I'm with the *Sun*."

"I used to think I'd like to be a journalist," she said and carefully did not add, *but I grew out of it.* Hayley was not going to be a smartass. She put her drink down, settled herself into the booth and waited for the oncoming questions.

Kim was pleased. The editor was interested. There'd been no shooting downtown for a week. People were tired of hearing about the economic crisis and the needle exchange. Even *Young Ghills Lake woman disappears* had been losing traction. But *Young GL woman reappears as ghost to wheelchair-bound wife* was about to revive the story. Though since they'd found the unlocked basement door at the Cosgrave house, the spirit had lost some credibility. So who wanted to kill Verlyn? Just about half the town, according to gossip. Glynis at Fashion Now had told her that they, of course, felt sorry for the woman. Maybe she told those stories as compensation, the kindly Glynis said, and perhaps, to give Verlyn her due, she was just smarter than the rest of them. It seemed that Candace Wilson was generally liked though the protesters despised her for going along with her husband's plans and Althea in the café despised her for cheating on her good, decent husband. Jealousy there. Even Ms Wilson's own sister seemed to have reservations. As for weepy Alys Steen, colleague, and apparently less talented co-worker, she was going to have to take stress leave if she kept on wallowing in her guilt. That might be one to watch. A couple of men had edged her out of Glenn, Barden and Tyler's this morning just as soon as they found out she hadn't come to fix their stupid computer system.

Someone else had to have seen CW on Friday morning besides the kid who'd watched her kick at the dentist's door. And that somebody was keeping totally quiet.

Denver/Hayley Cosgrave had said nothing bad about her mother but not much good either. Her own reasons for leaving town and rarely returning were glossed over.

Kim had found details in the young woman's apparently casual reference to her father, and to Jack Wilson, more interesting. What exactly was going on with the financing of Pine View Estates? Often in a murder, and Kim now knew that's what it had to be, it came down to money. Money, jealousy, despair. These were things that pushed the nice, ordinary person you might see in any café or library or office to decide that they had to eliminate wife, husband, friend, colleague. Absolute desperation. And then of course there were the evil men – and women – who killed because they liked it, because human life was of no more value to them than that of the housefly. She wrote that sentence down. From her reading, she knew that the wicked didn't wear their characters on their foreheads. But after this, when they gave her crime and moved that useless prick Adams to the book club desk, she'd study criminology, hang out with detectives and write her book. She had already figured out how to get information from people.

After Hayley Cosgrave had gone, she moved up to the bar to talk to Freddy, "So you've known her all her life, I guess."

"We all know Denver, calling herself Hayley now," he said. "Sorry she went to work in Vancouver. She was a great party girl. But I guess she finds the airport an interesting place."

"Airport?"

"Spa there. She's a whatdoyoucallit, does people's nails. Gives facials. All that stuff. One of those little places. You can pass the time while you're waiting for a flight. Get a massage, whatever. She did stay home to look after her mom for a while. Felt guilty, I guess. Not that the accident was her fault. She was in the back seat. Her dad was driving. It was the drunk in the other car who made a left turn too fast. Lucky for him, he died in the ambulance or they'd have sued his pants off."

"I'll have another Coke, please."

"Want rum in it?"

Kim looked down at the page in her book.

Ms Denver/Hayley Cosgrave had told her that she was a travel agent specializing in exotic destinations. She had told her that her mother's accident three years ago was caused when her dad let go of a ladder while Verlyn was cleaning windows. She had told her that she'd be on her way to Bhutan now had it not been for the trouble at home: An only child has to make sacrifices. She had told her a load of freaking garbage!

"Rum, Kim?" Freddy repeated.

"Yes," she said. "Yes, please." After all the paper was paying a per diem now.

Had any of these people told her the truth? The reverend Reaver, Jack's best friend at school, had told her that Candace was most likely in Europe with a rich man, money being important to her though, he had said in a forgiving way, there is nothing wrong with that. And since we don't know, we shouldn't conjecture. Jack was on the high school football team and certainly had a temper but that didn't mean there was violence. After ten minutes of forgiving everyone whose faults he'd named, he suggested she come to church. "I've only been here a year," he said. "Glad to come back to my old home. These are good people. And I can't believe there's anyone who would make away with Candace. Though of course even the people one knows best can surprise one."

Holy hypocrite, she thought after she'd left him there in the café, drinking tea that she'd paid for and eating a piece of cheesecake. Holy liar?

According to Wendy Price, Marcus Brandt was a saint whose late wife and two daughters had driven him almost to despair. King Lear wandering fool-less on the heath. On the other hand, someone else had said he was a doting parent but needed watching as he hung around the school too frequently though it was most likely only to pick up his grandchildren.

Kim left half the drink. It was vile stuff anyway. And she had work to do. It was well past visiting time but maybe she could sneak into the hospital and get a few words of sense out of the patient.

●

Verlyn clutched at the nice, clean sheet. She was gasping and trying to fake a heart attack, any kind of attack that would keep her here, safe in this hospital room even though she had to share it with two others.

How could she go home when the spirit or even the fleshly emanation of Candace lurked there ready to push her over or worse? Lying under the wheelchair, one handle pressing into her stomach, the cushion over her face, had been almost worse than the original accident. She'd only been able to flounder, hardly able to breathe, and listen for the sounds of the being who'd tipped her over lightly yet with great strength.

I cannot go back into that room, that house, that life or even, maybe, to that man, my husband in name only.

They could say what they liked about the basement door being open but they hadn't been there. It was no human that had appeared in the living room today.

If Denver had already been home then Verlyn might have suspected some kind of trick. But no! Denver didn't hate her mother. She was only an exasperated girl who hadn't found a clear way into life, which was probably her father's fault. Eventually she would be her old sweet self again. She had talked just now in a kind, caring way. At least for a sentence or two. So there was hope.

"I don't want to go home," she said aloud.

"I know what you mean," the woman in the opposite bed called out. "My old man's a slob. Never cleans up after himself. And do you think me lying here with a ruptured spleen is going to change that? The mess I'll be going back to, you wouldn't believe."

It was the ruptured spleen that did it. Verlyn couldn't bear to hear about it one more time. It made her sick to imagine it, that awful lump of bloody flesh. Spleen! The very word was gruesome. She couldn't arch her back. Contrary to fiction, the accident had not brought back the strength to her legs. There was no sudden, Behold, I can walk. But she could twist and turn and moan.

"Oooh," she cried, tossing the top part of her body about as well as she could. "Nurse!"

When the nurse eventually came, she said, "There, honey. There. I'll give you a little injection to ease the pain."

"I don't want an injection," Verlyn shouted. "And what took you so long. If I'd been having a heart attack, I'd've been dead by now. I want a drink."

"It won't hurt," the demon replied. She had a kind, round face and was wearing a floral top and blue pants. Where had starched white linen gone, and caps that hid the hair? These professional women and men dressed as if they bought their clothes at thrift shops.

The needle went in. Stupefied, they would send her home like a drugged bear returned to the wild. She gritted her teeth and tried with all her might to resist the drug. Well, if she had to go home, she would insist on having someone with her all the time, every hour, day and night. Hayden would have to dig deep into his pockets and pay for a companion who would be a friend and ally. Life could be sweet after all. The young man would be tall and strong, able to lift her onto the bed and do what Hayden was afraid of doing, have sex with her. There were ways.

"I'm not a statue," she said.

The nurse was straightening her sheets and saying, "We'll have you out of here in no time."

Not if I can help it.

Then the angel of mercy went across to Ms Spleen and touched her forehead and said, "You're a little hot, dear." She lowered her voice and Verlyn knew they were talking about her, about Candace. She strained to listen but only heard the words "crazy" and "murder".

Perhaps we, me and Hayde, she thought, can bribe our only child whose golden curls still shine in memory and photographs, to stay home and look after her loving parents.

Before she drifted off, she shouted across the space, "I'm not crazy and I didn't murder anyone and I don't believe my husband did either."

Kim caught the words as she looked into the room. The woman was falling asleep. Useless to try to talk to her. But she saw, or thought she saw, movement under the sheets lower down where Verlyn's legs had to be. She stared and was still staring when the woman in the corner bed beckoned to her and said, "You want to hear about my spleen, dear? The doctors say they've never seen anything like it."

•

Jack's intention had been to make the town proud, proud of him and Gary, proud of itself. This was the place where he'd grown up, played on the lakeshore, tried to build a boat with Hayden and Dan. The boat that sank as soon as they pushed it out onto the water. He'd never wanted to leave. Those two years trekking to Vancouver to go to UBC had been like exile. Only good part was the music. And the football. And Stefan. In Ghills Lake, the streets, the trees, the old houses, were all part of his background and he hadn't wanted another. But now the trees, the windows, the paving stones were all against him, all whispering. He'd reached beyond his capacity and the Fates had slapped him down. Hey, wait a minute, he said to himself, that's negative thinking, that's Greek myth stuff.

Yet Candace had disappeared and he might have to go away too, one way or another.

"All we wanted, me and Gary," he said to Marcus, as they sat in the old man's living room with its pocked walls and dusty furniture, "was to stay here and build something really good, you know. Make an improvement. Something new that people would point to and admire. And now, I'm a leper. I walk down the street and people disappear inside or they're staring in store windows. It's like they don't know me."

Marcus looked at his son-in-law and loved him. The boy had been brought down and it was unfair. He regretted his own fleeting moments of suspicion. Such things spread through the air like flu bugs and no amount of handwashing could stop them.

"I'll make a couple of tuna sandwiches, and then I want you to do something."

"How old's your mayo?" Jack asked.

"Leave the gift horse alone, boy."

While the old man was in the kitchen, Jack couldn't resist going to the wall and pulling at a few of the remaining coasters. There must have been hundreds. It was satisfying, ripping, tearing, bits of wall coming off, not caring about the white powder drifting onto his sweater. Maybe he should be out there destroying something instead of trying to build architecturally designed housing, elegant homes. Even the word elegant could add to the price. My home is no longer my home, he thought. He'd have to stay until there was no possibility of Candace returning. Six months? A year? And then hand over the company to Gary and head out east. That is if the cops hadn't locked him up. Another innocent in jail for twenty years.

"Saskatchewan," he said out loud. Winter in some isolated place where he was unknown.

Alone. A sad, solitary man. He didn't like dogs but maybe a

small one for company. He picked at the wall again, recognized self-pity and tried to block it out. Candace needed all his thought, all his effort, all his will.

"I don't know what made me put those there," Marcus said when he returned with sandwiches and beer. "Well, I do but I was sorry after. I did love her, you know, Sheila. She just became so kind of unusual. I realized some of it was my fault. You get to know that too late. There were things I could've done. Been a bit more responsive. Not gone off to the Arctic every summer like I did. She wanted to come too but I said it wasn't a suitable environment and there'd be nothing for her to do. And I wanted to get away from her besides. But she would've picked up some of the language, learnt a few Inuit things. She had that curiosity and it was never satisfied."

Listening, Jack became aware that this might be himself in a decade or two down the road, talking about Candace, and he shuddered. Though of course Candace, aside from one or two things, was a good woman, sane. Not at all like her mother.

"And now," Marcus said, "SHE haunts me. She talks to me. I might have to let Wendy move in to lay the ghost."

"For Chrissake," Jack said. And then he added, "Sorry. It's your affair." And didn't say anything would be better than doing it on the living room rug for everyone to see. But did wonder why the old man appeared to have no shame. Not a scrap.

They ate in silence for a few moments. There were green onions in with the tuna and mayo and the bread was fresh. The sandwich tasted better than anything he'd eaten in days. Even the steak. Especially the steak.

"What is it you want me to do?"

"Come out with me. I have to check something."

Jack was too tired to argue or to say that it was dark and raining and getting on for midnight. He put on his jacket and followed the old man down the path. They made for the lakeshore, the building site.

Was Marcus going to suggest that, to placate whatever gods had taken Candace, he should fill in the foundation and make the place into a theme park, a monument, or perform an act of contrition by jumping into the hole? Not that he hadn't considered it but there were others involved, not least the people who'd bought into the place. Gary and the investors. And Bill wasn't the only one looking to pay off his debts.

"This is where I was earlier," Marcus said when they were out of the car, walking near the lake. "Bill told me to clear off. I wasn't even close to the site. My umbrella jumped out of my hand."

He took a flashlight from his pocket and swung the light around. Inch by inch, he trod the ground. Jack, thinking they must look like a couple of idiots, nonetheless followed closely. There had to be room for instinct when everything else had failed. You couldn't dismiss intuition just because you yourself thought in concrete terms. He turned towards the water. Its lapping sound was an undercurrent to the rain. He heard a yell and when he looked back, Marcus was gone.

"Marcus!" he shouted.

A weak cry came from below the ground a couple of metres to his left beside the maple tree. He went closer and found he was on the edge of a hole, nearly slipped into it, and fell onto the muddy earth.

"She's here. Get help," came from below.

Jack cried out, "Is she okay?" He was shaking all over. Moments passed before his fingers were steady enough to key in the three numbers on his cellphone.

It was a nightmare and a dream all in one. There were ropes, lights, ambulances. The old man was hurt and Candace, Candace, she was unknowing.

TWELVE

Those who'd been loudest in their suspicions of him were now hinting that he'd pushed her into the hole and hoped she'd never be found. Others congratulated him and hugged him but Jack sensed ambivalence. He didn't know whether he should put a notice in the paper in his own defence or simply leave town and concede defeat. His mother bustling round the kitchen, quoting, "They say. Let them say" wasn't exactly a comfort.

"I'll stay till she's all right," she said.

"I think you should go back to the sunshine. The damp isn't good for your arthritis."

She sat down opposite him at the kitchen table.

"Jack, you've had a very difficult time. And what I'd like to do with some of the money Dad left is buy you some good furniture. We could set it up so that when Candace gets out of hospital, the house is all really nice."

Jack thought his voice must be coming out of him as a scream but his mother went on looking calm, sunburnt, eager, full of her generous idea.

"Mom. We have to leave that to her. She has to live here. We, Candace and I, have plans for the house. And she'll want to choose."

"It's been nine years," she replied.

"We're comfortable. We like space. It's easy to clean."

"You were brought up in a nice home."

Maybe that was it. The reason for the apparent lack of comfort. All the niceness in his childhood home had gone into the appearance of it. And his dad's surly moods and their quarrels

218

were acted out on a pleasing stage. It was a set where nothing was allowed to sink into shabbiness and the paint was always free of marks.

Rebellion came in many forms, and sometimes late.

"We'll sort it out, Mom. But thanks. That was real kind."

"While you were out that nice boy you were at school with came round. The clergyman."

"Did he?"

"I told him to come back when you're home."

"I wish you hadn't."

"There's no need to snap."

Where had it gone? The sympathy. The kid glove approach. Candace was found. It was as if the world were saying, "Good times are over, boy." But they had not been good times. His nerves were taut like piano wires and his heart was still leaping about. He was thrilled that she was safe but the letting go of fear had turned him to mush. And he had a deep sense that the worst was still to come. His mother gave him her disappointed look and before she could say any sad thing about only trying to help, he got up and said he was late.

"I'll come too."

"She'd love to see you, Mom. But right now it's only me and her dad and Erica."

After he'd put his jacket on, he went back to the kitchen and hugged his mother and told her he was very glad she was there.

●

Candace was more awake than they thought. A heavy kind of tiredness lay over her like a blanket. She watched the parade. Men and women in white jackets. Jack, Erica, her dad, wanting to atone for what had happened to her as if they'd all had a hand on her back when she fell. Mercifully, one doctor had said, she won't remember it all. But she would. The pain in her legs was a reminder of being crunched up in the dark place with rats, or was it bats. Of being wet and also dry. Of being afraid and then resigned when she knew she was forgotten and would die. Trying to conjure up pleasant images for her last hours on earth and finding none.

She bent forward and touched the bandage on her leg. The physiotherapist had told her to move it as much as possible but gently. That morning the doctor had smiled in approval as Candace wiggled her toes and bent her good knee. Warm blankets. The IV drip. Before long, Jack and others would arrive again, still looking at her as if she had risen from the dead. Another day, *they* murmured, and she might have been beyond recovery, though there were stories of people lasting weeks alone in desperate places.

At times she lay very still and pretended not to hear. Even after she came out of the first sleep, she'd kept her mouth closed.

They spoke, the people round the bed, and she had no answers for them. There was nothing to say. She had no language to express darkness, solitude or her new love for pebbles.

Then resentment entered her mind. Why had they let her stay in that hole for so long? What had she done to them that they were so cruel?

She saw, through half-closed eyes, the shape of Jack's face. That was him, the man she married. He was a man who dug holes in the ground and got no thanks for it. His face was thinner, he had a dark, fearful look. His eyes were wet. Had she chosen to live with a man with doggy eyes? But his wasn't the voice she thought she'd heard that morning. It had been a high-pitched woman's voice. And it could very well have been the last human sound she ever heard.

She made up her mind to listen for it.

●

Erica couldn't think why she'd picked a teddy bear to take as a gift. It had looked at her with its little glass eyes through the window of the hospital gift shop and now she was standing beside her sister's bed and holding the toy towards her. Candace, IV lines going into her arm and her stomach, glanced at it and said, "He's in one piece." She took the bear and held it, murmuring to it. Then Erica wanted to grab it back. The twinge of unexpected jealousy surprised her. Okay, she said to her other self, I'll buy you one on the way home, a bigger one.

"You're looking better," she said.

"Good. Nice."

Candace's thought processes didn't seem to have caught up with her yet. The doctors said that she would be normal in a few more days. She was remarkably resilient considering she'd spent four days in a dark hole. Solitary. A prisoner shut off from sight and sound. Once or twice over the past couple of days, Erica had sat very still in the dark and tried to imagine what it was like. Last night, she'd found Tannis sitting under her duvet doing the same. "It must have been horrible," the girl had said. "And nobody came for days and days. We didn't look hard enough, did we, Mom?"

Erica handed her sister the card the kids had made on the computer. Make it cheerful, their father had said and so it was. A mass of smiley faces and a blue bird with a speech balloon in its beak. *Welcome back.*

"Nice," Candace said and smiled. "Cute."

Erica asked how she was feeling.

"Fine. Sleepy, you know."

No. We didn't look hard enough. We weren't there when you were calling our names, sister. The guilt might wear off eventually but the sense of uncertainty, the fear, never will.

She took hold of Candace's hand and stroked it.

Simon, good Simon, had tried to depict Candace's experience

in paint but hadn't got further than a black background. He'd spent most of yesterday sitting in front of the canvas, waiting, he said, for the whole experience to settle into an image or a series of images. He spoke of the tree root that had apparently held onto the brown leather bag and then bent under its weight and let it drop, and of his lone walks in the October nights. If I were an artist, Erica thought, I'd paint a picture in swirling greys and blues like the map of an approaching tornado.

Looking back over the week since Friday the sixteenth, she shuddered. This was what people meant when they said they'd been through the wringer. "I've been flattened, all my previous self squeezed out of me. It'll take time to recover. And for you too," she whispered to her sleeping sister.

Candace opened her eyes and said, "Thank you for coming."

"Best not to tire the patient," the nurse said from the doorway.

Erica got up. There was something she had to do and she wasn't sure how to go about it: To tell Simon that she loved him, loved him in an eternal way that had nothing to do with sex. Perhaps if she said it every day, he would come to believe it.

●

By falling on top of Candace and breaking her arm, Marcus had become a hero. He had also opened a can of worms. How could they not have found her? What had the searchers been doing? Why had the police not examined the ground more closely? The hole was right there behind the maple. The police spokesperson, standing there in her uniform on TV had said, in a kind of apology, that they thought at first that Ms Wilson had simply left town as often happened in these cases. An anonymous caller had seen her on the bus to Vancouver. Only later had they focused on the site. The dog handler had been called away to another case and wouldn't be back till Tuesday. A laundry list of excuses! Near-fatal incompetence! And so his beloved daughter had been there all the time lying in her own mess, dehydrated, afraid and finally unconscious while the town got on with its usual life and her husband began to build his monument to the future of Ghills Lake. Rose had been sharp in her criticism of them all and the cops in particular. And she had given him a horrid shock when he'd seen her off on the airport express two days ago. At first she'd been solicitous about his sore legs, his bruised ribs. Then, sitting in the car, at the last moment, she'd said, and the words would never fade from his mind, "I came here thinking we could be brother and sister again and maybe live together and I'd keep the farm. But you're too dithery, Marcus. Just like when you were a kid. Always late too. You'd forget to feed the hens, forget to shut the gate. I need someone reliable. I hope you won't be hurt but I've been in touch with a guy on the Net. He lives in Vancouver now but he's coming for a month in January to see how he can stand the winter. You could come for a holiday sometime and bring that strong boy." That had been it! She got out of the car, took her bag off the back seat, waved and went to the waiting bus. She might as well have hit him with a two-by-four.

He glanced at the paper. It was odd how, while Candace was gone, wars, threatened elections, melting ice in the Arctic, had become unimportant, as if, with a click, he and the rest of the family, by ignoring it, had shut the world down. He turned the page. It was all still happening out there. The whole disturbing, gibbering, murderous mess. He felt the smallness, the ant-ness, of his own life; and wondered what colour he should paint the living room.

Wendy said, "If you're not going to eat the rest of that steak, I will."

He let her take it from his plate. He worried now that new rumours would be spreading around the streets, in and out of the cafés and homes and along the cyber highway.

"I don't think it's a good idea," he said, referring to her plan of bringing her things over next week. A few of her clothes, she said. A gradual takeover! "I have to finish decorating first."

She knew enough about men to understand that the last lick of paint would never be applied. It would always be ongoing. A lifetime project.

"I'll bring some of my stuff on Monday," she said. "We'll move into the back bedroom while we get the carpet cleaned in the other. Or do you think maybe we should go for nice flooring with rugs on top?"

Responding to his look, she said, "I'm not going to sell my place, only rent it out till we see how it goes, sweetheart. Think of it as a trial."

He did.

"And you'll teach me how to use the computer?"

"I'm not sure you want to get in there, honey. It's a morass."

"I'm not going to spy on you. I'll buy me a laptop and you can show me how to google. All my friends think I'm Betty Flintstone."

Everything that happened had attachments. One thing he'd learned in life: Nothing is straightforward.

"Why are you wearing your hat?"

"I forgot. I keep it on when I'm decorating."

She reached across and took the tuque from his head.

"Your hair!" she said.

"Newspaper photographer was coming so I cut it a bit but reaching up hurt my chest."

"You poor monkey. Wait a minute."

He moved his chair away from the table and sat there while she fetched a comb and scissors and draped a towel round his neck. There was a price to pay for not being lonely but it could be a bargain too. At least he'd never have to fork out for a haircut again.

"Mind my ear," he yelled.

And if there was to be blood, so be it.

●

Candace was becoming more aware. He had to attend to her. Dividing his day between the office and the hospital, Jack hardly had time to think, only to feel. She'd been out of the ICU for two days. The pneumonia that might have killed an older person, the doctor said, had receded. An older person or someone who didn't eat right and go to the gym would have died after four days in that chill, wet hole. Her survival was a miracle. That's what they kept saying.

Jack bought six red roses from the stall by the hospital door. Candace was propped up on pillows, her right arm in a cast. She looked at him and touched his hand. Fragile she was, like a glass flower. Her eyes seemed to be seeking something from him that so far he hadn't been able to give. And then, before he could stop them, the tears came again. She handed him the edge of the sheet but he found the box of Kleenex on her bedside table and mopped his face. When he came close, she drew his head to hers. "Love," she said.

"Yes," he replied.

The nurse found him lying beside her and shook her head.

"Too soon," she said. "Naughty."

"We weren't."

Standing behind the nurse was Marak, the man who had loved Candace in grade twelve. He was hugging a basket of fruit.

"Out both of you," the nurse ordered. "Visiting time's over."

●

"All's well that ends well," the cop said. "So, Jack?"

"Marak?"

"Do you want that couch back?"

"Give it to the thrift shop."

The two men stood together outside the ward, and the policeman apologized for taking the stuff out of Jack's freezer and knocking down part of the basement wall. They'd had an anonymous tipoff that Candace was in the house. So they'd waited till he left to go to his father-in-law's that night and then moved in to search the cellar.

"I'll be glad if you don't take that any further," Marak said.

"If you re-plaster the wall and buy me some meat."

"Your meat's okay. Don't push it."

They laughed for a moment a little hysterically, then Marak's beeper sounded. He patted Jack on the shoulder and hurried off down the corridor.

●

Verlyn poured coffee for herself and her daughter. Hayden had gone to Abbotsford. These mornings, he sped out of the house as if pursued. And he was pursued – by the thoughts of his wife and child.

"So you didn't mind, Mom?"

"Of course I minded, Hayley. That is a pretty name. I'm not going to apologize for calling you Denver. It seemed good at the time. I guess there's a kind of arrogance to people calling kids after themselves as if they're so wonderful they want the kids to be like them."

"You're digressing."

"I know this accident, this happening, whatever it was, didn't work a miracle like these things are supposed to. Or they do in books anyway. For a few hours I really thought I could move my foot. Imagination is a wonderful thing. But it does seem to have affected my mind. You might not think for the better."

"Mother!"

"Yes. Okay. I think it's a great idea. Your dad will be happy to pay for it. You might not think I can save money sitting around like this but I do. And you can drive me to Vancouver next week so we can shop for clothes. You will work hard?"

"They'll only consider letting me start in January if I commit to three and a half courses."

"I'll postpone my trip to Hungary. Your education is more important."

Denver/Hayley wasn't going to fall for that. Let her be a martyr, which in a way she was anyway. She could afford to go to Europe if she wanted. But she allowed her an element of goodness and said, "Thank you, Mom."

When, if ever, she qualified as a psychologist, she might be able to work it all out and understand why it had been so important to aggravate her parents, to leave home and spend her days filing other people's nails. Her own nails were chipped here and there and needed polish. It had been a hectic few days.

"I'll have to go back to Van and sort things out. I'll maybe hang on to the room. It's only a bus ride from the university."

"It sounds like a squalid place to me. You should be in residence."

"I'm going to fax this form from Dad's office. Is there anything you need?"

You. I need you, Verlyn thought. You're my daughter and I love you.

Hayley waved from the door and said, "I won't be long."

Verlyn wondered if it was possible to will yourself to forget. Maybe I should have told them that I saw Candace and called out to her moments before she disappeared. But Candace had been found alive and would be well so there was no need for guilt. And she truly had no idea there was a hole by the tree. Also, Jack was nowhere near at the time but there were still people who didn't want to know that. You could hit them over the head with the truth and they still preferred their own construction.

One of the things she remembered, or thought she remembered, was that just before she fell over, or was pushed, last Monday, she'd heard a man say he was Boris. Impossible! Boris lived in Antigua on a yacht with a crew of girls. Ears play funny tricks in times of stress. And she had moved, like a snake. Pushing herself with her arms, she'd got herself out from under the chair before Hayden found her lying there, face down.

HALLOWEEN

SITTING BESIDE CANDACE on the new sofa, an L-shaped object deeply cushioned, covered in imitation beige moleskin and taking up half the living room, Jack said, "What would you like for dinner?"

Erica had left cold salmon and salad, and the rest of the pie Ben's mother had given him was in the freezer.

It was her second day home and he was still afraid. She was pale and he'd been told she might have nightmares and that he shouldn't leave her alone for long periods. He touched her good arm gently; a reality check. She was here. The doctor had sent her home, he said, because there was less chance of infection there than in the hospital. A nurse would come in once a day to check on her and make sure she was having proper care. And to make sure perhaps that, in the minds of some, her husband didn't make another attempt to kill her.

Was it too soon to mention that far-off province where winter was for real and roads disappeared into the horizon and where they could start again, unknown.

"I think if we'd had a couch like this years ago –" she said, perhaps suggesting that she would never have had sex with Hayden, as if furniture had anything to do with fidelity.

"Mom insisted on buying it. It was the only way I could get her to go back to Florida."

"Jack, you could have asked her to stay a while longer." Was she was thinking that there would then have been womanly care?

"I told her we'd go there when you can travel. So dinner, sweetheart? What would you like?"

"Whatever there is, Jack. Not very much. Soup maybe, and crackers."

In the kitchen, he opened a can of cream of celery and tipped it into a bowl. Stirring in the milk, he felt a strange weakness and knew what it was.

He heated the soup in the microwave and tried to squash the lumps. He put the dish on the silver tray that had been a wedding gift, along with a spoon and crackers on a plate, and set it on the table beside her.

"I have to go out," he said. "I'll be back before the kids start coming. Don't go to the door yourself."

"You bought candy?"

"I'll go get some now."

Before he left, he fetched her a glass of water. It was important to keep her hydrated.

•

Candace listened. She heard the door close, the fridge humming in the kitchen, a car going by. Sounds had become precious to her. Even the spoon tapping against the side of the bowl was a kind of reassurance. As she ate the tepid soup, pushing the lumps to one side, Candace considered her resurrection. It had to mean something. There were always reasons if only a person could fig-ure them out. She remembered sitting at the picnic table pondering a new life. She'd tried to make a list. And the only item on that list was couch! Yet beyond 'couch' lay the whole wide world. The head office in Toronto beckoned. What kept her in this particular place? Friends? Hiking the coastal trails? Jack? The shock of being close to death had made her aware that this was her now-or-never time. She munched on the crackers. She needed strength before she could make a decision either to inhabit her life as it was or to move on.

They were out after all, the children. Marcus waited by the door. He'd bought a box full of little Mars Bars and KitKats and put them in the plastic pumpkin. While he was waiting for the first ring, he went to get something for dinner out of the freezer. The eye looked back at him. He couldn't remember now why he'd bought the pig's head except that Darren had more or less dared him to take it, suggesting that he had no idea how to cook it.

He would boil it and make the meat into pâté or cook cheeks and cabbage. There had to be a recipe somewhere.

Regarding Wendy. Advantage: There would be sex on tap.

First thing would be to shut down access to the chat room. He'd joined it to keep up with life out there and maybe to find friends. What he'd found was a sewer of gossip and banality. It was important to know what people were doing and saying, so he'd thought. Truth was he'd checked in out of loneliness. Kids didn't need him and there were long boring days. But Boris, playboy of the Caribbean, had to die. Boris had nearly killed Marguerite. He shouldn't have run off and left her like that but something in him didn't care at the time. It would shut her up for a couple of days. Had she known all along that she'd seen Candace that morning and kept quiet out of malice? Hard to believe. But if she'd spoken out, Candace might've been rescued much sooner. And there was what she'd said about Jack! Spreading lies and rumours the way she did was a crime in itself.

He'd only wanted to come up behind her and say he was Boris and that she must recant what she'd said about Jack. Then he'd tripped over the coffee table and it collapsed. He rushed out of the room. As he ran down the stairs, he heard another crash but hadn't gone back to see what it was. Like a coward, he'd slipped out the way he'd got in, through the basement door. The fault lay, really, with whoever had left that door unlocked. He'd tried the back door to the kitchen first and then gone down the steps to the cellar. He hadn't gone to the front door and rung the bell and confronted her face to face because he was angry and wanted to surprise her, startle her, frighten her a little. And so he had.

Erica said that some slight movement had returned to Marguerite's legs. Maybe, by chance, he'd wrought another miracle. So he decided to leave guilt to others and go on being a hero.

He looked at the dictionary, closed the heavy volume and patted the dark blue cover. A good companion, but for random use only in future.

●

The *Star* had sent a photographer with her to take a picture of the hole. Kim wanted to climb down into it so that she could describe what Ms Wilson had been through and maybe Sean could get a shot of her looking up in hope of rescue. But there was still yellow police tape round it. Engineers had said the sinkhole had come about because of the underground stream, the digging at the building site, erosion, a shifting of tectonic plates. It all added up to the fact that they had no idea. Sean said there was nothing here of any use, no prize-winning images. The maple tree in fall was a cliché. The best thing was for Kim to show him round town. There'd already been photos of the Wilson house, the new development, the characters involved, but maybe he'd see a different angle.

As soon as Ms Wilson was fit, Kim intended to return again to Ghills Lake and ask her what it was like down there alone, dark, peeing yourself, thirsty, calling out, getting weaker and weaker. And finally too weak even to be desperate. She felt tears coming and wiped her face, hoping Sean wasn't looking. So it was back to the city again. That Saturday when she'd first arrived in Ghills Lake, the town itself had seemed like a sinkhole, a dead place. A place for the dead inhabited by a people who were unhappy, drifting, clinging to the place because they didn't know

any better. She knew now that it was a small universe and she
needed time to think about that.

Two days after Candace had been found, she paid the bill
at the B & B and Maia the landlady gave her a jar of homemade blueberry jam and told her she was welcome any time.
Driving away down the highway that Wednesday, she'd men-
tally cast her regrets out of the window. Believing everything
she was told had been stupid. But it was all material for her
book: A fictionalized account of the brief disappearance of
Candace Alison Wilson.

•

Jack was hungry, as if he hadn't eaten since Candace went missing
two weeks ago. He pulled up at the supermarket and went in to
get little bags of pretzels and chips.

After that he stopped at Best Big Burgers and ordered a double cheese with fries to go.

While he waited, he considered luck, chance, divine interven-
tion. Candace was found. *Maybe there is a God.* He might choose
a church, even Reaver's, Reaver after all was only being what he
was, a clergyman, a shepherd, and go once in a while to offer up
thanks. Building was going ahead. Deliveries so far on time. It
would be done as they'd planned, Pine View. And then he and
Gary could move in on the strip mall.

He heard his name. Wilson. And listened. Two men in the
booth nearest the counter were talking.

"Sure. He pushed her in. Didn't expect she'd ever get out.
Why didn't he just fill it with dirt and be done with it?" That was
an older man, a voice he didn't know.

"Not Jack. He wouldn't do that. Some kind of a sinkhole, they
said. Can happen overnight."

"Or can be made to happen, right."

When he got home with his paper sack full of fatty food,

Candace was sitting up making a list, writing very slowly with her left hand.

"Should you be doing that, honey?"

"It's not strenuous. I want to go back to work next week."

"The doctor said a month, sweetheart. And you need to get the cast off your arm first."

He put the chips and pretzels into a bowl and set the bowl on a chair by the door. The outside light was on so maybe the kids would come, kids whose parents knew him for an innocent man.

He sat down beside his wife. Her cheeks were hollowish and her eyes flickered a bit. It would take a while.

In a week or two, he might ask her if she'd like to move to the Prairies. Standing at the Burger counter, he'd understood that he must leave this town and let Gary take over the project. He could start afresh in a new place where there was no suspicion. Those had been his thoughts all the way home. In his mind, he saw a green place, okay with a lousy winter, but new, and inhabited by kind men and women who were open-minded because they lived where the horizon was visible but distant. He could set up a company and build homes for those people to keep out the cold. Stefan had said, "When it's over, come out here. Join me. We'll work together."

And failing all else, he could get a job in the oil patch.

The question formed in his brain. Candace sweetheart, would you like to move away from here? He recalled the voice. He'd looked over at the booth: There was his foreman, Bill, talking to an older guy, one of the workmen. Betrayal was a word. Loyalty was another. And what was either of those words worth? Layoff had consequences. I'll lay the whole freaking lot off. That'll teach them.

He grabbed at the list Candace was making and his sharp movement made her wince.

The wobbly words said, Broccoli. Cheese. Apple pie.

"Sorry, Candy," he said. "We should've found you sooner. We thought we'd looked everywhere. If it hadn't been for that damn tree, you know. We let it stand in our way, and didn't go around it."

"You must have been worried."

Worried hardly covered it, he thought. Frantic, in a panic, terrified, accused. He smiled at her and said, "We were all out of our minds."

She was quiet. It seemed to take her a moment now to catch on to what he said.

"My mom insisted on buying the couch. Is it okay?"

"We might never have got one."

"It's ugly and it takes up half the space."

"It's so comfortable, I might never want to move."

They both laughed.

Jack tried to feel happy, settled. But the older guy's words wouldn't fade. So they still thought him capable of murder. Many people in this rotten town had, for four days, assumed he had murdered his wife, and now there were those who thought he'd tried and failed. He wanted to blow the place up entire, every house, every building, and reduce Ghills Lake to rubble.

And suppose, suppose, Candace too came to suspect him? Then he was finished, a dead man.

He had a clear choice: The coward's way led eastward to a new life, to Stefan. The other meant remaining here, biting his tongue often, not being vengeful, simply getting on with life as best he could.

The doorbell rang. Jack leapt up and went to answer it.

Candace heard a grown-up's voice, then a child's soft, "Trick or treat?"

When he came back, Jack said, "That was Alys with her kid. He's dressed as a vampire with bloody fangs. She wanted to come in and say hello but I told her it's too soon."

"I want to talk to her." Candace looked at the walls of the room, at Simon's painting of two lovers grasping, maybe stifling, the world. "I would've liked to see her." She stopped herself from asking if she was a prisoner now, a prisoner *again*. After all, this room did have an exit.

"If you feel up to it next week, love, we'll go for a drive. Maybe a trip to Vancouver."

"Okay," she replied. She could relax, remain in patient mode, till she felt ready to take hold of her life and shape her future.

"We really were all out of our minds," he said again.

"I expect there's a word for being afraid of Fridays."

"If there is, your dad will know it. I'll take every Friday off and stay with you. I'll cling to you like – like..."

"Like ivy?"

"A limpet. Shall I put some music on?"

"Anything. I'll never want silence again."

He went to the shelf and ran his hand over the top row of plastic covers and picked out the CD. It wasn't her favourite but he couldn't resist it because he'd been listening to it on the last day that the universe had felt safe to him.

The first notes of the *New World Symphony* filtered into the room.

His wife looked at him and said, "Hi."

He knelt beside her and said, "I washed the kitchen floor. It was hard. I've called Maids R Us. They're going to start on Wednesday. I'll do the shopping and make the bed. Mom did the laundry. I've found a place where we can get good ready-made meals, just need heating up, and weekends, I can cook for us on the barbecue."

Candace took hold of his hand, his large, hairy hand, and said, "Be quiet, Jack. Let's just listen to your music for now."

•

Verlyn looked out the window. She wiggled the toes on her left foot and felt a twitch in her calf muscle. The doctor said. The doctor hoped. The physiotherapist said to come in twice a week. Who knew? She wasn't going to let on yet. It would be a huge adjustment. There would be no more sympathy, no more allowances made. I will have to be better. I can love Hayden. I love all these people. They're not perfect and someone has to tell them their faults now and then. But it's my place, my town. In the dim light she watched the shadowy parade of animals, ghosts, supermen and superwomen, Harry Potters and Hermiones, two grim reapers and a minute fireman as they trotted down the street, going from house to house, giggling, shouting, "Trick or Treat."

Denver, or rather Hayley, was at the door wearing a witch hat, handing out candy. Verlyn smiled. The children had been allowed out again because their parents thought the streets were safe.

AKNOWLEDGEMENTS

It has been a pleasure to have Edna Alford as my editor again. I'm most grateful for her careful attention to my words, and for her sharp vision. My thanks also to all at Coteau for their encouragement and their care in producing this book.

ABOUT THE AUTHOR

RACHEL WYATT is an award-winning author of novels, short fiction, stage and radio plays, and non-fiction works. Her fiction includes the novels *Letters to Omar* (published in 2010 by Coteau Books) and *The Rosedale Hoax,* and the short story collections *The Magician's Beautiful Assistant* and *The Day Marlene Dietrich Died.* Her stage plays have been produced across Canada and in the US and the UK. She has also had over 100 plays produced by CBC and BBC radio. Rachel was director of the Writing Program at the Banff Centre for the Arts during the 1990s. She was awarded the Order of Canada in 2002, the Queen's Jubilee Medal in 2003 and the Queen's Diamond Jubilee Medal in 2012.

FSC
www.fsc.org

MIX

Paper from
responsible sources

FSC® C016245